"The first collection of Aira's stories might be his masterpiece."
—*Publishers Weekly* (starred review)

A DELIRIOUS COLLECTION OF SHORT STORIES

from the Latin American master of microfiction, César Aira—the author of at least eighty novels, most of them barely one hundred pages long—*The Musical Brain* comprises twenty tales about oddballs, freaks, and loonies. Aira, with his *fuga hacia adelante* or "flight forward" into the unknown, gives us imponderables to ponder and bizarre and seemingly out-of-context plot lines, as well as thoughtful and passionate takes on everyday reality. The title story, first published in the *New Yorker*, is the crème de la crème of this exhilarating collection.

"Aira is firmly in the tradition of Jorge Luis Borges and W. G. Sebald, those great late modernists for whom fiction was a theater of ideas."
—Mark Doty,
   Los Angeles Times

"Aira seems fascinated by the idea of storytelling as invention, invention as improvisation, and improvisation as transgression, as getting away with something."
—*The New York Review of Books*

"Aira conjures a languorous, surreal atmosphere of baking heat and quietly menacing shadows that puts one in mind of a painting by de Chirico."
—*The New Yorker*

"César Aira's body of work is a perfect machine for invention."
—Maria Moreno, *Bomb*

"This prolific Argentine writer has inspired a cult following."
—Scott Esposito, *Tin House*

W9-DFR-307

The Musical Brain
and other stories

The Musical Brain
and other stories

•

CÉSAR AIRA

Translated by Chris Andrews

A NEW DIRECTIONS BOOK

Copyright © 2013 by César Aira
Translation copyright © 2015 by Chris Andrews

Published in conjunction with the Literary Agency Michael Gaeb / Berlin.

All rights reserved. Except for brief passages quoted in a newspaper, magazine, radio, television, or website review, no part of this book may be reproduced in any form or by any
means, electronic or mechanical, including photocopying and recording, or by any information storage and retrieval system, without permission in writing from the Publisher.

Manufactured in the United States of America
New Directions Books are printed on acid-free paper.
First published clothbound by New Directions in 2015
Design by Erik Rieselbach

Library of Congress Cataloging-in-Publication Data
Aira, César, 1949-
[Short stories. Selections. English]
The musical brain & other stories / Cesar Aira ;
translated from the Spanish by Chris Andrews.
pages cm
ISBN 978-0-8112-2029-3 (alk. paper)
1. Aira, César, 1949– —Translations into English. I. Andrews, Chris, 1962– translator.
II. Title. III. Title: Musical brain and other stories.
PQ7798.1.I7A2 2014
863'.64—dc23   2014021279

10 9 8 7 6 5 4 3 2

New Directions Books are published for James Laughlin
by New Directions Publishing Corporation
80 Eighth Avenue, New York 10011

Contents

THE MUSICAL BRAIN
and other stories

A Brick Wall

AS A KID, IN PRINGLES, I WENT TO THE MOVIES A LOT.
Not every day, but I never saw fewer than four or five films a
week. Four or six, I should say, because they were double features; two for the price of one, and everybody watched both
films. On Sundays the whole family went to the afternoon session that started at five. There were two cinemas to choose
from, with different programs. As I said, they were double bills:
a B movie first, and then the main attraction (the "premiere,"
though I don't know why it was called that because they were
all premieres for us). Sometimes, almost always in fact, I also
went to the matinée session at one o'clock on Sunday, which
was a double feature, too, intended for children, although back
then they didn't make movies specially for children, so they
were westerns, adventure films, that sort of thing (and I got to
see some serials, including, I remember, *Fu Manchu* and *Zorro*).
A bit later on, when I was twelve, I started going in the evenings
as well, on Saturdays (the movies were different) or Fridays (it
was the same program as the afternoon session on Sundays, but
since there were two cinemas ...) or even on weekday nights.

And at some point one of the cinemas started continuous screenings of Argentine films on Tuesdays, all afternoon. How many movies would I have seen? Calculating like this is a bit silly, but four a week makes two hundred a year, at least, and if I kept going that often from the age of eight to the age of eighteen, that makes two thousand movies. It's even sillier to take the calculation to its ultimate conclusion: two thousand movies at an hour and a half each makes three thousand hours, or a hundred and twenty-five days, that is, four long months of uninterrupted viewing. Four months. A span like that is more concrete than a bare number, but it has the disadvantage of suggesting one excruciatingly long film, when in fact there were two thousand of them, each one unique, spaced out through a long childhood and adolescence, anxiously awaited, then criticized, compared, retold, and remembered. Above all remembered: hoarded like the manifold treasure they were. I can testify to this because those two thousand movies are still alive in me, living a strange life made up of resurrections and apparitions, like ghost stories.

People have often complimented me on my memory, or been amazed by the detail with which I remember conversations or events or books (or movies) from forty or fifty years ago. But the admiration or criticism of others is immaterial, because nobody else can really know what you remember or how you remember it.

It was precisely for that reason (because if I don't do it, no one else will), rather than as a remedy against "the tedium of hotel life," that I began to write this account of a curious incident that occurred last night in connection with a movie. I should point out that I'm in Pringles, in a hotel. It's the first time I've stayed in a hotel in my hometown. I came back to see my mother, who has had a fall and is confined to bed, and I've found a place on the Avenida because her little apartment is occupied by companions who are looking after her. Last night, as I was flipping through TV channels, I came across an old black-and-white English film (the steering wheels were on the right), which had started but only just (for a seasoned cinephile, a couple of shots are enough to identify the opening scenes of a film). There was something familiar about it, and when, after a few seconds, I saw George Sanders, my suspicions were confirmed: it was *Village of the Damned*, which I'd seen fifty years earlier, right here in Pringles, two hundred yards from the hotel where I'm staying, at the Cinema San Martín, which no longer exists. I hadn't seen the movie since, but it was very clear in my mind. Coming across it like that, without warning, was serendipitous. It wasn't the first time I'd seen a film that I remembered from childhood on television or video. But this time it was special, maybe because I was seeing it in Pringles.

The movie, as any buff will know (it's a minor classic), is about a village that is paralyzed by an unknown force: one day all its inhabitants fall asleep; when they wake up, the women are pregnant, and nine months later they give birth. Ten years pass, and the children begin to demonstrate their terrifying powers. They are all very similar: blond, cold, self-assured. They dress very formally, stick together, and never mix with the other kids.

Their eyes light up like little electric lamps and give them the power to dominate the will of the man or woman on whom they fix their gaze. They have no qualms about exercising this domination in the most drastic manner. A man with a shotgun is watching them; using telepathy, they force him to put the barrel of the shotgun in his mouth and blow his brains out.

George Sanders, who is the "father" of one of these children, realizes what is going on; his observations lead him to conclude that there is only one solution: to eliminate them. Meanwhile, the children make no secret of their intention to take over the world and annihilate the human race. As they grow, their powers increase. Soon they will be invulnerable; they almost are already, because they can read thoughts and anticipate any attack. (There was a similar case in Russia, which the Soviet authorities dealt with in their own way, killing the evil children along with the rest of the local population by carpet-bombing the village concerned.)

The protagonist is at home, wondering what to do. Or rather, how to do it. He knows that any plan he adopts will be present in his mind, which means that it will be visible to the children as soon as he approaches them. He tells himself that he will have to put a solid wall between him and them . . . As he says this, he is looking at the wall of his living room, next to the fireplace, which is covered with fake bricks. He murmurs: "A brick wall . . ."

At this point the camera follows his gaze and focuses on the brick wall for a moment. This fixed shot of a brick wall, with the voice off camera saying "A brick wall" was what fascinated me. In the movies I used to watch back then in Pringles, every image, every word, every gesture had meaning. A look, a silence, an almost imperceptible delay revealed betrayal or love or the existence of a secret. A mere cough could mean that a character would die or come to the brink of death, although she had seemed perfectly healthy up till then. My friends and I had become experts in deciphering that perfect economy of signs. It seemed perfect to us anyway, in contrast with the chaotic muddle of signs and meanings that constituted reality. Everything was a clue, a lead. Movies, whatever their genre, were really all detective stories. Except that in detective stories, as I was to learn at around the same time, the genuine leads are hidden among red herrings, which, although required in order to lead the reader astray, are superfluous pieces of information, without significance. In the movies, however, *everything* was invested with meaning, forming a compact mass that captivated us. To us, it seemed like a super-reality, or, rather, reality itself seemed diffuse, disorganized, deprived of that rare, elegant concision that was the secret of cinema.

So that "brick wall" prefigured the idea that would be used to save the world from the impending threat. But for the moment no one knew what the idea might be, and it was impossible to know. The wall wasn't easy to decode, like an actor's cough or the close-up of a sidelong glance. In fact, not even the character knew: for him the idea was still at the metaphorical stage. In order to carry out an effective attack on the diabolical children, he had to put a barrier between himself and them that would be impenetrable to telepathy, and the image that came to mind as a representation of that barrier was a brick wall. He could have chosen a different metaphor: "a steel plate," "a rock," "the Great Wall of China" ... His choice must have been determined by the fact that there was a brick wall right in front of him. But despite its visible materiality, the wall was still a metaphor. The children would surely have been able to read thoughts through walls, so a literal wall was not the solution. He was referring to something else, and that gave the shot a disturbing negativity, which made it unforgettable.

A brick wall ... the expression went on resonating.

I'm not the only admirer of this film, and I certainly didn't discover it as a cult classic. Nevertheless, I can claim a certain priority, since I saw it when it premiered. That was two or three years after it first came out, as was usually the case in Pringles, but it was still a "premiere" movie, and I was part of the target audience, who watched it without the distance introduced by cinephilia and historical perspective. We *were* cinephilia and history, both of which I would eventually convert into intellectual pursuits.

And there was something more: I was the same age as the children in the film. I probably tried to make my eyes light up with that electric gleam, to see if I could read people's minds. And Pringles was a small town, not as small as the one in the film, but small enough to suffer a "damnation" of that kind. For example, the mysterious paralysis of the opening scenes: our town was often empty and silent, as if everyone had died or left, during the siesta, say, or on a Sunday, or any day, really, at any time.

Still, I don't think anyone in the capacity audience at the Cinema San Martín on that Sunday long ago would have made the connection between the two towns and the two damnations. Not because there were no intelligent and cultivated individuals among the inhabitants of Pringles back then, but because of a certain decorous restraint, prevalent in those bygone days, which kept people well away from meanings and interpretations. Cinema was an elaborate and gratuitous artistic fantasy, nothing more. I don't mean that we were consummate aesthetes; we didn't need to be.

The priority that I mentioned owes less to these chance coincidences than to the fact that between my first and second viewings of the film, I accompanied its transformation from commercial product for a general public (that is, for the public, period) to cult object for an enlightened elite. And it was accompaniment in the fullest sense of the word: I was personally converted from public to elite. My life and *Village of the Damned* have followed the same path of subtle transformation, changing without having changed.

I suppose the same thing happened with the rest of the two thousand movies I saw in those years: the good and the bad, the forgotten and the rediscovered. It must have happened even with the classics, the great films that make it into Top Ten lists. They all crossed over from directness to indirectness, or withdrew to a distance, which is logical and inevitable, given the passing of time. Hitchcock's *North by Northwest*, which I also saw at the Cinema San Martín in, I'm guessing, 1960 or '61 (the film dates from 1959), is a case in point. In Argentina it was called *Intriga internacional*, or *International Intrigue*, and I probably didn't find out what it was called in English until twenty years later, when I began to read books about Hitchcock and think about his work in the light of my intellectual concerns. Perhaps because the original title is abstract, or because of the way the translation resonates for me, I still think of it as *International Intrigue*, though I know it's rather absurd; the translations of film titles were often ridiculously inappropriate in those days, and they've since become a source of jokes.

Few other films, none perhaps, made such an impression on Miguel and me. Miguel López was my best friend in early childhood, and as it turns out — another coincidence, though not a happy one — he died yesterday. They announced it on the local radio, and I heard only because I was in Pringles, otherwise it would have taken me months or years to find out, if I ever did. No one would have thought to tell me: we hadn't seen each other for decades; there weren't many people left who remembered that we'd been childhood friends; and here in town it's generally assumed that the locals have already heard and outsiders wouldn't care.

And yet, up till the age of eleven or twelve, we were inseparable. He was my first friend, almost like the big brother I never had. He was two years older than me, an only child, and lived across the road. Since we used to play in the street, or in the vacant lots between the houses, I'm guessing that our adventures began as soon as I could exercise a minimal autonomy, at the

age of three or four. From a very early age, we became serious
movie fans. So did all the other kids we knew, inevitably: the
movies were our major source of entertainment, the big out-
ing, the luxury at our disposal. But Miguel and I took it further:
we played at cinema, "acting out" whole movies, reinventing
them, using them as material for the creation of games. I was
the brains, naturally, but Miguel followed me and egged me
on, demanding more brains: being a physical, histrionic sort
of boy, he needed a script. I greedily consumed the inspiration
that each new movie gave me. *International Intrigue* was a great
inspiration, and more than that. I'd almost go so far as to say
that we made something out of that film that encompassed our
whole childhood, or what was left of it.

I couldn't say just what it was about *International Intrigue*
that made such an impression. Our enthusiasm was pure and
simple, without a trace of snobbery or prejudice: we didn't even
know who Hitchcock was (or maybe we did, but it made no difference), and it can't have been just because the film was about
spies and adventure, because we saw films like that every Sunday. Any hypothesis I hazard now is bound to be contaminated
by everything I've read about Hitchcock and the ideas I've had
about his work. Recently someone was asking about my tastes
and preferences, and when he came to cinema and my favorite
director, he anticipated my response: Hitchcock? I said yes. It
wasn't hard to guess. (I'm one of those people who can't imagine anyone having a favorite director *other* than Hitchcock.)
I said I'd be more impressed by his perspicacity if he guessed

(or deduced) my favorite Hitchcock film. He thought for a moment and then confidently proposed *North by Northwest*. This left me wondering what kind of visible affinity there might be between *North by Northwest* and me. It's a famously empty film, a virtuosic exercise in emptying the spy film and the thriller of all conventional contents. Thanks to the bungling of hopelessly incompetent bad guys, an innocent man finds himself caught up in a conspiracy without an object, and as the action unfolds, all he does is stay alive, without understanding what's going on. The form that encloses this emptiness could not be more perfect, because it's nothing more than form, in other words, it doesn't have to share its quality with any content.

That must have been what fascinated us. The elegance. The irony. Although we didn't know it at the time. Why would we have needed to know?

My earliest memory of Miguel dates back to when I was six: between a week and two weeks after my sixth birthday. The reason I can be so precise is that my birthday is near the end of February, and the school year begins at the start of March, and this happened on the first day of school. It was my first day ever (there was no preschool in Pringles back then), and my parents were taking it all very seriously. The teacher had given us homework, practicing downstrokes or something like that. After class, or maybe the next morning, they sat me down at a desk in a room facing onto the street, with my exercise book and pencil … Just then, Miguel's face appeared at the window, as it always did when he came to fetch me so we could go and play. It was quite a high window, but he had worked out how to jump up; he was very strong and agile (there was something feline about him), and tall for his age. My father went to the window and sent him packing: I had work to do, I had responsibilities, my days of going out to play at all hours were over ... He didn't say it in so many words, but that was what he meant. And there was something more as well, beneath (or above) the words he did say: I was beginning the middle-class journey that would turn me into a professional, and indiscriminate fraternizing with the kids on the street was no longer appropriate (Miguel was very poor— he lived with his parents in a single room in a sort of tenement). The second part of the prophecy was not fulfilled, because we went on being inseparable friends all through primary school, and the time I spent playing was hardly reduced because, given my natural brilliance, I could finish my homework in a flash and didn't need to go over my lessons.

I don't need to be reminded that every memory is a screen. Who knows what this memory—one of my earliest—conceals. It has been with me, perfectly vivid, all these fifty-six years, and, within it, Miguel's round smiling face on the other side of the glass. He wasn't offended by my father's abruptness; he just dropped back to the ground. And I wasn't bothered either; no doubt I was fascinated by the novelty of the exercise book and the pencil, and pleased, perhaps, by the fuss being made of me at home, and convinced, deep down, that I'd be able to go on playing in the street as much as I liked, because, timid and unassuming as I am, I've always ended up getting my own way.

It's strange: in the days that have followed Miguel's death, that fleeting vision of his face in the window has seemed like the last time I saw him: a farewell. Strange, because it wasn't the last time but the first. Although not really: it's just the first sight of him I remember. That's what I had in mind when I began to recount this memory. The reason my parents and I were so quick to interpret his presence was that he came to fetch me every day. That first memory, while still the first, is also a memory of what happened before, of what has been forgotten. Forgetting stretches away, before and after; my memory of the first day of school is a tiny, solitary island. There are a few other childhood memories, also discrete and isolated, erratic and inexplicable. Nevertheless, I treasure them, and I'm thankful for the screening mechanism that has preserved them for me. All the rest has been lost. This so-called "infantile amnesia," the total oblivion that swallows up the first years of our lives, is a remarkable phenomenon, and has been explained and understood in various ways. Personally, I subscribe to Dr. Schachtel's explanation, which runs, in essence, as follows:

Small children lack linguistic or cultural frames to put around their perceptions. Reality enters them torrentially, without passing through the schematizing filters of words and concepts. Gradually they incorporate the frames, and the reality that they experience is stereotyped accordingly, becoming linguistic and therefore retrievable in so far as it has adapted itself to being consciously recorded. That initial phase of immersion in brute reality is totally lost, because things and sensations have no limits or set formats. The immediate absorption of reality, which mystics and poets strive for in vain, is what children do every day. Everything after that is inevitably an impoverishment. Our new capacities come at a cost. We need to impoverish and schematize in order to keep a record, otherwise we'd be living in a perpetual present, which would be completely impractical. Even so, it's sad to realize how much has been lost: not only the capacity to absorb the world in its fullness, with all its riches and nuances, but also the material absorbed during that phase, a treasure that has vanished because it wasn't stored away in retrievable frames.

Dr. Schachtel's book, so persuasive in its dry, scientific eloquence, avoids what, in this context, could only be a false poetry. It also avoids giving examples, which would lead inevitably to poetic falsification. Poetry is made of words, and every word in a poem is an example of that particular word in its everyday use. To give a truly adequate example, every word would have to be accompanied by a chaotic enumeration encompassing, or at least suggesting, the entire universe. We see a bird flying, and at once the adult mind says "bird." The child, by contrast, sees something that not only does not have a name but is not even a nameless thing: it is (although the verb *to be* should be used with caution here) a limitless continuum involving the air, the trees, the time of day, movement, temperature, the mother's voice, the color of the sky, almost everything. The same goes for all objects and events, or what we call objects and events. It could almost be an artistic project, or the model or matrix from which all artistic projects are derived. What's more, when thought attempts to examine its own roots, perhaps it is trying, unwittingly, to return to a time before it existed, or at least trying to dismantle itself piece by piece, to see what riches it conceals.

This would change the meaning of nostalgia for the "green paradise" of childhood: perhaps the object of longing is not so much (or not at all) an innocent state of nature, but an incomparably richer, more subtle and developed intellectual life.

It is my belief that all the lost memories of my early years are recorded in the two thousand films I saw in that time. I will try to illuminate the nature of that vast archive by describing an invention that Miguel and I came up with. I said that *North by Northwest*—or *International Intrigue*, as we knew it—made an impression on us, no more perhaps than many other films, but in a different way. The day after seeing it, we decided to create a secret society dedicated to international intrigue. Now that I think of it, the sound of those two words might have been what triggered our initiative: *intrigue*, an intriguing word in itself, which could refer to just about anything; and *international,* indicating importance, the world beyond Pringles. Without secrecy, of course, there would have been no point. Secrecy was at the center of it all.

We were possessed of the easiest and safest means of keeping secrets, simply by being children and letting the adults think, rightly, that there was no need to investigate our games because they belonged to a sphere apart, separate from their reality. We must have known—it was obvious—that nothing we could do would be of the slightest interest to adults, which devalued our secrecy. In order for a secret to be a secret, it had to kept from someone. Since we had no one else, we would have to keep it from ourselves. We had to find a way to split ourselves in two, but that was not impossible in the world of play.

We named our society the "ISI" (for International Secret Intrigue), and its operations began immediately. The principle rule, as I said, was secrecy. We weren't allowed to talk to each other about the ISI; I wasn't supposed to find out that Miguel was a member, and vice versa. Communication was to take place via anonymous written messages placed in a "letter box" to be agreed upon. We agreed that it would be one of the cracks in the wooden door of a derelict house on a corner. Once we had established these rules, we pretended to have forgotten all about the ISI and started playing another game, although our heads were buzzing with plans for conspiracies, investigations, and stunning revelations, which we were scripting in advance. Both of us were itching to go home and write the first message, but we had to hide our impatience, so we went on playing more and more distractedly as the texts took shape in our heads, until nightfall. Only then, with some plausible excuse ("I have to do my homework" or "I have to have a bath"), did we go our separate ways.

The rules, as you can see, were purely formal. We didn't worry about the content: it would take care of itself. And as it turned out, there was no shortage of material. On the contrary, there was an excess. Writing and drawings filled up the sheets of paper; sometimes we needed two, and the folded wad was so thick we had trouble wedging it into the crack. We tore pages from our school exercise books: it was the only paper we had, and in those days of abundance they made it thick and tough to resist the assault of erasers. We learned the art of folding, and may even have discovered for ourselves that a piece of paper cannot be folded in half more than nine times.

What did we write? I can't remember how we began, no doubt by inventing some imminent danger, or giving each other instructions for saving the world, or indicating the enemy's whereabouts. It became more intense when we started accusing each other of blunders, denunciations, and betrayals, or simply of being dangerous enemy agents who had infiltrated the ranks of the ISI. Threats and death sentences were frequent. Meanwhile, we went on playing together, going to the movies, building tree houses, organizing stone-throwing battles in the vacant lot opposite the school (this dangerous game was a favorite among the local kids), and doing target practice with our slingshots. We never mentioned the ISI, of course. We were leading parallel lives. And we didn't have to pretend; it was something that came naturally. We had split ourselves in two.

Children quickly tire of games, and we were no exception. Even the games that excited us most were abandoned after a few days. The ISI lasted because of its peculiar format, though I'm not sure whether it was the splitting or the secret that made the difference. I should say that it wasn't entirely exempt from the general tendency, and the initial frenzy died away after a week or two, but the system of written communication guaranteed a continuity that was, in a way, independent of us.

We started forgetting to go to the old red door to see if there was a new message, and if by chance I passed and saw a folded sheet of white paper wedged into the crack, I would pull it out, only to discover, more often than not, that it was my last message, written and left there so long ago I couldn't remember what it said, so I would read it with interest before putting it back.

Or else the old message would be from Miguel. In any case, all the workings of the game would come rushing back into consciousness, and arouse a real enthusiasm in me (or him), a feeling of responsibility and loyalty, and admiration for the mind (whose mind?) that had invented such a brilliant source of fun. Development is rapid at that age, and although we were still children, we regarded the already distant creators of the ISI as infants with scant intellectual resources and were amazed by their precociousness; we couldn't have come up with it, in spite of our age and education. We couldn't believe it, our past selves seemed so remote and primitive ... Nevertheless, we'd quickly write a reply, of course, whichever one of us it was, pleased to have the chance to display what we had learned in the meantime. We'd put it into the crack, and for a day or two, we'd go back every half hour to see if there was a response, not realizing that the ISI was as far from the other player's mind as it had been from mine or Miguel's before he or I happened to see the message. And this preoccupation would soon be displaced by others and lapse into oblivion.

It's no exaggeration to say that these interruptions became extremely long. It was as if they corresponded to successive phases of our lives, as if all the body's cells had to be replaced before one of us could pass the peeling, weather-beaten door, notice a thin white strip in one of its cracks, and ask himself what it might be. Say it was me. Out of pure idle curiosity, and only because I wasn't in a hurry, I'd pull it out, with difficulty, because time and rain had lodged it firmly. It was a ragged, discolored wad of paper. It came apart along the creases when it was unfolded. There was something written on it, the ink had faded and run, but the message was still legible; the handwriting was childish, interspersed with maps and sketches, and warnings in stern capitals, with underlinings and exclamation marks. For a moment, and this would provoke a certain flutter of excitement, there seemed to be a possibility that it was about something serious like a kidnapping or a denunciation ... In that case, it would have to be shown to the police. But no, it was too absurd. And suddenly the memory would return, as if from very far away: The ISI! The dear old ISI ... That game we invented ... So many memories, so much nostalgia! But then I'd think: It's my turn to reply. He'll be so surprised to find that I'm still checking up, still ready to play!

Could it be true, as I seem to remember, that this scenario was repeated over and over? Maybe I'm mistaken. If it had really happened like that, my childhood, and Miguel's, would have lasted thousands of years, and we'd still be alive today.

JANUARY 22, 2011

Picasso

IT ALL BEGAN WHEN THE GENIE CAME OUT OF THE Magic Milk bottle and asked me what I would prefer: to have a Picasso or to be Picasso. He could grant me either wish but, he warned me, only one of the two. I had to think about it for quite a while; or rather, I made myself think about it. Folklore and literature are so full of stories about greedy fools who are punished for their haste, that it makes you think those offers are all too good to be true. There are no records or reliable precedents on which to base a decision, because this sort of thing happens only in stories or jokes, so no one has ever really thought about it seriously; and in the stories there's always a trick, otherwise it would be no fun and there would be no story. At some point, we've all secretly imagined this happening. I had it all worked out, but only for the classic "three wishes" scenario. The choice the genie had given me was so unexpected, and one of the options was so definitive, that I had to weigh them up, at least.

It was a strange choice but not inappropriate; in fact, it was particularly apt. I was leaving the Picasso Museum, in a state of rapture and boundless admiration, and at that moment I could not have been offered anything, or any two things, that would have tempted me more. I hadn't actually left the museum yet. I was in the garden, sitting at one of the outdoor tables, having gone to the café and bought a little bottle of the Magic Milk that I'd seen tourists drinking everywhere. It was (it is) a perfect autumn afternoon: gentle light, mild air, and still a while to go before dusk. I took my notebook and pen from my pocket to make some notes, but in the end I didn't write anything.

I tried to put my ideas in order. I silently repeated the genie's words: to have a Picasso or to be Picasso. Who wouldn't want to have a Picasso? Who would turn down a gift like that? But on the other hand, who wouldn't want to have been Picasso? Was there a more enviable fate in modern history? Not even the privileges of supreme worldly power are comparable to what he had, because they can be removed by political events or wars, while the power of Picasso, transcending that of any president or king, was invulnerable. Anyone else in my place would have preferred the second option, which included the first, not only because Picasso could paint all the Picassos he liked, but also because it's well known that he kept a lot of his own paintings, including some of the best (the museum I'd just visited had been set up with his personal collection), and in his later years he even bought back works that he'd sold as a young man.

This inclusion did not of course exhaust the advantages of being transformed into Picasso, not by a long shot: the "being" went far beyond the "having," taking in all the protean joys of creation, stretching away to an unimaginable horizon. "Being

Picasso," in the wake of the real-life Picasso and whatever he was really like, meant being a Super-Picasso, a Picasso raised to the power of magic or miracle. But I knew my geniuses (*je m'y connaissais en fait de génies*), and I could tell or guess that it wasn't quite so simple. There were good reasons to hesitate, and even to recoil in horror. In order to become someone else, one has to cease being oneself, and no one willingly consents to that surrender. Not that I considered myself to be more important than Picasso, or healthier, or better equipped to face life. He was fairly unstable — I knew that from the biographies — but not as unstable as me, so by becoming him I would improve the state of my mental health to some degree. Still, thanks to a lifetime's patient efforts, I had made peace with my neuroses, fears, anxieties, and other handicaps, or at least reached a point where I could keep them under control, and there was no guarantee that this partial cure would work with Picasso's problems. That was more or less my reasoning, although I didn't put it into words; it was just a series of hunches.

Fundamentally, this was an extreme case of the problem of identification, which is raised not only by the master of Málaga, but by every artist one admires or venerates or studies. The problem goes beyond Picasso, and yet remains within him too. Identification is one of those things that can't be generalized. There is no identification in general, as a concept, only identification with this or that figure in particular. And if the figure is Picasso, as in this case, there can be no other. The concept turns itself inside out, as if we were to say (although it's a clumsy way to put it) that it's not about "identifying with Picasso" but about "Picassifying identification."

Few individuals have inspired so much writing; everyone who came into contact with Picasso left a testimony, an anecdote, or a character sketch. One is almost bound to find a common trait. For example, I've read that he had a problem with action. He would see a piece of paper lying on the floor of his studio, and it would bother him, but he wouldn't pick it up, and the piece of paper could lie there for months. Exactly the same thing happens to me. It's like a tiny, incomprehensible taboo, a paralysis of the will, which keeps me from doing what I want to do, indefinitely. Picasso overcompensated for this with his frenetic production of art, as if by painting picture after picture he could make the piece of paper pick itself up.

Whatever the reason, there was no doubting the continuity of his production, through all his metamorphoses. Picasso was only Picasso insofar as he was a painter, so if I were Picasso, I could paint all the Picassos I liked, and sell them and get rich, and maybe (since the rich can do anything these days) stop being Picasso if I felt trapped in a life I wasn't enjoying. That's why I said that the gift of "being" included that of "having."

Picasso once said: "I'd like to live in peace like a poor man, only with lots of money." Setting aside the deluded belief that the poor have no problems, there's something odd about the remark: he was rich already when he made it, very rich. But not as rich as he would be now, thirty years after his death, with the rise in the price of his paintings. Everyone knows that painters have to die, and therefore stop producing, for their work to become really valuable. So there is an economic gulf between "being Picasso" and "having a Picasso," as there is between life and death. The remark about living in peace, leaving aside its facile ingenuity, could be applied to the situation in which the genie had placed me; it was a message from beyond the grave, sent in the knowledge that my dearest wish was for a truly peaceful life, without problems.

Given the current prices, and the relative modesty of my aspirations, a single painting would be enough to make me rich and allow me to live in peace, writing my novels, relaxing, and reading ... My mind was made up. I wanted a Picasso.

No sooner had the thought formed in my mind than the painting appeared on the table, without anyone noticing; by then, the people who had been occupying the neighboring tables had got up and walked away, and the others had their backs to me, as did the waitresses at the café. I held my breath, thinking: It's mine.

It was splendid: a medium-size oil painting from the thirties. For a long time I gazed at it intently. At first glance it was a chaos of dislocated figures, a superposition of lines and wild but fundamentally harmonious colors. Then I became aware of the beautiful asymmetries that leaped out at the viewer, then hid, then reappeared elsewhere, then concealed themselves again. The impasto and the brushwork (it had been painted *alla prima*) were a masterful demonstration of the assurance that can only be achieved by unself-conscious virtuosity.

But the painting's formal qualities were merely an invitation to explore its narrative content, which began to reveal itself little by little, like the meaning of hieroglyphics. First there was a flower, a crimson rose, emerging from the multiple Cubist planes of its petals; facing it, like a mirror image, was a jasmine in virginal whites, painted in Renaissance style, except for the right-angled spirals of its tendrils. In a collision of figure and ground, typical of Picasso, the space between was filled with little snail-men and goat-men, wearing plumed hats, doublets and breeches, or armor, or a fool's cap and bells; there were nude figures too, dwarf-like and bearded. Over this court scene presided a figure who must have been the queen, to judge by her crown: a monstrous broken-down queen, like a damaged toy. Rarely had the distortion of the female body, one of Picasso's trademarks, been taken to such an extreme. Legs and arms stuck out of her any old how, her navel and her nose were chasing each other across her back, the windmill of her torso was inlaid with the multicolored satins of her dress, and one foot, encased in a big high-heeled shoe, shot up skyward ...

Suddenly the plot revealed itself to me. I was looking at an illustration of a traditional Spanish fable, or rather a joke, and a joke of the most primitive and puerile variety; it must have come back to Picasso from his early childhood. The joke is about a lame queen, who's unaware of her handicap, and whose subjects don't dare tell her about it. The Minister of the Interior finally comes up with a strategy for tactfully letting her know. He organizes a floral competition, in which all the kingdom's gardeners compete with their finest specimens. A jury of experts narrows the field down to two finalists: a rose and a jasmine. The final decision, the choice of the winning flower, is up to the queen. In a grand ceremony, with the whole court in attendance, the Minister places the two flowers before the throne, and, addressing his sovereign in a clear, loud voice, says: "*Su Majestad, escoja*," which means "Your Majesty, choose," but also, if the last word is broken up, "Your majesty is lame."

The tale's humorous tone was translated visually by the multicolored tangle of gaping courtiers, by the stocky minister raising his index finger (which was bigger than the rest of him), and above all, by the queen, composed of so many intersecting planes she seemed to have been extracted from a pack of cards folded a hundred times over, refuting the proven truth that nine is the maximum number of times a piece of paper can be folded in half.

The fable had some intriguing features, which gave Picasso's decision to turn it into an image further layers of significance. First, the fact that the protagonist was lame and didn't know it. It's possible to be unaware of many things about oneself (for example, to take the case at hand, the fact that one is a genius), but it's hard to imagine how this could extend to an obvious physical defect like lameness. Perhaps the explanation lay in the protagonist's regal condition, her status as the One and Only, which prevented her from judging herself by normal physical standards.

The One and Only, as there had been only one Picasso. There was something autobiographical about the painting and about the idea of basing it on a childish joke that he must have heard from his parents or his schoolmates, and even about the implicit use of his mother tongue, without which the joke wasn't funny and made no sense. The picture dated from a time when Picasso had been in France for thirty years and had completely adapted to the language and the culture; it was curious, to say the least, that he had resorted to Spanish to provide the key to a work that was otherwise incomprehensible. Perhaps the Spanish Civil War had renewed a patriotic streak in him, and this painting was a kind of secret homage to his homeland, torn apart by the conflict. Perhaps, and this need not exclude the previous hypothesis, the root of the work was a childhood memory, which had lived on as a debt to be repaid when his art had acquired a sufficient degree of power and freedom. By the thirties, after all, Picasso had been recognized as the pre-eminent painter of asymmetrical women: complicating the reading of an image by introducing a linguistic detour was just another means of distortion, and in order to underline the importance that he attached to this procedure, he had chosen to apply it to a queen.

There was a third hypothesis, on a different level from the first two, which took the painting's supernatural origins into account. Up until then, no one had known that it existed; its enigma, its secret had remained intact until it materialized before me, a Spanish speaker, an Argentine writer devoted to Duchamp and Roussel.

In any case, it was a unique piece, singular even among the works of an artist for whom singularity was the rule; it could hardly fail to fetch a record price. Before embarking on one of my habitual fantasies about future prosperity, I took a little more time to enjoy contemplating the masterwork. I smiled. This crooked little queen, who had to be put together again from a whirl of tangled limbs, was touching, with her biscuit-like face (once you found it), her golden chocolate-wrapper crown, and her puppet's hands. She was the center of a centerless space. Her entourage, a veritable court of painterly miracles, was waiting for her choice; the evanescence of the flowers was a reminder of time, which for her was not a duration but an instant of understanding, a final realization, after a lifetime of illusion.

A crueler version of the joke can be imagined: the queen has always known that she's lame (how could she not know?), but good manners have prevented her subjects from broaching a topic that she prefers to avoid. One day her ministers dare one another to say it to her face. This may be more realistic, but it's not what the painting represented. No one would make that queen the butt of a joke; no one would mock her. The courtiers all loved her, and wanted her to know it. Beneath the surface message ("choose"), the hidden message ("is lame") was meant for her: she would hear it and then, in a flash of insight, understand why the world rocked when she walked, why the hems of her dresses were cut on the diagonal, and why the lord chamberlain rushed to give her his arm each time she had to descend a staircase. They had resorted to the language of flowers, that eternal vehicle for messages of love. She had to choose the most beautiful flower in the kingdom, just as I had been obliged to choose between the two gifts offered by the genie ...

At that moment I too had my flash of insight, and the smile froze on my face. Why this hadn't occurred to me before, I couldn't understand, but all that mattered was that it was occurring to me now. As in a nightmare, an insoluble problem loomed, engulfing me in anxiety. I was still inside the museum: sooner or later I would have to leave; my life as a rich man could only begin outside. And how could I leave the Picasso Museum with a Picasso under my arm?

NOVEMBER 13, 2006

Athena Magazine

WHEN WE WERE TWENTY, ARTURITO AND I LAUNCHED
a literary magazine called *Athena*. With youthful enthusiasm
and a fervent sense of mission, we devoted ourselves body and
soul to the work of writing, layout, printing, and distribution
… or at least the diligent planning of those activities, the sched-
uling and budgeting. We knew nothing about the publishing
business. We thought we knew all about literature, but were
happy to confess our almost total ignorance of the concrete
mechanisms that convey literature to its readers. We'd never
set foot in a printing works, and didn't have the vaguest idea of
what had to happen before and after the printing. But we asked
and we learned. Many people gave us helpful advice, warnings,
and guidance. Poets with long experience of self-publishing,
editors with ten short-lived magazines to their credit, booksell-
ers, and publishers, they all made time to tell us how it worked.
I guess we seemed so young to them, just a pair of kids, so keen
to learn and make it happen, they must have been moved by
a fatherly concern, or by the hope that our naïveté would al-
chemically transmute their own failures, and bring about the
long-delayed triumph of poetry, love, and revolution.

Of course, once we gathered all the necessary information and began to do the sums, we saw that it wouldn't be so easy. The obstacle was economic. The rest we could manage, one way or another; we didn't lack self-confidence. But we had to have the money. And no one was going to give it to us just like that, as we realized when our first timid appeals came up against an impenetrable barrier. In those days, there weren't any funding bodies that you could apply to for publishing grants. Luckily, our families were well off and generous (up to a point). We had another advantage too: intrepid youth, without burdens or responsibilities, taking no thought for the far-off tomorrow. We were prepared to stake everything we had, without hesitation. That's what we were doing all the time, in fact, because we were living from day to day.

We managed to scrape up enough money to pay for the first issue. Or we anticipated that we would have the right amount when the moment came to pick up the copies from the printer. Reassured on that account, we set about gathering, organizing, and evaluating the material. Since our ideas and tastes coincided, there were no arguments. We let our imaginations run wild, invented new provocations, discovered new authors, laid claim to the forgotten, translated our favorite poets, composed our manifestos.

But although we were deeply absorbed in the intellectual aspect of the enterprise, we didn't forget about the money. Not for a moment. We couldn't have, because everything depended on it, not just the existence of the magazine, but also its physical appearance, the illustrations we could include (in those days, anything other than type required the use of costly metal plates), and especially the number of pages, which was essential for any calculation. At the printers they'd given us a provisional "cost schedule" for various sizes and quantities of pages, in different combinations. The quality of the paper, it turned out, made very little difference. There could be thirty-two pages, or sixty-four, or ... The printers worked with numbers of "sheets," which was something we never fully understood. Mercifully, they simplified the choices for us. We took it on ourselves to complicate them.

We thought long and hard about the frequency of publication: monthly, biannual, triannual? Had it been simply up to us, dependent only on our zeal, we would have made it fortnightly or weekly ... There was no shortage of material or enthusiasm on our part. But it all depended on the money. In the end we adopted the view of Sigfrido Radaelli, one of our obliging advisers: literary magazines came out when they could. Everyone accepted that; it was the way things were. When we accepted it ourselves, we realized that irregularity would not oblige us to give up our idea of selling subscriptions. All we had to do was change the formula from a period of time ("yearly subscription") to a number of issues ("subscription for six issues").

Recounting all these details now, they seem absurdly puerile, but they were part of a learning process, and maybe a new generation is repeating these lessons today, *mutatis mutandis*, as the love of poetry and knowledge is eternally reborn. The prospect of having subscribers and, more generally speaking, the desire to do a good job led us into an area of greater complexity. The general perspective was important: we felt that whether or not our readers were subscribers they were entitled to a product that would continue over time. The subscribers would be *more* entitled, of course, because they would have paid in advance. Continuity mattered to us too. We were depressed by the mere thought that our magazine might decline or dwindle with successive issues. But we had no way to insure against it. In fact, there was no guarantee that we'd even be able to get enough money to print a second issue. With admirable realism, we left sales out of our calculations. Even more realistically, we anticipated a diminution of the energy that we'd be able to devote to bothering our families and friends for money ... Basically, the question was: Would we be able to bring out a second issue of *Athena*? And a third? And all the following issues, so as to build up a history? The answer was affirmative. If we could get the first issue out, we could get the others out as well.

I don't know if we hypnotized each other, or were led to believe what we wanted to believe by our fervent commitment to literature, but we ended up convincing ourselves. Once we were sure our venture would continue, we felt we could indulge in some fine-tuning. Our guiding principle was a kind of symmetry. All the numbers of the magazine had to be equivalent to the others, in number of pages, amount of material, and "specific gravity." How could we ensure that? The solution that occurred to us was curious in the extreme.

We'd noticed that literary magazines often brought out "double issues": for example, after number 5, they'd bring out 6–7, with twice as many pages. They usually did this when they got behind, which wouldn't be the case for us, because we'd already opted for irregularity. But it gave us an idea. Why not do it the other way around? That is, begin with a double issue, 1–2, not with double the pages, though, just the 36 we'd already decided on. That way, we'd be covered: if we had to make the second issue slimmer, it could be a single issue: 3. If, on the other hand, we maintained the same level, we'd do another double issue, 3–4, and we'd be able to go on like that as long as the magazine prospered, with the reassuring possibility of reducing the number of pages at any time, without losing face.

It must have occurred to one of us that "double" was not an upper limit; it could be "triple" too (1–2–3), "quadruple" (1–2–3–4), or any other multiple we liked. There were known cases of triple issues: rare, admittedly, but they existed. We hadn't heard of anything beyond triple. But there was no reason for us to be deterred by a lack of precedents. The whole aim of our project was, on the contrary, to innovate radically, in the spirit of the times, producing the unusual and unheard-of. There were practical reasons, too, why the double-issue solution didn't merit our immediate adhesion. From a strictly logical point of view, if we had to cut back, who was to say that we would have to cut back by exactly half? It would have been very strange if we did. Our publishing capacity could have been reduced by lack of funds, inflation, fatigue, or any number of accidents, all unforeseeable in their magnitude as well as their occurrence, so we might well have had to cut back to less than half ... or more. That's why starting with a triple issue (1–2–3) gave us more flexibility: we could cut back by a third, or by two thirds, so the second issue could be double (4–5) or single (4). But if, as we hoped, we managed to sustain the momentum, the second issue would be triple again (4–5–6). There was something about this speculation, so lucid and irrefutable (given the premises), that excited us and carried us away, as much as, or even more than, the rushes of literary creation itself.

We wanted to do a good job. We weren't as crazy as it might seem. After all, editing a literary magazine, the way we were doing it, is a gratuitous activity, rather like art with its unpredictable flights of inspiration, or play, and for us it served as a bridge between the future and the childhood we'd just left behind. Though we hadn't left it behind entirely, to judge from our abstract perfectionism, so typical of children's games. To give you an idea ...

The triple issue ruled out the possibility of cutting back by exactly half. That possibility, with its strict symmetry, was, we had already decided, very unlikely to correspond to reality, but we were sad to be deprived of it, even so. Especially since there was no reason to deprive ourselves of anything: all we had to do was start with a quadruple issue (1–2–3–4), that way we'd still have the possibility of cutting back by half (the following issue would be double: 5–6), or if our means were not so far reduced, we could cut back by just a quarter (and follow the inaugural quadruple issue with a triple: 5–6–7), or if our laziness or lack of foresight or circumstances beyond our control obliged us to do some serious belt-tightening, the second issue would be a single: 5. If, however, providence was kind, we would bring out another normal, that is, quadruple issue: 5–6–7–8.

It's not that we thought, even for a moment, of producing a first issue three or four times thicker than the one we had at first envisaged. Those initial plans remained intact, and they were very reasonable and modest. We never thought of making it any bigger; our first issue, as we had designed it, with its thirty-six pages, seemed perfect to us. The texts were almost ready, neatly typed out; there were just a few unresolved questions concerning the order (should the poems and the essays be grouped separately or should they alternate?), and whether or not to include a particular short story, whether to add or remove a poem ... Trifling problems, which, we were sure, would resolve themselves. If not, it wouldn't matter much: we wanted *Athena* to have a slightly untidy, spontaneous feel, like an underground magazine. And since there was no one breathing down our necks, we took our time and went on calculating for the future.

All this was notional, which gave us free rein to speculate boldly. It was like discovering an unsuspected freedom. Maybe that's what freedom always is: a discovery, or an invention. What, indeed, was to stop us from going beyond the quadruple issue to make it quintuple, or sextuple ... ? Beyond that, we didn't know the words (if they existed), but that in itself was proof that we were entering territory untouched by literature, which was the ultimate aim of our project. We were embarking on the great avant-garde adventure.

If we presented the first issue of *Athena* as a "decuple" issue—that is, numbers 1–2–3–4–5–6–7–8–9–10—we would, at one stroke, secure a marvelous flexibility with regard to the size of future issues. We'd be covered against all contingencies, able to cut back in accordance with our straitened circumstances, without having to resign ourselves to gross approximations. If the cost of the first issue was a thousand pesos (an imaginary sum, solely for the purposes of demonstration), and it was a decuple issue, and if we ran short for the second and could muster only seven hundred pesos, we'd make it a "septuple issue" (11–12–13–14–15–16–17). If five hundred pesos was all we could get, it would be a quintuple issue (11–12–13–14–15); but if we raised a thousand pesos again, it would be another decuple (11–12–13–14–15–16–17–18–19–20). And if our utter idleness prevented us from collecting more than one hundred pesos, we'd make the next issue a single: 11. The "single" issue, containing a single number, would be as low as we could go. Whatever the first issue was would be "normal."

We found these fantasies exhilarating, as I said, and it's true. Even today, so many years later, writing these pages, I can still feel some of that exhilaration, and I still understand it as we did back then: this was the world turned upside down, and we were venturing into it with the exuberance that the young bring to everything that happens in their lives. Wasn't that the definition of literature: the world turned upside down? At least, of literature as we imagined it and wanted it to be: avant-garde, utopian, revolutionary. We delighted in the idea of swimming against the current: dreams are usually dreams of grandeur, but ours were of smallness, and they were dreams of a new kind: dreams of precision and calculation, poetry adopting the unprecedented format of real equations. We thought of our project as the first literary version of Picabia's mechanical paintings, which we adored.

We continued on this route, spurring ourselves on. Why should we be limited by the number ten? There was, perhaps, a practical, concrete reason. It determined a minimum number of pages if we had to economize drastically: three. A magazine of fewer than three pages (which is how many it would have if, at some point, compelling economic considerations forced us to bring out a single issue) would not be a magazine. A practical, concrete limit wasn't going to hold us back, but we complied with it provisionally, and put it to the test. We found two holes in the reasoning that I have set out schematically here. First, there *could* be a magazine of fewer than three pages. It could consist of a single page. And, more important, a tenth of our decuple issue wouldn't be three pages, but 3.6, since the inaugural issue of *Athena* would conform to the printers' standard format that we had adopted as our norm: thirty-six pages.

So, predictably, we began to consider a first issue that would be thirty-six-fold, so to speak. An issue made up of numbers 1–2–3–4–5–6–7–8–9–10–11–12–13–14–15–16–17–18–19–20–21–22–23–24–25–26–27–28–29–30–31–32–33–34–35–36. That would allow for an almost total flexibility. Why hadn't we thought of it before? Why had we wasted our time with "triples" and "quadruples" and "decuples" when there was such an obvious solution right under our noses? The printer's "sheet" should have shown us the way right from the start, from the moment we discovered its existence, the famous "sheet" that was unfolding now before our eyes, like a rose in time.

The problem was how to fit those numbers on the cover. Would there be enough room for them all, and the dashes, between the title and the date? Wouldn't it be a bit ridiculous? There was the option of replacing them with an austere "Nos. 1–36," but for some reason we found that unsatisfactory. Defiantly, we decided to go the opposite way: filling the cover with numbers, big ones, in nine rows of four. Without any explanation, of course: we'd never have dreamed of explaining our contingency plan to the readers.

This confronted us with a serious problem: whether or not we provided explanations, people would look for them anyway—that's just how the human mind is made. And a thirty-six-fold issue would suggest an obvious explanation, which everyone would find convincing: that the numbers on the cover had something to do with the number of pages. As they did, in fact, but not in what would seem to be the obvious way. This connection completely spoiled the fun of the idea, which we abandoned immediately. At that point I think we felt that we'd never really been satisfied with thirty-six.

Freeing ourselves of that bad idea freed us completely. We

leaped to really big numbers, first a thousand, then ten thousand, which had a special prestige because of its Chinese associations. China, with the Cultural Revolution in full swing, was much in vogue at the time.

Any more moderate number would have seemed insufficient. Ten thousand. But no more than ten thousand. We could have gone wild and continued up into the millions, or the billions; but we were engaged in a very concrete and practical task—producing a magazine—not in wild speculation. We weren't intending to abandon realism, though a mediocre, storekeeper's realism had never been a part of our intellectual outlook. Ten thousand guaranteed total originality, without tipping over into unworkable folly. We made sure of this with pencil and paper, setting it all out in black and white.

Making an issue composed of ten thousand numbers meant that the "single" issue would be 0.0036 of a page. We weren't math wizards. We had to do the calculations step by step, visualizing it all. This made the process infinitely more interesting; it became an adventure among strange and novel images. How did we arrive at 0.0036? Like this: if we reduced the magazine by a factor of ten, it would have 3.6 pages; if we reduced it by a factor of one hundred, it would have 0.36 pages, that is, a bit more than a third of a page or three tenths of a page; if the factor was a thousand, the magazine would be 0.036 pages long, that is, a bit more than three hundredths of a page; and if we increased the factor to ten thousand, thus reducing the magazine to a "single" issue, that issue would consist of 0.0036 of a page, in other words a little more than three and a half thousandths of a page. We had to visualize this too, to get a clear idea of what it meant. Referring to the budget prepared for us by the printers, we saw that the page size we had chosen for the first issue, in accordance with our means, was 8 by 6 inches. So the area of each page would be 48 square inches. Divided by ten thousand, that gave 0.0048 square inches, which had to be multiplied by 3.6 (that is, by the number of ten thousandths produced by the previous calculation). The result was 0.01728 square inches ... Should we round up? No, exactitude was the key, or one of the keys, to the enchantment that transported us. And unless we were mistaken (we covered a lot of paper with our calculations), 0.01728 square inches was the area of a rectangle 0.1516 inches high and 0.1140 inches wide. That wasn't so easy to visualize. It was futile trying to use the imagination as a microscope to see that molecule, that speck suspended in a moment of sunlight (it didn't seem heavy enough to settle.) We had leaped beyond the sensory and the intuitive into the realm of pure science, and yet—this was the supreme paradox—it was there that we found the true, the real *Athena*, in the form of a "single" issue, springing from our heads just as the goddess whose name we had borrowed had sprung from the head of her father.

MAY 21, 2007

The Dog

I WAS IN A BUS, SITTING BY THE WINDOW, LOOKING
out at the street. Suddenly a dog started barking very loudly
nearby. I tried to see where it was. So did some other passengers.
The bus wasn't very full: the seats were all occupied, but there
were just a few people standing up; they had the best chance of
seeing the dog, because they were looking from higher up and
could see out both sides. Even for someone sitting, as I was,
buses provide an elevated view, as horses did for our ancestors:
la perspective cavalière. That's why I prefer buses to cars, which
carry you so low, so close to the ground. The barks were coming from my side, the sidewalk side, which was logical. Even
so, I couldn't see the dog, and since we were going fast I figured it was too late; we would already have left him behind. He
had provoked the mild curiosity that always surrounds an incident or an accident, but in this case, except for the volume of
the barking, there was little to indicate that anything had happened: the dogs that people walk in the city rarely bark except
at other dogs. So the attention of the passengers was already
beginning to dissipate ... when suddenly it was refocused: the

barking started up again, louder than before. Then I saw the dog. He was running along the sidewalk and barking at the bus, following it, racing to keep up. This really was strange. In the old days, in country towns and on the outskirts of cities, dogs would run beside cars, barking at their wheels; it's something I remember well from my childhood in Pringles. But you don't see it anymore; it's as if dogs had evolved and grown used to the presence of cars. And besides, this dog wasn't barking at the wheels of the bus but at the whole vehicle, raising his head, staring at the windows. All the passengers were looking now. Had the owner got onto the bus, perhaps, forgetting the dog or abandoning him? Or maybe it was someone who'd attacked or robbed the dog's owner? But no, the bus had been driving along Avenida Directorio without stopping for several blocks, and it was only in the current block that the dog had begun his chase. More elaborate hypotheses—for example, that the bus had run over the dog's owner, or another dog—could be set aside, because there'd been nothing like that. It was a Sunday afternoon and the streets were relatively empty: an accident could not have gone unnoticed.

The dog was quite big, and dark gray in color, with a pointed muzzle, halfway between a purebred and a street dog, though street dogs are a thing of the past in Buenos Aires, at least in the neighborhoods we were passing through. He wasn't so big that the mere sight of him was scary, but he was big enough to be threatening if he got angry. And he seemed to be angry or, rather, desperate and distraught (for the moment, anyway).

The impulse that was driving him was not (or not for the moment, at least) aggression but an urgent desire to catch up with the bus, or stop it, or ... who knows?

The race continued, accompanied by barking. The bus, which had been held up by a red light at the previous corner, was accelerating. It was driving along close to the sidewalk, on which the dog was running, losing ground. We'd almost reached the next intersection, where it seemed the pursuit would come to an end. But, to our surprise, when we got there, the dog crossed to the next block and went on chasing us, accelerating too, and barking all the while. There weren't many people on the sidewalk, otherwise he would have bowled them over, charging along like that, his gaze fixed on the windows of the bus. His barks became louder and louder; they were deafening, drowning out the noise of the motor, filling the world. Something that should have been obvious right from the start was finally sinking in: the dog had seen (or smelled) someone who was traveling on the bus, and he was after that person. A passenger, one of us ... This explanation had evidently occurred to others; people started looking around with inquisitive expressions. Did someone know the dog? What was it about? An ex-owner, or someone the dog had once known ... I was looking around too, and wondering, Who could it be? In a case like this, the last person you think of is yourself. It took me quite a while to realize. And the realization was indirect. Suddenly, moved by what was still a vague presentiment, I looked ahead, through the windscreen. I saw that the way was clear: ahead of us a row of green lights stretched off almost to the horizon, promising rapid, uninterrupted progress. But then, with anxiety rising inside me, I remembered that I wasn't in a taxi: a bus has fixed stops every four or five blocks. It was true that if there was no one at the stop and if no one rang the bell to get off, the bus would keep going. No one had approached the back door, for the moment. And with a bit of luck there would be no one at the next stop. All these thoughts occurred to me at once. My anxiety continued to mount and was about to find the words with which to declare itself. But this was delayed by the very urgency of the situation. Would chance allow us to drive on without stopping until the dog abandoned his chase? Having averted my gaze for barely a fraction of a second, I looked at him again. He was still keeping up, still barking as if possessed . . . and he was looking back at me. Now I knew: I was the one he was barking at, the one he was chasing. I was seized by the terror that attends the most unexpected catastrophes. I had been recognized by that dog, and he was coming to get me. And although, in the heat of the moment, I was already resolving to deny it all, and not confess to anything, deep in my heart I knew that he was right and I was wrong. Because I had once mistreated that dog; what I'd done to him was truly, unspeakably disgraceful. I have to admit that I've never had very firm moral principles. I'm not going to try to justify myself, but the lack can be explained in part by the ceaseless battle that I've had to fight, from the tenderest age, simply to survive. It has gradually dulled my sense of rectitude. I've allowed myself to do things no decent man would ever do. Or would he? We all have our secrets. Besides, my misdeeds were never all that serious. I didn't commit actual crimes. Nor did I forget what I had done, as a real scoundrel would have. I told myself I'd make amends, though I never really stopped to think about how. This was the last thing I was expecting: to be recognized in such a bizarre way, confronted with a past that had been buried so deeply it seemed forgotten. I realized that I had been counting on a certain impunity. I had assumed, as anyone in my place might have done, that a dog being first and foremost a dog, its individuality would be reabsorbed by the species and finally disappear. And with that disappearance my guilt would vanish too. My despicable betrayal had individualized the dog for a moment, but only for a moment. There was something supernatural and terrifying about the idea that the moment had lasted so many years. But, as I thought it over, a hope appeared, and I grasped at it: too much time had passed. Dogs don't live that long. If I multiplied the years by seven ... These thoughts were tumbling in my head, colliding with the muffled barks that kept getting louder and louder. No, it wasn't true that too much time had gone by; doing the sums would just have been a way of prolonging my self-deception. My last hope was the classic psychological reaction of retreat into denial when faced with something that is too much to bear: "It can't be, this can't be happening, I'm dreaming, I must have misinterpreted the data." This time it wasn't a just psychological reaction; it was real. So real I couldn't look at the dog; I was scared of what he might be expressing. But I was too nervous to pretend to be indifferent. I looked straight ahead. I must have been the only one; all the other passengers were following the race, including the driver, who kept turning his head to look, or using the rear-view mirror, and joking with the passengers at the front. I hated him for that: the distraction was making him slow down; otherwise how could the dog have kept pace all the way to the second intersection? But what did it matter if he was keeping up? What could he do, apart from bark? He wasn't going to get onto the bus. After the initial shock, I began to assess the situation in a more rational way. I had already decided to deny that I knew the dog, and I held firmly to that decision. An attack, which I thought unlikely ("his bark is worse than his bite"), would cast me in the victim's role and prompt onlookers, and the forces of order if necessary, to come to my aid. But, of course, I wouldn't give him the opportunity. I wasn't going to get out of the bus until he disappeared from sight, which was bound to happen sooner or later. The 126 goes right out to Retiro, along a route that twists and turns after it leaves Avenida San Juan, and it was inconceivable that a dog could follow it all that way. I dared to glance at him, but immediately looked away again. Our gazes met, and what I saw in his eyes was not the fury I'd been expecting but a limitless anguish, a pain that wasn't human because it was more than a human could bear. Was the wrong I'd done him really so grave? It wasn't the moment to embark on an analysis. And anyway, there could be only one conclusion. The bus went on accelerating. We crossed the second intersection, and the dog, who'd fallen back, crossed too, in front of a car that had stopped for the lights; but if the car had been moving, he would have crossed just the same, he was running so blindly. I'm ashamed to admit it, but I was hoping he'd be killed. Such things have been known to happen: there's a film in which a Jew in New York recognizes a kapo from a concentration camp forty years before, starts chasing him, and is run down and killed by a car. Remembering this depressed me, rather than affording some relief as precedents usually do, because it happened in fiction and made the reality of my situation all the more evident, by contrast. I didn't want to look at the dog again, but the sound of his barking indicated that he was falling behind. The bus driver, no doubt tiring of the joke, had put his foot to the floor. I dared to turn around and look. There was no risk of drawing attention to myself because everyone else in the bus was doing the same; on the contrary, it might have seemed suspicious if I'd been the only one who wasn't looking. I was also thinking it might be my last glimpse of him; a chance encounter like that wouldn't occur again. Yes, he was definitely falling behind. He seemed smaller, more pitiful, almost ridiculous. The other passengers began to laugh. He was an old, worn-out dog, on the brink of death, perhaps. The years of resentment and bitterness that lay behind that outburst had left their mark. The race must have been killing him. But he'd waited so long for that moment to arrive, he wasn't going to give up. And he didn't. Even though he knew he'd lost, he kept on running and barking, barking and running. Perhaps, when he lost sight of the bus in the distance, he'd go on running and barking forever, because there would be nothing else he could do. I had a fleeting vision of the dog's figure in an abstract land-scape (infinity) and felt sad, but it was a calm, almost aesthetic feeling, as if the sorrow were seeing me in the far distance as I imagined I was seeing the dog. Why do people say the past doesn't return? It had all happened so quickly, I'd had no time to think. I'd always lived in the present because simply taking it in and reacting to it used up practically all my physical and mental energy. I could manage the immediate, but only just. I always felt that too many things were happening at once and that I had to make a superhuman effort and summon more strength than I possessed simply to cope with the now. That's why whenever an opportunity arose to free myself of a burden in any way at all, I didn't bother with ethical scruples. I had to get rid of anything that wasn't strictly necessary for my sur-vival; I had to secure a bit of space, or peace, at any cost. How this might harm others didn't trouble me because the conse-quences weren't immediate, so I couldn't see them. And once again the present was ridding me of a troublesome guest. The incident left a bittersweet taste in my mouth: on one hand, there was relief at having escaped so narrowly; on the other, an understandable remorse. How sad it was to be a dog. To live with death so close at hand, and so implacable. And sadder still to be *that* dog, who had thrown off resignation to the destiny of his kind, but only to show that the wound once inflicted on him had never healed. His silhouette against the light of a Buenos Aires Sunday, in a state of constant agitation, racing and barking, had played the role of a ghost, returning from the dead or, rather, from the pain of living, to demand ... what? Reparation? An apology? A pat? What else could he have wanted? It can't have been revenge, because he would surely have learned from experience that he was powerless against the unassailable world of humans. He could only express himself; he'd done that, and all it had achieved was to strain his weary old heart. He'd been defeated by the mute, metallic expression of a bus driving away, and a face watching him through the window. How had he recognized me? I must have changed a lot too. His memory of me was obviously vivid; perhaps it had been present in his mind all those years, never fading for a moment. No one really knows how a dog's mind works. It wasn't beyond the bounds of possibility that he'd recognized my smell; there are amazing stories about the olfactory powers of animals. For example, a male butterfly smelling a female miles away, through all the thousands of intervening smells. I was beginning to speculate in a detached, intellectual way. The barking was an echo, varying in pitch, now higher now lower, as if it were coming from another dimension. Suddenly I was jolted from my thoughts by a hunch that I could feel all through my body. I realized that I had been too quick to declare victory. The bus had been speeding up, but now it was slowing down again: it was what the drivers always did when the next stop came into sight. They accelerated, gauging the distance still to go, then lifted their foot, and let the bus glide to the stop. Yes, it was slowing down, pulling over to the sidewalk. I sat up straight and looked out. An old lady and a child were waiting to catch the bus. The barking was getting louder again. Could the dog have kept running? Hadn't he given up? I didn't look, but he must have been very close. The bus had already stopped. The child jumped in, but the woman was taking her time; that high step was difficult for a lady of her age. I was silently shouting, Come *on*, old bag! and anxiously watching her movements. I don't normally speak or think like that; it was because of the stress I was under, but I got a grip on myself immediately. There was really no need to worry. Maybe the dog would make up some lost ground, but then he would lose it again. In the worst case, he'd come and bark right in front of my window in a very obvious way, and the other passengers would see that I was the one he was chasing. But all I had to do was deny any knowledge of the animal, and no one would contradict me. I gave thanks for words and their superiority over barks. The old woman was lifting her other foot onto the step; she was almost in. A burst of barking deafened me. I looked out to the side. He was coming, quick as a shot, fur flying, loud as ever. His stamina was incredible. Surely he must have had arthritis, at his age, like all old dogs. Maybe he was firing his last rounds. Why keep anything in reserve if he was closing the circle of his fate by venting his resentment, having found me after all those years? At first (this all happened in a crazy shattering of seconds), I didn't understand what was going on, I only knew it was strange. But then I realized: he hadn't stopped in front of my window, he'd kept going. What was he doing? Could he be ...? He'd already drawn level with the front door and, agile as an eel, he turned, leaped and dodged. He was getting onto the bus! No, he was on the bus already, and without having to bowl the old lady over—she just felt something brush against her legs—he turned again and, barely slowing down, still barking, ran down the aisle ... Neither the driver nor the passengers had time to react; the cries were rising in their throats but hadn't yet come out. I should have said to them: Don't be afraid, it's not about you, it's me he's after ... but I didn't have time to react either, except to freeze and stiffen with fear. I did have time to see him rushing at me, and I could see nothing else. Close up, face on, he looked different. It was as if when I'd seen him before, through the window, my vision had been filtered by memory or my idea of the harm I'd done to him, but there in the bus, within arm's reach, I saw him as he really was. He looked young, vigorous, supple: younger than me and more alive (the life had been leaking out of me all those years, like water from a bathtub), his barks resounding inside the bus with undiminished force, his jaws with their dazzling white teeth already closing on my flesh, his shining eyes that had not, for one moment, stopped staring into mine.

MARCH 16, 2008

In the Café

A CUTE LITTLE THREE- OR FOUR-YEAR-OLD GIRL WAS running around among the tables, laughing, playing on her own, hiding from her mother, who was chatting with a friend, and responding to the greetings of the customers by smiling and dashing off again. An old couple called her over; she went, and the man presented her with a little boat that he had made by folding a paper napkin. She ran to show it to her mother, who admired it and asked her if she had said thank you to the nice man. The girl ran back to do that, and played with the boat, which was very flimsy because of the fineness of the paper and soon came apart in her hands. But by then another man, sitting alone at another table (he was reading the soccer pages of *Clarín*) had called her over and given her a little plane, also made from a paper napkin. As before, the girl ran to show it to her mother, and then she ran to show it to the man who had given her the boat, and her trills of pleasure made faces at other tables turn and smile. A child requires so little to be happy. So little, and yet, at the same time, so much, because the little thing that fills the child with innocent happiness lasts no longer than a sigh and then must be replaced by another. Sensing this, perhaps, a third customer, with eyes half closed and a look of intense concentration, had begun to fold a napkin. He was an older man, really old, in fact, and he must have been concentrating in an effort to remember; no doubt he'd done this for his grandchildren many years before, but not for his great-grandchildren, whose preference for electronic games had disheartened him. Now, in the café, where he came to kill time, he could reuse that modest skill, acquired so many years ago, to make another child happy; an unexpected opportunity, handed to him on a platter, to employ a metaphor in keeping with the scene. For a moment he feared that it had been too long, that forgetfulness had triumphed, as it had already in so many parts of his brain, disconnected by old age. And then there was the growing stiffness of his hands, the loss of coordination in his fingers, whose poor aching bones were inelegantly twisted out of line. But memory stubbornly threaded its way through the ruins of old age, and the man saw a little doll of fine, almost transparent paper appear shakily before him, trembling in its elementary disjointedness. The girl didn't mind; she was happy just to receive the gift, to which she'd been drawn as if by a special sense. The paper figure, a silhouette with a tutu, made only by folding, without a single cut, was supposed to have joints in the arms and the legs, but because of imperfections resulting from the man's memory lapses and alterations, and from the inadequate, ultra-fine paper, it came out like a limp puppet. Even so, the little girl recognized the shape and, with a spontaneous gesture that drew smiles from the customers all around the café who were observing this scene, cradled it in her arms, singing "Rock-a-Bye Baby," and carried it to where her mother was sitting with her friend. A sweet sensation flooded through the old man, but the success of his creation must have been regarded as suspect, partly because its crude sexism was demagogic and facile (a doll for a girl, a ball for a boy), partly because that tattered scrap of paper paid scant honor to the venerable art of figurative origami. The response was already being prepared at a table occupied by a middle-aged man and a young couple. The difference in age wasn't great enough for him to be their father; he looked more like a teacher with his students, or a boss with two young employees. Their table was covered with papers, which could have been pages of notes, lists, dispatch slips, bills, or computer printouts, but now they were focused on the fine paper napkin to which the young man was applying himself, under the gaze of the girl and the older man, who was commenting abundantly, gesturing to stress an authority based on age rather than skill, because it was clear that the boy was the one with the know-how. In his hands the rectangle of paper, folded and unfolded over and over, became a hen, with a plump, maternal body, a crescent of triangular tail feathers, a raised head and an open beak. A cheerful cock-a-doodle-doo from the hen's creator attracted the little girl, who in turn attracted the wandering attention of the customers, curious to discover the new offering, which could have been anything, given the wide range of possibilities afforded by the material. The need to renew this improvised amusement was urgent because the little doll was already lying on the floor. The fate of the previous creation foreshadowed, of course, what was to come; and, if only at a speculative level, the question arose as to whether it might have been a waste of effort. But even without an explicit reminder that "Nothing is lost, all is transformed," the atmosphere was suddenly charged with gain, not loss. The little girl's rapid consumption of novelties was accepted as something natural, even exciting. This is how it should always be, some people were thinking, philosophically: getting and losing, enjoying and letting go. Everything passes, and that's why we're here. Eternity and its more or less convincing simulacra are not a part of life. The girl, who was life and nothing but, was delighted by the hen, which served as a pretext to dash off again, holding it up as if to make the bird fly, although, because of her unsteady, beginner's steps—she was perpetually about to fall, perpetually recovering her balance—it flapped more like a butterfly. She clearly wasn't bothered by the fact that hens don't fly, or at least not like that. In the simple zoology of children, one animal shape covers a range of species, geographies, and epochs, and can even encompass night and day, since the little flying hen was also flying like a bat and, given the inherent ambiguity of all chunky forms, might in this case have been taken for one, except that a bat would have been completely out of place in the hands of candor incarnate. And speaking of candor, the color of the paper napkins conspired against that interpretation too: their white was irreversible. In any case, all that flying and the erratic pressure of the child's little pink fingers proved to be utterly destructive: the hen's round body became a pyramid in ruins, the proud triangles of the tail were soon all askew, and by the time the junior test pilot remembered to show it to her mother (a ceremony to which she seemed to attribute the gravity of a certification), it was already in tatters. But obviously no one minded, and they wanted to go on indulging her. Two girls who were having a lively conversation and had not appeared, up till then, to be paying attention to what was going on, waved something white, which, like a red rag to a bull, brought the interested party rushing over: it was a clown made by ingeniously folding a small paper napkin. Presumably, then, they had been inattentive to the girl's forays because they were attending to the little work in progress. And it was a remarkable work, superior in quality to what had been produced so far: the clown had a round hat, a disproportionate protuberance to represent his rubber nose in the middle of the paper circle that was his face, a tail coat, baggy pants and the classic shoes that reach all the way to next door. To judge from appearances, neither the girl who was now handing the clown to its eager recipient nor her companion would have seemed capable of such an exploit: they looked like airheads, good for nothing but idle chatter (which is what they had seemed to be engaged in, at least for those out of earshot). The only explanation that bridged the gap was that they were kindergarten teachers, or one of them was, and her training must have included an obligatory or optional unit on making paper figures. A clown! Every child's best friend, who keeps his little charges company even when they close their eyes, tucked into bed, and never forsakes them, not even in their worst nightmares; on the contrary, that's where he takes the lead role, in order to prevent others—monsters, for example—from stepping in. This inoffensive little clown, made of paper so fragile a gaze could tear it, had been marked somehow by his contact with monsters in the world of dreams. But how? The trace was perceived subliminally, and in no other way, because the continual movements of the clown's possessor—her dashes and sudden displays—prevented any detailed observation. It was, in fact, a stain: the paper clown's white was not immaculate like that of the earlier figures. Not a very noticeable stain, just a dirty brown smudge, of indeterminate shape, which, because of the folding, appeared on various separate parts of the body. Coffee, from the lips of one of the girls. So they must have folded a used napkin. That was strange. Given a choice, why pick faulty materials for a delicate and difficult piece of work? Maybe they had started folding just to see (could it be done with this sort of paper and a sheet of this size?), using the first napkin that came to hand, and by the time they realized it was possible, the work was so far advanced that it wasn't worth getting a new napkin and starting all over again. If they really were kindergarten teachers, as it seemed from the general impression they gave—the loud voices, the dyed hair, the spontaneity—satisfying childish desires with whatever came to hand was what they did every day. Now might be the moment to say a few words about the napkins that were being used to make these gifts for the little girl. A well-stocked napkin dispenser sits on every café table in Buenos Aires. The classic rectangular, elongated nap-

kins in the equally classic metal dispenser with a spring to push
them up have gradually been replaced by square napkins, made
of slightly tougher paper, on which the name, logo, and address
of the café are printed. (There are triangular ones too, but they
are less common.) And the new dispensers are plastic or
wooden stands of one sort or another. The café in which the
events recounted here took place had not been modernized in
this regard: they were still using the old metal dispensers with
their elongated napkins, folded twice, resting on a metal plate
pushed up from underneath by a spring: a system that had disappeared, at that point in the city's history, from all but the
lowliest establishments. It was an anomaly, all the more striking
since the café had recently been renovated in a way that aspired
to elegance and modernity. Either the owners had a large number of old dispensers in good condition and had decided to
avoid the cost of buying new ones, or, more likely, this was simply a detail that they had overlooked. These possibilities were
not mutually exclusive, and they were complemented, not excluded, by a third, which actually included them: perhaps the
owners regarded the old dispensers as superior, not only from
a practical point of view, but also because of that vague, unconscious fondness that we have for objects we have lived with for
a long time, or all our lives. The refurbishing of the old cafés,
which had to be done in order to attract a new generation of
customers and compete with the new cafés, contributed to the
ceaseless transformation of the city and the consequent obliteration of memories. Preserving something in the midst of
change was a reflex to ensure survival or continuity, operating

on a tiny detail that would then irradiate the whole. But in this case there was something more: this large, renovated café was situated on an invisible urban frontier: to one side lay the local shops and businesses; to the other, near the movie theaters, a space traversed by workers and domestic staff, who lived in the poor suburbs to the west, coming from or going to the Flores railway station, just two hundred yards away. The old napkin dispensers linked not only the present and the past but also the coexisting social strata, which were not mutually exclusive either, since poverty was a thing of the past. In any case, the division of a city's population into socioeconomic classes is a crude simplification because every person belongs to a stratum of his or her own: there are as many strata as individuals. One such individual, a man of impressive sartorial elegance, who looked like an executive, was sitting at a table on which he had opened business files, and was making marks and notes on the pages with a stylish pen; his cell phone was lying among the papers, and his briefcase was open on the chair beside him. He must have been getting ready for an important meeting, absorbed in his figures and arguments, but not entirely, to judge from what happened next. Absently, without looking, he plucked a napkin from the metal box. The way he did it spoke of a long familiarity with the apparatus (with a neat flick of his thumb and index finger he extracted the napkin without creasing it at all) and hence of a life spent in cafés; perhaps he had once been a sales rep, selling pharmaceuticals or some other product, stopping at a café halfway through his daily round to take the weight off his feet and catch up with his paperwork. If so, he had progressed through the ranks, but as always—this is how progress works, fundamentally—he still retained the habits of the world that he had left behind. He had put down his pen and stopped reading his documents, and in the few seconds it took the girl to destroy the little clown inadvertently, his clever folding produced the next gift. It was—surprise!—a coffee cup with its saucer. This was a qualitative leap with respect to all the previous folded offerings, and since there had already been one such leap in the series, it was a leap with respect to a leap. The cup was simply perfect in its Bauhaus simplicity, and its curves, produced without breaking the basic rule of creating shapes solely by means of folding and unfolding, were a tour de force. So was the way it was all in one piece, although the real thing was made up of two: the cup and the saucer, indissolubly united in this case by the paper. The little girl, who still hadn't learned to be shy, came over happily, without needing to be called, to accept this new tribute to her grace and beauty. Another votive offering to her innocence. She took it in her clumsy little hands and, laughing triumphantly, ran to show it to her mother, except that this time she stopped at each table along the way and reached up on tiptoe to place it next to a real coffee cup where possible, so that everyone could see the resemblance. Many of the customers—all of them, no doubt—would have been able to appreciate the full worth and difficulty of that work, but she took it for granted; it was as natural to her as a flower or a stone, something a nice man had given her as a token of admiration;

there was no need for *her* to admire it. By the time she reached her mother, the cup was already halfway back to being a napkin again. Her mother, still chatting, spared her the briefest mechanical glance. After the first little figure, the first of what was beginning to look like an infinite series, she had immediately switched off, as adults do when their children are playing. Nobody loses out, because, from that moment on, the children enter a dimension of their own, composed of repetitions and intensities. Something like that had happened in the café. The girl had achieved a kind of invisibility, in which she was moving like a fish in water. The life of the café continued as normal. The waiters—there were six of them, each attending to his own group of tables—circulated with their trays, took orders, served, and collected money. The customers came and went, greeted one another, took their leave; those arriving late apologized and blamed the traffic. And even those who had made the ritual folded-napkin offering switched off after that and got on with their own lives. But the series, if that's what it really was, did not come to a halt; it was as if the flow of ordinary time were yielding to the peremptory nature of childhood. A lady with dyed-red hair, who was drinking tea, wearing a violet and yellow tracksuit, caught the girl's eye with a smile and presented her with what she had constructed from a little paper napkin. This new creation was a masterful, prize-worthy piece of work, which took the very concept of the qualitative leap to a whole new level. It was a bunch of flowers, a profusion of tiny roses, arum lilies, gladioli, daisies, and carnations, crowned by a chrysanthemum, and filled out with ferns. All this had sprung from half a dozen folds in the miserable little napkin, and expert unfolding to fluff it into shape. All the flowers, with their almost microscopic details, were recognizable. The only thing they lacked was color; the white of the paper made them ghostly. The qualitative leap wasn't necessary in itself, since the only thing that mattered from the girl's point of view was the continuation of the game, regardless of crescendos or decrescendos, but the leap's own necessities favored subtle forms; as a result, one had to look at this bouquet twice, or three times, to make out the flowers, otherwise it might have been mistaken for a ball of crumpled paper. This escalation was inevitable; other kinds of gift-objects—birthday or wedding presents, offerings made to a bountiful god—could also evolve toward ever-greater subtlety and ultimately assume the appearance of trinkets, or of nothing at all. When that happens, people say, with a condescending smile: "It's the intention that counts." But it's true: the intention counts so much it disappears into the gift, just as a smaller number, 843, say, disappears into a bigger one like 1,000 and, lying hidden there, is extremely hard to find, as hard as winning the lottery. Brandishing the bouquet of paper flowers, the girl set off, spinning like a bee, as if she were sending a coded message to all the little girls in the world, indicating the direction of the garden. Her handling accentuated the ephemeral nature of flowers: before she had finished transmitting her message, the delicate posy, bouncing crazily as she leaped about, had totally lost its shape. If anyone regretted the rapid destruction of these fugitive playthings, it certainly wasn't her. She was riding the succession of novelties, which, in turn, because they were novelties, were riding on time, which was emitting speed and unpredictability, like sparks streaming off in two different directions. The late bouquet lay on the floor, where countless shoes would step on it, while, with her winning smile, the girl laid claim to what was already coming her way from a table occupied by four men, not all that young but "still young" all the same, rock fans or bikers, one of whom had folded and refolded a paper napkin (who knows where and how he'd learned to do this) to make a quivering replica of the Guggenheim Museum in Bilbao, with all its bold intersecting planes, every single one. Trills and laughter from the recipient, the squealing of a happy little creature: she was delighted, although she had no idea what it represented—but that might have been, and no doubt it was, precisely what delighted her. Children have a very special attachment to the incomprehensible; there's so much they don't understand at that age, they have no choice but to love it, blindly, like an enigma, but also like a world. It teaches them what love is. It traces out the vacant shape of their lives, heralding the marvelous variety of forms. Incomprehensible objects are keys to the word *incomprehensible*, and that's why children are so fond of the word, which holds the promise of an object to be opened and entered into. They live, provisionally, in that correspondence. With the imaginative flexibility particular to her age, the girl entered the museum and walked through its rooms, among the works of contemporary art, those supremely strange works that, for the uninitiated, belong to the realm of the incomprehensible. Arbitrary objects and excessive complications reversed themselves for the benefit of innocence. But the almost transparent paper of the napkin from which the museum was made was so flimsy, and the tensions that held it all in place were so delicately balanced that it was already coming apart under the clumsy pressure of the girl's little fingers, and the renowned curved surfaces were flexing with a pliability that no architect, least of all Frank Gehry, would have been able to foresee. Folding, enfolding, and unfolding were all gathered into the abstraction of a geometrical point. And at that point a question arose spontaneously: how could it be that the set of customers who happened to have come to one of the multitudinous cafés scattered around the city at that hour of the afternoon included so many people who had so thoroughly mastered the art of paper folding? Was it an almost miraculous coincidence? A gratuitous conspiracy? A moment's inspiration? But folding paper into recognizable shapes is not a skill that requires long study, or travel to the Far East for classes with a master. It would have been more surprising to find that among the customers sitting in a café at a certain time, there were twenty podiatrists or sociolinguists, sitting on their own or in pairs or little groups at each table, who didn't know each other and had come to the café at that time for twenty different reasons—*that* would have been truly jaw-dropping. Up to a point, figurative paper-folding is a natural and spontaneous activity, but only up to a point: the starting point, that is, the making of little boats or planes. And yet, because of the natural tendency to elaborate and the spare time that, in retrospect, we generally turn out to have had, in this case the idle pastime had given rise to escalating transformations. And that was precisely where the solution began to emerge. The question at issue could not, in fact, be answered by comparing or juxtaposing paper-folding with other activities, or considering fortuitous groupings of things or people. The answer lay in the reason for the activity of folding, which was originally to fold the spatiotemporal coordinates in which coincidences occurred. These coincidences gave rise to many misunderstandings and arguments, which were never resolved. Were they coincidences or were they reality? Here, two incompatible modes of thought—statistical and historical—entered into conflict. Representative figures made by folding paper must have first appeared when someone discovered that a sheet of paper cannot, however hard one tries, be folded in half more than nine times, no matter how large or thin the sheet is. Faced with this limit, what had been simply a piece of folded paper flowered into something that resembled a piece of the world. The work of folding, in other words, bounced off the wall of the incomprehensible and opened into the figurative. The discovery of the ninefold limit had taken place in the legendary time of origins. The Dawn of Humanity, it must have been, since the limit was a mathematical absolute. But it turned out that paper had been invented at a relatively late stage in History, before which it was already impossible to fold a sheet of paper more than nine times, although there was no paper. What this meant for Humanity was that the ingenious and amusing figures achieved by folding were, as they say, "within everyone's reach." Doubt once dispelled, the series continued and soared away from the simple and the clichéd. And so it was that the next gift, which the little girl received from a short man with an impressive quiff of black hair combed back and held in place with brilliantine, who was eating a sandwich and drinking a beer, realized the possibilities of a little paper napkin in the most elaborate way. It was a boat, not a schematic representation like the first gift, but an elegant sailing ship decked with flags, and the folding continued out from the keel to show the wavy water of a river and the banks on either side, and houses on the banks, and stores, a church, gardens, and people crowding the streets along the waterfront, waving to the passing ship. On board, the crew was busy working the sails, while the passengers admired the view and waved back to the locals. The group of passengers, who were obviously important people, in eighteenth-century attire (wigs, ermine stoles, braid), was dominated by the majestic, rotund figure of a queen, disproportionately large and clearly in command. Standing slightly apart from the group, and just as prominent as the queen, was a handsome, prepossessing man in full military regalia, with a plumed hat, a fur cape, and a sword hanging from his belt. An almost microscopic fold of the tortured napkin used to construct this panorama showed that he had only one eye. That detail was enough to identify him and situate the scene, for this was, in fact, the depiction of a very particular historical event. In 1786, Potem-kin, Prince of Tauris, favorite of Catherine the Great, com-pleted the conquest and pacification of the Crimea, and in the spring of the following year, he arranged for the sovereign to visit the peninsula, as well as Ukraine, which had also been an-nexed to her empire. She traveled in grand style, with all the court and the diplomatic corps, and hundreds of servants, cooks, musicians, and actors, plus a portable theater and salons, libraries, and pets. Each stage of the journey was celebrated with magnificent parties held at castles along the way, attended by the local aristocrats and dignitaries. Coaches, berlins, carts, and sleds were left in Kiev, and the voyage continued over the water: eighty luxuriously fitted-out ships set off on the Dnieper, and this was the moment that had been captured by the napkin: the tsarina in the flagship, surrounded by the ambassadors of all the European powers, and Potemkin at the prow, making sure that the grand spectacle that he had orchestrated was go-ing according to plan. (He had lost an eye in a brawl with the brothers Ostrov, who were also among Catherine's lovers.) It was all his creation: the prosperous cities they could see on the riverbanks, thrown up overnight to be displayed to the visitors; the plump, multitudinous cattle, brought in specially; the con-tented peasants cheering the tsarina, in reality a corps of care-fully instructed extras. In the diplomatic reports that were later sent to various courts, it was clear that none of the ambassadors were entirely convinced by this playacting, but all admired the industry of the favorite who, in a few short months, had mocked up an entire country from scratch. The leap from the legendary tsarina to the delightful little girl had traversed every kind of representation. The minuscule diorama, treated with a regal indifference, began to unfold as soon as she touched it, and by the time she reached her mother's table, after making all manner of unnecessary detours and digressions with her new treasure on display, the destruction was almost complete: the queen was sinking into the waves of the river; the courtiers and ambassadors were collapsing onto each other in an involuntary orgy; Potemkin was on top of a church tower, standing on his head; and the ship looked like a bicycle. The ruin, reverting to the condition of a crumpled napkin, sank in a puddle of Coca-Cola, and the little girl ran to the other end of the café. A bespectacled youth had set aside his laptop for a moment to join in the folding game, and was offering her a paper version of Rodin's *Thinker* (if the almost impalpable material of the cheap napkins in those metal dispensers can be dignified with the name of paper). She greeted it with her indiscriminate trilling and laughter, although, for a child of her age, it was hardly an appropriate toy. It was probably the only thing that the youth had learned how to make by folding paper. Or perhaps he had once made other things, but this was the one that had turned out best, and from then on he had specialized. Or perhaps, as his use of a computer suggested, he was committed to going paperless and saving the planet's forests. If he'd made an exception in this case, it was because he wanted to take part in the competition along with all the others and not be left behind; to insist on saving a tiny napkin made of the lightest paper would clearly have been a symptom of the fanatical rigidity that discredits a good cause. But there was something else, which had to do, precisely, with *The Thinker*. The only paper-saving that made sense was the kind that depended on mental work, on concentration (so finely represented by Rodin's masterpiece), which enabled a thinker to skip the intermediate steps, and thus avoid the need to waste reams of paper on those rough drafts, the works of the philosophers. The girl was a stranger to philosophies and concentration, and all she could recognize was a human figure, which she cradled in her arms, singing a simplified lullaby. The customers smiled as she went past their tables, and there was perhaps—or almost certainly—an element of vindictive pleasure in the smiles of those who had inwardly condemned the gift as inappropriate, a form of cultural showing-off quite out of place in that context. The next object the little girl received (folded by a priest in a break from his conversation with two contractors about an extension to the parish soup kitchen) seemed to have been intended to contrast with the incongruous *Thinker*. It did this by signaling its origins in infantile zoology and storybook illustration, and its resemblance to a toy with moving parts. Using only the obligatory material (the little paper napkin), the priest, by means of ten cunning folds, had made a kangaroo. A mother kangaroo, with a joey's head emerging from the ventral fold. Before handing it over, he gave the girl instructions, or just the one, which was very simple and required no words since it took the form of a practical demonstration: by pulling on the kangaroo's long, curved tail, he made the joey's head pop out of the pouch and pop back in again. It can't have been the first time the priest's white hand had tugged on a kangaroo's tail. The little girl was charmed by the joey's shy peeping, and ran off at once to show it to her mother. The priestly origin of this ingenious folding was lost along the way, as the fragile mechanism was destroyed by the girl's clumsy jerks. But didn't this gift allude to the higher Maternity and the Child who appeared and disappeared at the miraculous edges of the world? That priest had practiced with communion wafers, so similar to the napkins in their texture and fineness. No one really knows what a wafer looks like before the ceremony in which it plays the leading role. The origins of the host are surrounded by a multitude of legends. For example, the legend of the tenth fold. There was no time to repair the tail-lever because the girl's mother was already standing up, along with her friend, and looking around, not realizing at first that her daughter was right there beside her, then taking her by the hand to go. Suddenly she was in a big rush: there'd been so much to say, they'd talked so long; time had flown, and the hairdresser was about to close. At the last minute the little girl let go of her mother's hand and ran a few steps to take something that was being held out to her. Her mother called her impatiently, holding the door open, and it was only when they were out on the sidewalk that she saw what her daughter was holding: a polyhedron made by folding a little paper napkin.

JUNE 12, 2011

God's Tea Party

I

ACCORDING TO AN OLD AND IMMUTABLE TRADITION IN the Universe, God celebrates His birthday with a magnificent and lavish Tea Party, to which only the apes are invited. Nobody knows or could know, in those timeless regions, when this custom began, but it has become a fixture in the great year of the All: it seems that the patiently anticipated day will never come, but come it does, precisely on time, and the Tea Party takes place. It is said, plausibly enough, that the original reason for the ceremony was negative: the idea was not so much to invite apes as to not invite humans. Apes are a sarcastic joke, a kind of deliberate and spiteful (or, at best, ironic) slight on the part of the Lord, aimed at a human race that has disappointed Him. It may well have begun like that. But as soon as the arrangement was in place, it was accepted as an ancestral tradition, without a clear meaning, but saved from blatant absurdity by the hefty weight of precedent.

Traditions cannot be separated from the societies that created them. A community's traditions function like a sympathetic nervous system. They tend to be rather irrational, because their historical components were produced by an intricate web of causes that not even the most careful study would be able to disentangle. The case of God's Tea Party, however, should be simpler, because it's a tradition of the Universe, so there was nothing particular or historical about its origin; instead of a causal network, there was the gong of the absolute, no less. Yet, whether simple or difficult to grasp, its origin and reason for being remain obscure, perhaps just because the theologians never took the ceremony seriously, or were afraid of compromising their reputations by attending to something so grotesquely silly.

Nevertheless, to clarify, it can be said that it's not a natural occurrence like the spring thaw or an eclipse or the migration of ducks. It's a social event. It doesn't have to happen, should the Master of the house decide that He doesn't feel like having a Tea Party. Up until now, the custom has been observed and will, most likely, continue for all eternity. Even He respects the old established traditions, perhaps simply out of habit.

Like every social occasion, this one has its formalities. The first, which is really a sine qua non, is the issuing and distribution of the invitations. (This too could be different. Were the judgment to be rescinded or the sentence commuted one day, the guests might be human.) The invitations, addressed "To

Evolution," are automatically transmitted to the ape's instincts, like the sound of a doorbell. They are sent out all at once, en masse, and the operation may consist of no more than the divine enunciation of the word "apes." That is enough for all concerned to know that the day has arrived.

But what day is it? When does the uncreated Creator celebrate His birthday? Any time at all. It could be today. Except that "today" could be a lapse of countless eons or a slice of a microsecond—it depends what plane you're on—since His universe is a puzzle of days, hours, months, and centuries, all of different shapes and sizes, locked together in a polyhedron without end, on whose faces dawns and midnights, emptiness and plenitude, ends and beginnings coexist. Naturally, He who created time has the right to celebrate His birthday if He so desires. All the same, "God's birthday" has an odd ring to it, and the slight surprise provoked by the expression is the reason why the whole thing is so odd.

II

MORE THAN ODD, IMPOSSIBLE: A FIVE O'CLOCK TEA IMpossibly happening outside of time, in a realm of pure fantastic invention. Were a witness present, he'd see a sheer frenzy of senseless movement. The apes can't keep still. They leap up and down as if possessed, on their own chairs and those of the others. Incapable of staying put, after barely a moment in one place, they're looking for somewhere new. They squeeze in wherever they can, and there's always a space, because the others keep shifting too. They are possessed, truly possessed, by an enthusiasm without object, as if they knew that, just for a while, eternity was theirs to play havoc in, and were determined not to waste the opportunity. With their giddy diagonal leaps across the table, they knock over cups, send the spoons and forks flying; their stamping feet scatter the pastries, their tails swipe at the cream-laden cakes and come away spotted with white. What do they care! Their faces, hands, and chests are sticky with cake, tea, crumbs, and chocolate. The cups of fine porcelain implode in their clumsy grips, and to counteract the scalding tea they splash themselves with cold milk. They're constantly fighting; there's always some pretext, and if they can't find one they go ahead and fight all the same. Sometimes it looks like a battlefield: they bombard one another with sugar cubes, spit marmalade, hurl trays of scones. Inevitably one of them rises above the melee by swinging from the chandelier, until he gets distracted, lets go, and comes crashing down in the middle of the table, devastating the china and scattering the confectionery. And how they scream! The racket is so deafening, a fire truck's siren would be inaudible.

Exercising His omnipotence, God pours tea into all the cups at once. And while He's at it, He repairs some of the breakages. In a circus like this, of course, His good intentions only aggravate the chaos, giving it a velocity it wouldn't have in the natural order of causes and effects. The cataclysm becomes as inextricable as a tangled-up thread a million light years long.

And yet it's as if there were an order of ceremony, because every time God has a Tea Party, the same things happen. Every leap, every stain on the tablecloth, the trajectory of every slice of strawberry tart thrown from one end of the table to the other, exactly repeats what happened the time before and anticipates what will happen next time. The whole thing is identical. But there's really no reason to be amazed, because, after all, every event is identical to itself.

This identity explains why the party is repeated over and over. Without it, God may well have decided not to invite the apes to tea again, having seen what an awful mess they can make and just how badly they can behave. But yielding the initiative to the automaticity of the same takes all the risk out of repetition. The bad manners of the guests become a given configuration of reality, like a landscape. Nonetheless, the question of whether manners are subject to evolution does arise. Detached one by one from the apocalyptic block in which they manifest themselves at God's Tea Party, and isolated like signs, perhaps they could develop, becoming part of a story, and after a great many centuries or millennia, we would arrive at a divine, unprecedented spectacle: a gathering of apes sitting quietly around a table, lifting their teacups in one hand, their little fingers pointing at the surrounding void, dabbing at the corners of their mouths with napkins, perfectly demure and genteel.

III

THE PROBLEM OF THE BAD BEHAVIOR MIGHT BE DUE TO the fact that God doesn't preside. Or rather, He does and He doesn't. As we know, God is omnipresent, which turns out to be very handy for carrying out His functions, but it has the drawback of preventing Him from being visibly present in a particular place, for example sitting at the head of the table, keeping things under control. His absence (if His omnipresence can be counted as an absence) could be regarded as a discourtesy that legitimates all the subsequent discourtesies of his guests: a host who fails to turn up to his own party thereby authorizes his guests to behave as they like (this is the household version of the well-known saying "If God does not exist, everything is allowed.") But taking a wider view should allow us to see that His behavior is the transcendental form of the solicitude that characterizes the perfect host, who "thinks of everything" in order to guarantee the well-being of his guests, ensuring that plates, cups, and glasses are never left empty, all the provisions are of the finest quality, sweet and savory, hot and cold are balanced, the lighting and the temperature are just right, the tablecloth is well ironed and doesn't smell of mothballs, and the conversation never languishes or strays toward inappropriate topics. There are so many details to attend to! Only God could keep track of them all.

By making an appearance He could put a stop to the uproar, but if He were to be in one place He would cease to be in others and would thus betray His essence. So one of the apes stands in for Him. This King of the Apes is a legendary personage. Nobody believes in his real existence, for good reason: he exists only for the duration of God's Tea Party. He does what God would do were He to take a fleshly form, but he does it as the misshapen caricature that he is. Standing on the chair at the head of the table, frantic and raucous, intoxicated by his own impatient and capricious majesty, he distributes punches and kicks, yells his head off, hurls everything within his reach, and in his determination to impose order ends up being the most disorderly of all. Sometimes he is so maddened by his own energy that he is the one who starts a new brawl or launches a new campaign of destruction, which he then insists on quashing with renewed violence. The other apes, displaying an atavistic respect that seems to have been instilled in them by the light of divine reason, refrain from challenging the king's authority (not that it has much effect on their behavior). Indeed, if Supreme Command is diffusely present everywhere, it follows that it must be present in the King of the Apes, and it could even be argued that, while remaining evenly distributed, it is, in a sense, more present in him than elsewhere. However mechanically or automatically God's representative is designated, a Will is involved, and Will is beyond the reach of calculation and conjecture.

The king is the one who shouts the most, and who shouts the loudest. He prefigures the invention of the loudspeaker. He would like to have a thousand arms, so he could slap all the guests at the same time. Still, he manages pretty well with the two he has by leaping about unpredictably and keeping on the move. Apes are naturally endowed with exceptional agility, but he surpasses his physical limits. It's as if he were pure mind, and his mind is twisted and perverse, bitter and sadistic, sick with power. Like so many others, "he thinks he's God." He persecutes the slowest and most vulnerable apes, and especially the timid ones, at the bottom of the pile; he sprays lemon juice in their eyes, dips their fingertips into the boiling tea, plugs their ears with candy and their noses with marmalade, pushes silver spoons into their anuses ... In the breaks, he downs gallons of tea, to fuel his causeless fury. There must be something in that tea.

IV

ON ONE OCCASION A CURIOUS BEING INTERRUPTED God's famous Tea Party. As a rule, people who join a gathering to which they have not been invited try to go unnoticed; they don't draw attention to themselves; they keep a low profile and try to blend in. That's the interloper's logic. It doesn't always work, and some adopt the opposite strategy: assuming they'll be found out sooner or later, they decide to make it sooner and justify their presence by being "the life of the party."

In this case, the intruder apparently chose the first approach, for which she was unsurpassably equipped by her natural attributes. For a start, she couldn't have been smaller, because she was a subatomic particle. One of those pieces of a part of an atom that were left over when the Universe was formed and have been floating about ever since. To her the Void and the All were one; she roamed them both, in free fall, idle and unattached.

Millions of galaxies had seen her go by; or hadn't, but she'd gone by all the same. A well-informed observer would have been able to recognize her as an archaeological trace of the dimensions that had ceased to exist, or one of time's wandering milestones, or a messenger from the origin. Her tiny little body, on which not even the finest brush could have inscribed a single letter, nonetheless contained a long history. The most advanced cyclotrons would have been required to decipher that diminutive hieroglyph, but the eminent scientists who operated those costly instruments were busy with more important and beneficial projects. In any case, it would have been hard for them to capture or even locate her, because there were no maps showing her trajectory, and she didn't draw attention to herself. Discreet to the point of stealth, she slipped away quietly; before she'd finished arriving she was gone. She was there and not there.

The same was true of her path. It couldn't really be called capricious because all things obey the laws according to which they were created, but when a thing is as small as she was, literally off the scale (when, that is, it exists on a plane that is prior to measurement), there's no predicting which way it will go, or when. To give an idea of her size (although it's an inconceivable idea), if you took as many of those particles as there are atoms in the Universe and stuck them together, they still wouldn't make up the volume of an atom.

This intensified tininess gave her a quality that would have been extraordinary in a normal-size being: she didn't need to change course and never bumped into anything because she went right through whatever happened to be in her way. It would be misleading to liken this to a bullet's trajectory because she made no holes; she didn't need to. From her point of view, solid bodies were not solid. The atoms of a stone, which to us seem so tightly packed, were, for her, as far apart as the sun and the moon. So she glided through a meteorite of nickel and iron as a bird crosses the blue sky on a spring morning. She traversed a planet without even noticing. With the same oblivious fluidity, she passed through an atom. Or a sheet of paper, a flower, a boat, a dog, a brain, a hair.

For the particle, there was no such thing as a closed door. So to find her appearing (as it were) at a party to which she hadn't been invited, or at all the parties, could hardly come as a surprise. She was the prototypical interloper. Her gate-crashing was systematic, unstoppable, and supremely elegant. So many might have envied her! All the outcasts, the embittered, the paranoiacs, eaten up by jealousy, left at home alone while the others gather to enjoy themselves in the glittering salons of the Universe. But the envious would have had to consider the price the particle was paying: diminution, insignificance. Was it worth it, under those conditions?

V

AND EVEN GRANTING THAT NO SPACE WAS EXEMPT from the little wanderer's intrusions, it's still hard to accept that she could have snuck into the most exclusive gathering of all: God's Tea Party, the legendary party held to celebrate His birthday. It was a bit too much, even for her. Not just because the whole point of the gathering was to exclude the uninvited, but also because it was governed by an absolute. It was, in other words, a kind of fiction or artistic construction, and as a result each of its details, whether big or small, subtle or crude, had to correspond to a meaning or an intention. And the particle was not a detail in a story; she didn't contribute any information or advance the plot: she was an accident and nothing more.

On the other hand, it was bound to happen. Because the particle was one of a countless multitude, falling through the Universe. That's why it's called a "rain of particles," and although the analogy is misleading (this "rain" is falling in all directions, and never ends, and doesn't wet things), it does at least quash any hopes of detailed monitoring, because even the briefest local shower is composed of more drops than anyone could count, let alone name. And since these particles are so numerous and intrusive, why should it be surprising to find one passing through the scene of God's Tea Party?

Perhaps it wasn't an exception. It hasn't occurred to anyone to look into this question systematically, but it's entirely possible that particles are attracted by parties. Why would that be

strange? Or to put it the other way around: parties may well
be a natural sieve for particles. (The resemblance between the
words is not a mere coincidence.)

Coquettishly, the particle identified as a geometric point,
which meant that her manifestation in reality was linear, because over time a point will always trace a line. And since a
line is the intersection of an infinity of planes inclined at different angles, when this line entered God's Tea Party, something
like a windmill of superfine screens appeared, screens tilted at
various, changing angles, over which the apes went slipping
and sliding, tumbling over and getting up, finding themselves
somewhere else altogether, climbing a slope only to realize that
they were actually descending, or whizzing down a slide that, to
their surprise, was going up. Since there were so many planes, it
was very rare for two apes to be on the same one, which didn't
stop them fighting—on the contrary. Their leaps became mul-
tidimensional, as if they wanted to jump through spaces that
space did not contain. Suddenly they would discover that the
floor beneath their hairy feet was also beneath the feet of an
ape on the other side, defying the law of gravity. Or the space
across which they stretched their extralong arms, reaching for a
profiterole, was narrowed by the pressing in of two spaces from
neighboring planes, squeezing the arm into a superthin ribbon.
Or the tea they spilled flowed upward, downward, sideways,
backward, and forward, like a thousand-pointed liquid star.
All this intensified their silliness and drove them crazy; they
treated the phenomenon as a theme park specially built for

their amusement, and that's when chaos *really* began to reign. They started moving like wonky robots loaded with explosives. They jumped in all directions, put their hands and feet in the tea and their tails in the pompoms of Chantilly cream on the cakes; they yelled as if competing in a noise contest, choked, vomited, and crawled under the tablecloth, sending the dishes flying, as you can imagine.

It was amazing that such a tiny being could produce such far-reaching effects. The particle seemed to be everywhere at once, although, of course, she wasn't. At each moment she was in one place only, but present there as a cause, so her effects were simultaneously present in many other places, and while they were still being produced, she was already generating new planes and scrambling the apes into new configurations. The size of a cause doesn't matter: a cause is a cause, whether big, medium, or small. Even when it's the cause of madness.

VI

WITH ITS BAROQUE LAYERING OF NECESSARY ACCI-dents and accidental necessities, the Tea Party was, it seemed, complete both as an event and as a symbol. The birthday was duly celebrated, and rather than passing unnoticed, the date was marked, if not with the ecclesiastical pomp that might have been expected, at least with the animal (not to say bestial) energy and joy of the primitive and the authentic.

But, driven on by an obsessive perfectionism appropriate to His status and function, God wanted to add one last stitch, or sew on a final button, and tie off the end of the thread. He still had to give the particle an origin. He had to make her come from somewhere. Or, to put it more precisely, he had "to make her *have* come from somewhere." This was a preliminary task, which should come as no surprise, since all God's tasks are preliminary; otherwise, the completeness of His world would be compromised. It wasn't a problem, given His habitually bold approach to space and time. The problem came afterward, as we shall see, not that it was really a problem (partly because for Him *before* and *after* had no meaning).

God's Tea Party would have been incomplete without the story of the particle. Because the Party was a story, and every story is made up of stories, and if it's made up of anything else it ceases to be a story. We will never know whether it was a weakness on God's part, one of those forgivable little vanities, or a matter of logic, but He dearly wanted the birthday party to make a good story, a "once upon a time," every repetition of which would be a perfectly accomplished rehearsal. He couldn't allow the anonymity of the furtive interloper to spoil everything.

The nature of the object meant that his work was already half done: it couldn't be hard to find the origin of a particle because the word itself indicated that it was part of something. All He had to do was find that something, or invent it. God had made far more arcane discoveries, in the course of His long career. How many times had He found a needle in a haystack, just to satisfy His creatures' appetite for metaphors or proverbs!

In this case, it could have been anything, literally, and more than literally: the particle could have come not only from a material object but also from an event, a lapse of time, an intention, a thought, a passion, a wave, a form … By virtue of its size, it belonged in the primordial roundabout, from which the paths of mass and energy depart, with their respective mutual metamorphoses. The particles were at the heart of the action. Which didn't mean that the origin of this one in particular had to be sought exclusively at the beginning: she could have emanated from any state of the Universe, even the most recent. The infinitesimal birth of that nosy little globule could have taken place in a flare from the surface of Alpha Centauri or a pan used to fry a dove's egg in China, in a child's tear or the curvature of space, in hydrogen, blotting paper, a desire for revenge, a cube root, Lord Cavendish, a hair, or the unicorn … The catalog that God had to flick through, so to speak, was inordinately long. Not for the first time, it was borne home to Him that omnipotence is limited by *l'embarras du choix*. Words were his only guides in that great chaotic enumeration. At bottom, it was a question of language. There weren't any things in reality, only words, words that cut the world into pieces, which people end up taking for things. God didn't need to use words Himself, but when He had to intervene, when, as in this case, He wanted to imprint something on human memory, He had no choice but to take part in the linguistic game. He regarded it as a challenge.

It was quite a bit harder for Him than it would have been for a grammar teacher, because He had to consider all languages, living, dead, and potential (each of them carved the world up differently, and, viewed from above, their coincidences, divergences, and overlaps formed a superintricate patchwork).

Cutting to the chase: it has taken longer to formulate the problem than He took to solve it. As if He'd pressed a button, the particle had her birth certificate, which also served as an invitation to the party, to which she would return for her debut. And here, the Creator made an exception: He who keeps no secrets kept one on this occasion. He didn't tell anyone what He had chosen as the particle's origin. And that, ever since, has been the profound little mystery that runs through God's Tea Party.

The Musical Brain

I WAS A KID — I WOULD HAVE BEEN FOUR OR FIVE YEARS old. This was in my hometown, Coronel Pringles, at the beginning of the 1950s. One night, it must have been a Saturday, we'd gone to have dinner at the hotel; we didn't eat out often, not that we were really poor, though we lived pretty much as if we were because of my father's austere habits and my mother's invincible suspicion of any food she hadn't prepared herself. Some obscure combination of circumstances had brought us to the hotel's luxurious restaurant that night and seated us, stiffly and uncomfortably, around a table covered with a white cloth and laden with silver cutlery, tall wineglasses, and gold-rimmed porcelain dishes. We were dressed up to the nines, like all the other diners. The dress codes in those days were relatively strict.

I remember the continual to-and-fro of people getting up and carrying boxes full of books to a small table like an altar at the far end of the room. Most of them were cardboard boxes, though there were wooden boxes too, and some were even painted or varnished. Sitting behind the table was a little woman wearing a shiny blue dress and a pearl necklace, with a powdered face and white hair combed into the shape of a feathery egg. It was Sarita Subercaseaux, who later on, throughout my time there, was the high school's headmistress. She took the boxes and examined their contents, making notes in a record book. I was following all this activity with the keenest attention. Some of the boxes were too full to be properly closed, others were half empty, with only a few books knocking around inside, making an ominous sound. Yet it wasn't so much the quantity of books that determined the value of the boxes, though quantity did matter, as the variety of titles. The ideal box would have been one in which all the books were different; the worst (and this was the most frequent case), a box containing nothing but copies of the same book. I don't know who explained this rule to me, maybe it was the product of my own speculations and fantasies. That would have been typical: I was always inventing stories and schemes to make sense of things I didn't understand, and I understood almost nothing. Anyway, where else could the explanation have come from? My parents weren't very communicative, I couldn't read, there was no television, and the kids in my gang of neighborhood friends were as ignorant as I was.

Seen from a distance, there's something dreamlike about this scene with the boxes of books, and the way we're dressed up as if for a photo. But I'm sure that it happened as I've described it. It's a scene that has kept coming back to me over the years, and in the end I've worked out a reasonable explanation. Plans must have been afoot at the time to set up the Pringles Public Library, and someone must have organized a book drive, with the support of the hotel's proprietors: "a dinner for a book," or something along those lines. That's plausible, at least. And it's true that the library was founded around that time, as I was able to confirm on my most recent visit to Pringles a few months ago. Sarita Subercaseaux, moreover, was the first Head Librarian. During my childhood and adolescence, I was one of the library's most assiduous patrons, probably the most assiduous of all, borrowing books at a rate of one or two a day. And it was always Sarita who filled out my card. This turned out to be crucial when I began high school, since she was the headmistress. She spread the word that in spite of my tender years I was the most voracious reader in Pringles, which established my reputation as a prodigy and simplified my life enormously: I graduated with excellent grades, without having studied at all.

During my most recent visit to Pringles, hoping to confirm my memories, I asked my mother if Sarita Subercaseaux was still alive. She burst out laughing.

"She died years and years ago!" Mom said. "She died before you were born. She was already old when I was a girl . . ."

"That's impossible!" I exclaimed. "I remember her very clearly. In the library, at school . . ."

"Yes, she worked at the library and the high school, but before I was married. You must be getting mixed up, remembering things I told you."

That was all I could get out of her. I was unsettled by her certainty, especially because her memory, unlike mine, is infallible. Whenever we disagree about something that happened in the past, she invariably turns out to be right. But how could she be right about this? Perhaps I was remembering Sarita Subercaseaux's daughter, a daughter who as well as being the spitting image of her mother had followed in her footsteps. But that was impossible. Sarita had gone to her grave unmarried and she was the archetype of the unmarried woman, the town's classic old maid: always meticulously groomed; cool and remote, the very image of sterility. I was quite sure of that.

Getting back to the hotel. The movement between the tables in the restaurant and the little altar where the boxes were piling up was not entirely fluid. Everyone there knew everyone else — that's how it was in Pringles — so when people got up from their tables to take their boxes to the far end of the room, they stopped at other tables on the way to greet and chat with their acquaintances. The acquaintances were careful not to talk too much, politely supposing that the people who had stopped were carrying boxes of considerable weight (even if the contents were, in fact, woefully meager). The carriers, in turn, responded more politely still by chatting on, making it clear that the pleasure of the conversation amply compensated for the effort of bearing the weight. These little transactions, informed as they were by a sincere curiosity about the lives of others, which was common to all the inhabitants of Pringles, turned out to be rich in information, and that is how we learned that the Musical Brain was being exhibited next door, in the lobby of the Spanish Theater. Otherwise, we probably wouldn't have known, and would simply have gone home to bed. The news was an excuse to finish with the dinner, which all of us were finding tedious.

   The Musical Brain had appeared in town some time earlier, and an informal association of residents had taken charge of it. The original plan had been to lend it out to private homes, for short periods, following a procedure that had been used with various miraculous images of the Virgin. Requests for those images had come from people with illnesses or family problems, while the reason for borrowing this new magical device was sheer curiosity (although perhaps there was also a touch of superstition). Since the association had no religious framework, and no authority to regulate the rotation, it was impossible to stick to a schedule. On the one hand, there were those who tried to get rid of the Brain after the first night, with the excuse that the music kept them awake; on the other hand, there were those who built elaborate niches and pedestals, and then tried to use their expenses as a pretext for prolonging the loan indefinitely. The association soon lost track of where the Brain was, and those who, like us, had never seen it came to suspect that the whole thing was a hoax. That's why we were overcome by impatience when we found out that it was on display just next door.

   Dad asked for the bill, and when it came he reached into his pocket and took out his famous wallet, for me the most fascinating object in the world. It was very large and made of green leather, marvelously embossed with complex arabesques, the back and front adorned with glass beads that composed colorful scenes. It had belonged to Pushkin, who, according to the legend, was carrying it in his pocket the day he was killed. One of my father's uncles had been an ambassador in Russia at the beginning of the century and had bought many works of art, antiquities, and curiosities there, which his widow had distributed among her nephews and nieces after his death, since the couple had no children of their own.

The Spanish Theater, which was part of a complex belonging to the Spanish Provident Society, abutted the hotel. And yet we didn't go straight there. We crossed the street to where the truck was parked, walked around it, and then crossed back. This detour was for my mother's benefit: she didn't want the diners at the hotel, in the unlikely event that they should look out of the windows and actually be able to see something, to suppose that she was going to the theater.

We walked into the lobby, and there it was, placed on a box, an ordinary wooden one that Cereseto (the manager of the theater) had disguised with strips of shredded white paper, the kind used for packing. The presentation was quite effective: it was like a big nest, and suggested both the fragility of eggs and that of objects packed with care. The famous Musical Brain was made of cardboard and it was the size of a trunk. It resembled a brain quite closely in shape, but not in color, because it was painted phosphorescent pink and crisscrossed with blue veins.

We formed a semicircle. It was one of those things that leaves you at a loss for words. Mom's voice interrupted our rapt contemplation.

"What about the music?" she asked.

"Yes, of course!" Dad said. "The music …" He frowned and leaned forward.

"Maybe it's switched off?"

"No, it's never switched off, that's what so strange about it."

He leaned farther forward, so far that I thought he'd fall onto the Brain, then stopped suddenly and turned to look at us with a conspiratorial grin.

My sister and I came closer. Mom shouted, "Don't touch it!"

I felt an overwhelming desire to touch it, if only with a fingertip. And I could have too. We were completely alone in the lobby. The ticket vendor and the usher must have been in the theater, watching the play, which seemed to be nearing its end.

"How could you hear it, with all this racket!" Mom said.

"It's barely a whisper. To think that people give it back because they find the noise annoying! It's a disgrace!"

Mom nodded, but she was thinking of a different disgrace. Dad was enthralled by the Brain—he was the only one who'd heard its music—while Mom was looking around and seemed more interested in what was happening in the theater. Thunderous laughter was coming from inside, shaking the whole building. It must have been a full house. Leonor Rinaldi, Tomás Simari, and their troupe were performing one of those vulgar, broad comedies that used to tour the provinces for years on end; people never seemed to tire of laughing at them. The secret, tremulous music supposedly emanating from the Brain could hardly compete with all the guffaws and stomping.

My mother, proud heir to a line of sophisticated music lovers, reciters, and tragedians, disdained those products of popular taste epitomized by Leonor Rinaldi. Indeed, she actively campaigned against them. The theater, for her, was disputed territory, a battlefield, because it was there that the classes of Pringles waged their cultural wars. Her brother directed an amateur dramatic society called The Two Masks, which was devoted to serious theater; the town's other club, directed by Isolina Mariani, specialized in comedies of manners. All of Isolina Mariani's devotees must have been in the stalls that night, keen to learn, admiring Leonor Rinaldi's demagogic stagecraft, absorbing her mannerisms like an invigorating syrup.

Mom's aversion was so extreme that on several occasions, when one of those popular companies was coming to town, she made us have dinner early, then drove us to the theater just as the play was about to start and parked the truck near the entrance (but not too close, choosing a place hidden in the shadows), so that she could check on who was going in. Usually there were no surprises: the audience was made up of poor people from the outer suburbs, "the great unwashed" as my mother used to call them, hardly worth a dismissive remark such as "What can you expect of ignorant fools like that?"

But occasionally there was someone "respectable" among them, and then she became zealous. She felt that her spying had been worthwhile, and that from now on she'd "know the score" when dealing with certain cultural hypocrites. Once, she went so far as to get out of the truck and rebuke a cultivated dentist who was climbing the steps of the theater with his daughters. She told him how disappointed she was to see him there. Wasn't he ashamed to be supporting that vulgarity? And bringing his daughters! Was that his idea of education? Luckily, he didn't take her too seriously. He replied, with a smile, that for him theater was sacred, even in its most debased forms, and that his primary objective was to expose his daughters to popular culture at its crudest in order to give them some perspective. Needless to say, his arguments made no impression on Mom.

Anyway. To return to the memorable evening of our encounter with the Musical Brain. We got into the truck and off we went. We had a yellow Ika pickup. Although the four of us could fit in the front, I usually sat in the back, in the open air, partly because I liked it, partly to keep the peace—I was always getting into noisy fights with my sister—but mainly so that I could spend some time with my good friend Geniol, the family dog. Geniol was very big and white, of indeterminate breed, and he had a large head (like the man in the Geniol ads, hence the name). We couldn't leave him home alone because he howled and made such a racket the neighbors complained. But in the back of the truck he was well behaved.

There was also a more arcane reason why I liked to travel in the back: since I couldn't hear what they were saying in front, it meant I didn't know where we were going, and the itinerary would take on an unpredictable air of adventure. I knew where we were going when we set out, if I'd been paying attention, but as soon as Mom climbed into the truck she was bound to be overcome by a sudden curiosity and ask Dad to make a detour down one street or another so she could see a house, a store, a tree, or a sign. He was in the habit of humoring her, which meant that instead of going a few hundred yards in a straight line, we'd often end up driving five miles, following a tortuous, labyrinthine route. For my mother, who had never left Pringles, it was a way of expanding the town from within.

That night, all we had to do was turn the corner and go three blocks to our house. But we turned the other way, which didn't surprise me. It was very cold, but there was no wind. The street lights at the intersections, suspended by four diagonal wires attached to the posts on the corners, were still. And, above us, the Milky Way was all lit up and full of winks. I settled Geniol on my legs and hugged him to my chest. He didn't resist. His snow-white fur reflected the starlight. We continued straight ahead to the square and then took the boulevard. Sitting with my back against the cab, I could see the square tower of the city hall receding into the distance and I assumed that we were heading for the station, to satisfy one of Mom's whims. The station was far away, and the mere supposition that we were going there made me drowsy. Geniol had already fallen asleep. A few blocks down the boulevard, the buildings began to thin out, giving way to big vacant lots taken over by mallows and thistles. Those mysterious plots belonged to no one. My eyes were beginning to close ...

Suddenly Geniol shook himself, jumped off my lap, went to one side of the truck and growled. His agitation startled and bewildered me. Struggling free of the muddle of sleep, I looked too, and understood why we'd made the detour, and why Dad was slowing down now, bringing the truck almost to a standstill: we were passing the circus. My sister was leaning out the window in front and yelling in her half-articulate way, "César! The circus! The circus!" I knew, of course, that a circus had come to town; I'd seen the parades in the streets, and our parents had already promised to take us the following day. I stared, entranced. Points and lines of bright light showed through the canvas of the marquee, which seemed as big as a mountain, and the whole thing glowed with the light inside. A performance was under way: we could hear blaring music and the cries of the audience. The smell of the animals had made Geniol nervous. Behind the marquee, in the darkness, I thought I could see the silhouettes of elephants and camels moving among the wagons.

Many years later, I left Pringles, as young people with artistic or literary inclinations often leave small towns, hungry for the cultural offerings promised by the capital. And now, many years after that emigration, it strikes me that perhaps I was lured away by a mirage, because nights from my childhood in Pringles come back to me, each so vivid and manifold, that I can't help wondering if I didn't exchange riches for poverty. The night I am reconstructing is a good example: a book drive, a theatrical performance, and a circus, all at the same time. There was a range of options to choose from, and you had to choose. And yet there were capacity crowds everywhere. The circus was no exception. As we drove past the entrance, we had a brief glimpse of the boxes crammed with families and the stands groaning under the weight of the spectators. In the ring, the clowns had built a human pyramid, which came tumbling down, provoking roars of laughter. Almost everyone was at the circus. The inhabitants of Pringles must have thought it was the safest place.

Here an explanation is required. The circus had come to town three days earlier, and almost immediately the troupe had been rocked by a tremendous scandal. Among the attractions were three dwarfs. Two were men: twin brothers. The third, a woman, was married to one of the twins. This peculiar triangle apparently had a defect that made it unstable and led to the crisis that occurred in Pringles. The woman and her brother-in-law were lovers, and for some reason they had chosen our town as the place in which to make off with the savings of the cuckolded husband. We might never have been aware of this bizarre intrigue if it weren't for the fact that a few hours after the disappearance of the lovers, the husband vanished too, along with a 9mm pistol and a box of bullets belonging to the owner of the circus. His intentions could not have been clearer. The police were notified immediately, in the hope of averting a tragedy. The witnesses (clowns, trapeze artists, and animal trainers) all agreed on how furious the husband had been when he found out, and how determined he was to exact a bloody revenge. His threats were taken seriously, because he was a violent little man, known for his destructive fits of rage. The weapon he had stolen was lethal at close and long range, and there was no need to know how to use it. The police mobilized all available manpower, and in spite of the circus authorities' vehement insistence on discretion, the news got around. It was unavoidable, because the whereabouts of the runaways—that is, both the lovers and their pursuer—could be discovered only with the help of the public. At first, it seemed a simple task: the town was small and it was easy to give a clear description of the individuals in question, simply by using the word "dwarf." Police officers were positioned at the railway station, the long-distance bus terminal, and the two roundabouts at opposite ends of the town, from which the outgoing roads diverged (they were unsealed at the time). These measures served only to confirm that the dwarfs were still in Pringles.

Not surprisingly, they were the sole topic of conversation. What with the joking, the betting, and the collective searching of vacant lots and empty houses, the prevailing mood had initially been one of cheerful agitation and delicious suspense. Twenty-four hours later, the atmosphere had changed. Two fears had begun to creep in, one vague and superstitious, the other very real. The first arose from the fact that the case remained perplexingly unsolved. With ample justification, the inhabitants of Pringles had assumed that the town was socially and geographically transparent. How could something as conspicuous as three dwarfs go unnoticed in that tiny glass box? Especially since the dwarfs did not compose a single mass, but were split into a hiding pair and a third individual in pursuit, hiding in turn from the authorities. The episode began to take on a supernatural coloring. The dimensions of a dwarf turned out to be problematic, at least for the unsettled collective imagination. Perhaps they should have been turning over stones, examining the undersides of leaves, peering into cocoons? Mothers started looking under their children's beds, and children took their toys apart to check inside.

But there was a more realistic fear. Or, if not entirely realistic, it was at least presented as such to rationalize the other one, the fear without a name. Somewhere out there was a deadly loaded gun, in the hands of a desperate man. No one was worried about him carrying out his plan (and this can be explained without accusing the inhabitants of Pringles of being especially prejudiced; caught up in the general panic, they regarded the dwarfs as a species apart, whose lives and deaths were matters to be settled among themselves and were of no interest to the town), but shots do not always find their mark, and at a given moment anyone might happen to get in the way of a bullet. Anyone at all, because no one knew where the dwarfs were, much less where their encounter would take place. The source of the anxiety was not so much the husband's aim as the elusive tininess of the adulterers. The same fantastic miniaturization that accounted for the failure of the search led people to imagine that every shot was bound to miss. How could he hit a hidden atom, or two? Anybody, or their loved ones, could be cut down by a hail of stray bullets at any moment, anywhere.

Another twenty-four hours later, the two fears had become tightly intertwined, and the town had succumbed to an acute delirium of persecution. No one felt safe at home, still less in the street. But there was something reassuring about public gatherings, the bigger the better: other people could serve as human shields, and since altruistic scruples go out the window when terror reigns, no one spared a thought for those whose bodies would be riddled with bullets. That must have been why we'd gone out to dinner, something we virtually never did. And on another level of motivation, in the realm of magical thinking, it must have been why Dad had brought Pushkin's famous wallet, which he saved for special occasions. As you will remember, Pushkin was killed by a shot to the heart.

Here I close the explanatory parenthesis and return to the story. But in doing so, I notice that I have made a mistake. The action continues in the lobby of the theater, which means that the drive along the boulevard past the circus must have happened earlier, when we were on our way to the hotel. And in fact, when I think about it more carefully, it seems to me that the sky behind the city hall and above the circus tent was not entirely dark: it was the "blue hour," with some remnants of dusky pink, and a layer of phosphorescent white along the western horizon. The black starry sky must have been an interpolation, suggested by the hair-raising events that were to take place later, on the roof of the theater. My confusion may be due, in part, to the story's particular strangeness: although there is a compelling logic to the order in which the various episodes follow one another, they also exist independently, like the stars in the firmament that were the only witnesses to the final act, so the figures they compose may seem to owe more to fantasy than to reality.

It happened more or less like this: Having satisfied their curiosity about the Musical Brain, my parents headed for the street, partly because there was nothing more to see and partly to be gone before the audience started coming out of the theater. The performance must have been over; the applause hadn't stopped, but it couldn't go on for much longer, and Mom didn't want to be seen leaving along with "the great unwashed." People who didn't know better might think she had sunk to the cultural depths of the Peronists.

She turned and began to walk out in such a decisive manner that I felt the moment had come: it was safe now to indulge my desire to touch the large pink object. Without a second thought, I reached out. The tip of my right index finger touched the surface of the Brain for a bare fraction of a second. For reasons that will soon become clear, that momentary contact was something I would never forget.

My naughtiness escaped the notice of my parents, who went on walking toward the lobby doors, but not of my sister, who was two or three at the time, and imitated everything I did. Emboldened by my daring, she wanted to touch the Brain too. But, clumsy little devil that she was, she didn't go about it daintily. For her, there was no such thing as a fingertip. Drawing herself up to her full height—she was barely as tall as the box on which the Brain was sitting—she raised her little arms and pushed with all her might. Sensing what was about to happen, she held her breath, then released it in a scream as the Brain began to move. My parents stopped, and turned, and I think they took a step or two toward us. For me, the whole scene had taken on a phantasmagorical precision, like a play rehearsed a thousand times. The Musical Brain slid heavily over the edge of the box, fell to the floor, and broke.

My sister burst into tears, more upset by guilt and fear of

punishment than by the sight that had appeared before our eyes, which was probably beyond her powers of comprehension. I, however, was old enough to intuit what had happened, though struggling in the throes of a horrified confusion, which my parents must have shared.

The pink crust of the Musical Brain had shattered on impact, a sign of its fragility, since it had fallen only a few feet. Inside was a solid, glassy mass, like gelatin, perfectly molded by the shell. A certain flattening, and perhaps a certain wobble from the aftershock (though I may have imagined this), suggested that the substance wasn't hard. The color was unequivocal. It was semi-coagulated blood, and it wasn't hard to figure out its origin, or origins, because two dead bodies were suspended in the middle of the mass, in fetal position, head to toe: the male dwarfs, the twins. They were like playing-card images, dressed in their little black suits, faces and hands as white as porcelain; the color contrast made them visible through the dark red of the blood, which had escaped from wounds in both throats like open, screaming mouths.

I said that I saw this scene with supernatural clarity and that is how I see it now. I see more now than I did then. It's as if I were seeing the story itself, not as a film or a sequence of images, but as a single picture, transforming itself by freezing repeatedly rather than by moving. And yet there was plenty of movement: it was a whirl, an abyss of irrational atoms.

Mom, who was prone to hysteria, started screaming, but her screams were drowned out by a sudden uproar coming from

the theater. Something unexpected was happening. The great
Leonor Rinaldi had already received her ovation, and the cast
had taken seven curtain calls. The actors were about to walk off
after the final bow, and the members of the audience were already rising from their seats. At that moment, as the characters
began to fade from the skins of the actors, who were standing
all together in a line across the stage, each face and body still
identifiable as a part of the comedy, but a comedy whose plot,
with its surprises and errors, was jumbled in that row of smiling, bowing figures, as if it were up to the spectators now, as
they clapped and ran their eyes along the line, to recompose
the story and bid it farewell as the fiction it was, along with
the make-believe living-and-dining room, the armchairs, the
fake staircase, the painted windows, the doors that had opened
and closed in a cascade of comic revelations, and all the rest of
the set ... just then, as the festivities drew to a close, the large
plaster effigy of Juan Pascual Pringles that adorned the apex of
the proscenium arch burst open. The features of the founding
father exploded like a nova of chalk, and in their place the as-
tonished audience beheld the strangest creature ever produced
by a theatrical deus ex machina: the female dwarf. That had
been her hiding place, and no one would ever have found her.
It might have seemed accidental: perhaps the vibrations caused
by the clapping and the shouts of "Bravo!" had loosened the
aging molecules of the heroic grenadier's plaster head; but that
supposition soon had to be abandoned when it became clear
that the bursting of the effigy had been produced by an inter-

nal cause—namely, an increase in the size of the dwarf. Once impregnated, this killer chrysalis had withdrawn to a safe hiding place in order to allow nature (of which monsters are also a part, after all) to take its course. And, by chance, the process had reached completion just as the actors were about to walk off; a few minutes later and the creature would have emerged into a dark, empty theater.

As it happened, this provided an encore of a kind never witnessed before or since. Two thousand pairs of eyes saw a large head appear from the niche, a head without eyes, nose, or mouth, but crowned with curly blond hair, then two chubby arms ending in claws, and a pair of opulent pink breasts with eyes where the nipples should have been. The creature kept coming out, horizontally, up near the high roof, like a gargoyle ... until, with convulsive shudders, she freed her wings, first one, then the other—enormous iridescent membranes that made a sound like cardboard when they flapped—and was airborne. The rear part of her body was a bloated sac covered with black fur. At first, she seemed to be falling into the orchestra pit, but then she stabilized herself at medium altitude with a series of rapid wing-beats and began to fly around erratically.

Terror broke loose. A fire would not have caused as much panic as that flying mutant: there was no telling what she might do. The aisles were jammed, the exits blocked; people were jumping over the seats; mothers were looking for their children, husbands for their wives, and everyone was screaming. Frightened by the commotion, the dwarf flapped around aimlessly;

she, too, was looking for a way out. When she lost altitude, the screaming in the stalls intensified, and when she climbed again, the loudest cries came from the boxes, where spectators were trapped by the choked stairways. In desperation, some people climbed onto the stage, which the actors had already deserted. Some refugees from the front boxes also climbed down and crossed the semicircle of footlights. Noticing this, other members of the audience, who had been shoving their way down the aisles, but could see that it would be impossible to get through that chaotic human mass, turned, ran frantically back and leaped onto the stage. It was like breaking a taboo: invading the space of fiction, which is precisely what they had paid not to do; but the instinct for survival prevailed.

As for the winged dwarf, the giant dragonfly, after crossing the theater's airspace several times with her terrifying flap-flap, picking up speed, and repeatedly bumping into the ceiling and the walls, she too plunged toward the mouth of the stage, which was, after all, the most reasonable thing to do. She was swallowed by Leonor Rinaldi's bourgeois stage set, and all the drop scenes came tumbling down.

The audience finally fled the theater, but naturally no one wanted to go home. Calle Stegmann was seething with an agitated crowd. Diners came out of the hotel's restaurant, some with their napkins tucked into their collars, many still holding forks. The news had spread all around town; an unofficial messenger had taken it to the big top and arrived just as the show was ending, so the circus audience transferred itself en masse. When the police arrived, with sirens blaring, they had trouble making their way through the crowd, like the ambulance from the hospital, and the firefighters, who came on their own initiative.

Pouring out through the lobby, the crazed horde had thoughtlessly trampled the globe of blood. When the owner of the circus came to collect the bodies of the dwarfs, he was given two wrinkled silhouettes, which the clowns identified, handing them around. There hadn't been time for the clowns, or any of the other circus performers, to change out of their costumes. Riders, trapeze artists, and fakirs rubbed shoulders with actors from Leonor Rinaldi's company, and with Tomás Simari and la Rinaldi herself, and all mingling with the mingled audiences, not to mention curious onlookers, neighbors, and assorted night owls. There had never been anything like this, not even at carnival time.

The first search of the theater, conducted by the police with pistols drawn, and led by Cereseto (only he knew all the ins and outs), proved fruitless. The creature had disappeared again, wings and all. There was a rumor that she had found a way out and flown off. The hypothesis should have provided some relief, but people were disappointed. By now everyone was in the mood for a show, hanging out for more. Hopes were revived by an unexpected event: from the imposing mass of the theater countless bats and doves came flying out in all directions. Because doves don't usually fly at night, they gave this exodus a fantastic twist. Those little creatures had obviously sensed a monstrous presence and cleared out helter-skelter.

There was a moment of suspense, then a shout, a pointing hand. Every head rocked back, and all eyes converged on the pseudo-Gothic crenellations of the theater's facade. There, crouched between two turrets, was the monster, with her wings outstretched and her body seized by a tremor that was visible even at a distance. The fire truck's powerful spotlight lit her up. Down in the street, two of the clowns, with their motley costumes and painted smiles, climbed up on car hoods and waved the flattened bodies of the dwarfs over their heads, like banners.

Although the inhabitants of Pringles had never seen a mutant of this kind, they were mainly country folk, familiar with the principles of procreation. However odd the forms that nature's children take, the basic mechanisms of life are common to them all. So it was soon obvious to the crowd that the dwarf was about to "lay." All the signs pointed to a reproductive process: the sexual encounter, the period of seclusion to allow for the metamorphosis, the crimes, the enormous abdominal sac, the choice of an inaccessible place, and now the hunched posture, the air of concentration and the trembling. What no one could predict was whether she would lay one egg or two, or several, or millions. The last hypothesis seemed the most likely, because her closest morphological affinities were with the insect world. But when the furry silk of the sac began to split, what appeared was a single, white, pointed egg, the size of a watermelon. An enormous "Oohh ..." of wonder ran through the multitude. Perhaps because every gaze was fixed on the slow extrusion of that fantastic pearl, the surprise was all the greater when another figure appeared beside the winged dwarf: slowly it entered the circle of light, becoming entirely visible only when the egg had fully emerged and was balanced upright on that vertiginous cornice. It was Sarita Subercaseaux, with her big beehive hairdo, her pink, abundantly powdered face, her blue dress, and her little wedge-heeled shoes. How had she got up there? What was she trying to do? She was just inches from the creature who, having now finished her labor, turned her eyeless face to look, as it were, at Sarita. They were the same size, and both had the same aura of supernatural determination. A confrontation seemed inevitable, perhaps even a fight. The whole town held its breath. But something quite different happened. Shaking herself, as if waking from a dream, the creature stretched her wings as far as they would go, and, with a single flap, lifted herself a few yards into the air. With a wing-beat she turned, with another she began to pick up speed, and then she was flying, like a pterodactyl, toward the stars, which were shining like mad diamonds for the occasion. She disappeared among the constellations, and that was that. Only then did the gazes of the crowd return to the roof of the theater.

Sarita Subercaseaux was unperturbed by the departure of the mutant. Now she was alone with the egg. Moving very slowly, she raised one arm. She was holding something in her hand. An ax. Contradictory cries rose from the crowd. *No! Don't! Yes! Break it!* Opinion was, of course, divided. No one wanted to subject our quiet town on the pampas to the unforeseeable consequences of a monstrous birth, and there was something precious about the mere fragility of an egg. On the other hand, it seemed a pity to forego the possibilities offered by that unrepeatable occasion.

But when the movement of Sarita's arm brought the ax clearly into view, it turned out to be not an ax but a book. And her intention was not to break the egg but to balance the book on top of it, delicately. In the legendary history of Pringles, the curious figure thus produced has come to symbolize the founding of the Municipal Library.

JULY 26, 2004

A Thousand Drops

ONE DAY THE MONA LISA DISAPPEARED FROM THE LOU-
vre, provoking a public outcry, a national scandal, and a media
frenzy. It wasn't the first time: almost a hundred years earlier,
in 1911, a young Italian immigrant, Vincenzo Peruggia, who had
free access to the building because he was working there as a
painter and decorator, walked out with the masterpiece under
his workman's apron. He kept it hidden for two years in his garret, and in 1913 took it to Florence, with the intention of selling
it to the Uffizi gallery, justifying the robbery as a patriotic act,
the restitution of a national treasure. The police were waiting
for him, and the *Mona Lisa* returned to the Louvre, while the
thief, who by this stage was going by the name of Leonardo Peruggia, went to jail for a few years (he died in 1947).

This time it was worse, because what disappeared was the
painting, literally: the thin layer of oil paint that constituted
the famous masterpiece. The board underneath was still there,
and so was the frame, but the board was blank, as if it had never
been painted. They took it to a laboratory and subjected it to
all sorts of tests: there was no evidence that it had been scraped

or treated with acid or any other chemical; it was intact. The paint had evaporated. The only signs of force were a number of tiny, perfectly circular holes, a millimeter in diameter, in the reinforced glass case that separated the portrait from its viewers. These little holes were also examined, although there was nothing to examine; no traces of any substance were found, and no one could understand what kind of instrument could have been used to make them. This gave rise to journalistic speculation about extraterrestrials: some gelatinous creature, perhaps, that had applied a sucker equipped with perforating cilia, etc. The public is so gullible! So irrational. The real explanation was perfectly simple: the layer of paint had reverted to the state of live drops, and the droplets had set off to travel the world. After five centuries in a masterpiece, they were so full of energy that no sheet of glass, however well reinforced, was going to stop them. Nor could walls or mountains or seas or distances. The drops of color could go wherever they liked; they were endowed with superpowers. If the investigators had counted the little holes in the glass, they would have discovered how many there were: a thousand. But no one could be bothered to undertake that simple task; they were all too busy coming up with far-fetched and contradictory theories.

The drops scattered themselves over the five continents, eager for adventures, action, and experience. For a while, at the start, they stayed on the edges of daylight and toured the planet several times in the same direction, fanning out, moving at a range of speeds, some in the subtle grays of dawn, others in the passionate pinks of evening, many in the bustling mornings of the great cities or the drowsy siestas of the countryside, in the spring meadows or the autumn woods, in the polar ice fields or the burning deserts, or riding a little bee in a garden. Until one of them, by chance, discovered the depths of the night, and was followed by another, and another, and from then on there were no limits to their voyages and discoveries. When the urge to keep moving petered out, they were able to settle wherever they liked and display their inexhaustible creative ingenuity.

One ended up in Japan, where he set up a factory to make scented candles. They were called Minute Candles, and they smelled of Moon. Protected by strict patents and favored by the night, they were a huge success. Vast dance venues began to use Minute Candles, and so did temples, mountains, woods, and the whole realms of various shoguns. They were sold in boxes of six, twelve, twenty-four, and a thousand (everyone bought the boxes of a thousand). The multiplication of their little pink flames created a shadowless half light in which near and far, before and after were abolished. Not even the longest winter nights, it transpired, could hold so much intimacy. Drop San, rich as Croesus, had two geisha wives, who lugged around bundles of swords and performed dancing duels to entertain their husband. Absorbed in the study of ballistics, Drop San paid them less and less attention, and finally forgot all about them. Their reactions revealed a stark difference between the two girls, so similar in other ways that everyone got them mixed up. One remained faithful, and loved Drop San even more than when he had been attentive to her; the other looked elsewhere for the love she could no longer find at home. One was "forever," the other "while it lasts," and when she felt it had already lasted long enough she said, That's it, and took up with a photographer. Mr. Photo San was always traveling to Korea for business. One day, when he was away, the Drop family picnicked in the rain, with a big stripy umbrella, various boxes of Minute Candles, and a basket of shrimps. They drank tea, ate, admired the silhouettes of the trees against the violet sky, and then amused themselves with a curious toy: a foldable cardboard tennis court the size of a chessboard, on which four frogs dressed in white played a match of mixed doubles with little raffia racquets. The frogs were real, and neither alive nor dead. They were activated by electrodes, which was rather inconvenient. In addition, since neither Mr. Drop nor his wives knew the rules of tennis, the match was somewhat chaotic. But events took a tragic turn when one of the frogs, subjected to an excessive voltage, jumped onto Drop San's shoulder, put his head in the magnate's ear and uttered a single word: *cuckold*. One disadvantage of having two wives is that in cases of adultery you have to work out which is the culprit. In the frenzy that overcame Drop San, there was no stopping to think: he was going to kill them both. He jumped on the one who was closest and strangled her. As bad luck would have it, she was the faithful wife; the unfaithful one got away, mounted on the frogs' little tennis ball, believing it would take her to Korea (in fact it went to Osaka). The cuckolded avenger was left looking at the dead body. His status as a supernatural traveling drop exempted him from the consequences that any conventional criminal would have had to face. Or so he believed, in any case. But in fact no being in the universe is immune to bad luck. A suave and tuneful music opened slowly over the picnic, like a second umbrella. The candles were, it's true, Debussy-scented.

In Oklahoma, far from the land of chrysanthemums, a drop confronted Turpentine in one-on-one combat. Turpentine was a skinny little blond guy, who looked very much like Kant, fashionably well dressed, but not in a showy way. The only showy thing about him was his quiff, which rose without gel (an aid he disdained), by dint of sheer sculptural skill, to the great height of half an inch. This may seem a meager achievement, but only to those who are unaware that Turpentine was an inch tall, or an inch and a half, with the quiff. Among the whirls of dust whipped up by the prairie winds, Joe Peter Drop shouted: "It's him or me!" One of the two had to die. Deep in his oil-painterly soul, it pained him to destroy so fine a creature as Turpentine—an exquisite living trinket in a world of barbarity—but it had to be done. The world is big and there's room for us all—if anyone knows that it's a wandering drop—but there are situations in which incompatibility becomes acute. Not that it's such a great tragedy. Death for some means that others can live, while life for some, the simple, plain life we're living—that routine, boring, meaningless life—gradually brings about the death of some brilliant, storybook other. And perhaps repentance gave some meaning to that drift. Turpentine, trusting to his elegance, which up until that day had invariably ensured his triumph, rushed at his adversary with a little cactus pistol, emptying the magazine. Joe Pete Drop had a perfectly spherical nose; in fact it was a rubber ball, which absorbed the nine bullets. The counterattack was a dream that enveloped Turpentine in a Precambrian pastoral, and when his friends from the bridge club came looking they couldn't find him. He was never seen again. Joe Pete Drop went on running his plant for extracting cactus pink, which he exported to Korea in a gelatin solution, to be used as a photographic developer. He was wealthy, fulfilled, and married, but from time to time Turpentine's ghost visited him in the form of a sad little tune. He dealt with this by telling himself that all music was sad and that the general weariness he'd been feeling was natural; but in his franker moments, he admitted that by killing Turpentine he'd also killed the elegance he once had, and that elegance is a form of energy.

When it rained, the drop called Euphoria accelerated; she became a brain drop. When all the others fell, she rose. Gravity watched her thoughtfully, wondering, How could she be of use to me? What benefit could I extract from her? Euphoria flew through the clouds shouting, "I am a drop of Extreme Unction!" Water and oil never mix. All their weddings are followed by divorce.

When it rained on the Pope, the Great Bachelor, Gravity deigned to lower the ladder and let his retarded little sister, Mysticism, come down to earth.

One drop, hitching rides with the rain, infiltrated the Vati-

can, the Holy Vat and Can, and tried to go farther and enter the
Calendar of Pluvial Feast Days. He had an affair with the Pope,
a passionate romance that couldn't last. The Pope offered to
name him Primate of Turkey, so he could prepare the forth-
coming tour; it would be the first time a pope had visited the
Anatolian tablelands. They planned it all carefully, but it was
really just an excuse to get rid of the drop; the Pope was tired
of him. After anal coitus, man is sad.

Once the drop reached Ankara, he opened a school and convinced the Cooperative Association to set up a pencil factory
to finance the purchase of teaching materials. In his correspondence with the Eucharistic Synod he hinted at the possibility
of a coup d'état. It was set to take place on the thirteenth of
June, the day on which Gravity celebrated the anniversary of
his symbolic Pact with the Pope. Each year he threw a party and
invited the raindrops. Not all of them. He didn't have enough
glasses: just a delegate from each shower. Every twelfth of June
there were elections to determine the delegates. The votes were
cast in the tears of a young girl, Rosa Edmunda González.

In Turkey, the Pope's decision to name a drop as Primate
had caused perplexity and not a little suspicion. There was a
rumor going around that the drop had lived for a whole year in
the Pope's colon, and the new Primate's shape and size made
the story credible. One thing led to another, and the drop decided to canonize himself without waiting for the papal visit. In
the minutes before his ascension, he dictated a memo setting
out how the pencils were to be sold: there would be boxes of

six for poor children, boxes of twelve for the middle class, and of twenty-four for the rich. Plus specially produced boxes of a thousand, for the children of heads of state. At some point, the pencils in the boxes of six turned into burning Minute Candles, to the terror and distress of the children. The child who suffered most was Rosa Edmunda González, whose mother, a humble hairdresser, had made a great sacrifice to purchase one of the smallest boxes.

Shortly afterward, a Japanese delinquent named Photo San published compromising photographs, developed in pink: spherical cubist photos that showed the Pope kissing Drop.

Irresponsible and inhuman, the drop, made up of a thousand drops of the most beautiful colors, was everywhere. It's the End of Art! announced the eternal alarmists, claiming that in the future the only thing left to do would be to shut oneself in a garret, cut photos from magazines by the light of a Minute Candle, and make collages. But the pieces would never fit back together. There would never be a *Mona Lisa* again, because once the drops had tasted the salt of liberty, they would never return to the Louvre. And even if, by some supremely improbable coincidence, they did return, how likely was it that each one would go back in through the right hole?

In the city of Bogotá, there was a black dog wandering around in the streets, a great big beast made of black vanilla pods. He scavenged in the trash, slept in the sun, and sheltered from the rain in doorways. His size made him threatening and no one came near him, but he was gentle. Every stray is looking for a master, and the black dog found his in a drop that had come to visit that cold and rainy capital. They became friends. They obeyed each other; neither gave orders. It was a master-slave relation without a master or a slave, a marriage more than a friendship. They bought a little car, and last thing on a Friday evening they would set off for their cabin on the Lake of the Scented Candle. Their petit-bourgeois habits brought the End of Art down to the level of the Weekend.

One drop ended up in the luxuriant vegetation of a tropical land, among emerald leaves covered with dew, and mallows, fennel, and chard. The dew balls with which the drop played billiards had hearts of ice and hair of sun. And in that drop, evolution was stirring: she grew two pairs of rubber antennae; the top ones were long, the bottom ones short, and they were all retractable. She moved over the leaves, ate a green cell, digested it at the speed of light, and expelled a black dot, a suspension point. She turned gray, became almost transparent, and took on an elongated form, with something like a head (and antennae) at one end, a pointed tail at the other, and a hump in between. The excess nutrients that she had not metabolized for the purposes of movement were secreted from the hump as a hard, yellowish layer, forming a hollow spiral, which she began to use as a shelter, retreating into it to sleep.

Some children discovered her by chance and took her home. They put her in a plastic container and adopted her as a pet. They made holes in the lid with a pin so she could breathe. They called her Snailie, and every now and then they said: I wonder what Snailie's doing? They went to see. They guessed or invented her states of mind, the desires, dreams, and adventures that made up her minimalist life enclosed in transparent plastic. They fed her with moistened blades of grass, celery, and polenta.

And then one day, when they went to look, she was gone. She had turned back into a drop of oil paint from the *Mona Lisa* and escaped through one of the holes, repeating an ancestral pattern. It was proof that life in this world is not all of one kind; there are many varieties, each functioning according to its own logic, and evolution is not enough to unify them.

Other children, who lived in the city and were playing in the living room of a sixth-floor apartment, saw a wandering drop that had flown onto their balcony and couldn't find its way out again. The balcony had those wire-mesh guards that parents put up when they have small children.

"Daddy! Daddy! A little bird with a moustache!"

In that little space full of potted ferns and geraniums, the drop flew around as if afraid, back and forth, doing figure eights, loop-the-loops, and spirals, unable to escape. The children in the apartment, on the other side of the glass, were no less agitated. They sensed that the divine fly would not stay, and even though they lived in the fleeting instants of their attention, as children do, they were overawed by the eternity of the flight. They would have liked to keep the drop as a pet. They would have made a little paper house with doors and windows, an igloo, and a tiny bicycle for him to ride.

But suddenly he was gone.

"He escaped! Daddy! Mummy! He escaped! He was round! He was *so* cute!"

No one believed them, of course.

Meanwhile, in Norway, a drop was heading for the icy north in search of the nightingale of the snows. She ventured into a vast endless day in pursuit of a dubious legend. Dawns of never-ending pink were reflected in a crystalline lake, on the floor of which a Minute Candle in a diving suit burned without consuming itself. Indolent eagles with horses' heads glided over an endless grid of cold. The drop traveled in a Sherman tank, which crunched through the frost, leaving broad tracks. The natives were terrified. All Norway shook in fear before the advance of the Armored Drop. How far would she go? According to the local legends, which had never been contested, if the nightingale sang, the candle at the bottom of the lake would go out, and the inspiration of the artists would be extinguished along with that flame. In return, they would receive the scent of eternal melancholy.

Inevitably, war broke out. The tank multiplied and became a thousand tanks, each in a glass hexagon, advancing over transparencies of ice. It was a war entirely made up of mirages and phantasmagoria. The Snow multiplied too. She was a fat, white princess, the daughter of King Pole, and rivalry for her hand led to hostilities among the Scandinavian powers. Her lineage was especially illustrious. But when the Snow Princesses began to proliferate, perspectives in those icy wastes were thrown into confusion. General Panzer Drop Kick commanded the operation, enclosed in an engraved dropper. The battles were an incredible spectacle: millions of soldiers on bicycles plowing up the polar ice cap, the eagles growing visibly, and, always there in the background, the silver nightingale in its tabernacle of atoms. And all because of a drop!

Then a crack in the glass of the dropper allowed it to fill with mist. When, on the orders of the Norwegian Prime Minister, the mist was extracted with a pump, it turned out that the drop was no longer inside. It reappeared at the bottom of the lake, suspended over the tip of the candle's flame. The heat softened and deformed it, brightened its colors and made it give off a strange smell of old flowers.

On the wide grasslands of China, a drop set up a news agency. Village life, with its immutable cycles of yin and yang, was unsettled by the din of the transmissions. The DropToday agency bought a basketball team and the inaugural match (both for the team and for the luxurious stadium built in the wilds of outer Mongolia) was against an NBA all-star selection. The North Americans were keen to conquer the Yellow Empire's massive sports market, and the visit was managed by the State Department. The Pope promised to attend the event. The team was made up of China's tallest and strongest men, and Mr. Drop, who had been appointed coach, adopted a novel procedure for the training sessions. Or not so novel, in fact, because it had already been used by the ancient Romans, and was still being used by Hawaiian surfers. It consisted of practicing with a very heavy sphere of bronze instead of a normal ball. In this way the athletes developed powerful reflexes that would enable them to handle the ball like a dream when it came to a real match. The first day they used a twenty-kilo bronze ball, the second day it was twenty-five kilos, and on the third day it was thirty. The Chinese giants buckled under the weight of that hefty projectile. Drop went to the next level: he made them train on a court that was six miles long and two miles wide. Its dimensions were proportioned to the weight of the bronze ball. Drop was very adept at calculating proportions, and he didn't need to use graph paper. He applied the same skill to news stories, enlarging them while maintaining their proportions. This was the reason for the success of his agency; he pioneered the "Chinese news" technique and made it popular around the world.

It goes without saying that this aggravated exercise drew big drops of sweat from the athletes. It was inhuman, heaving that ball around and racing constantly from one hoop to the other. Heedless of the cost, Drop had hired a consultant: Gravity, who'd come to China to await the arrival of the Pope, with whom he was to be united in marriage. It was the story of the century. The newspaper headlines had quoted Gravity, the Universal Playboy, taking leave of the Holy Father after their first night of love: "SEE YOU ON THE BALTIC!" That northern sea was to be enclosed by a wall of red marble, which was under construction; one of its wings would join up with the Great Wall, making a thunderous crash.

Drop went so far as to get the five giant team members out of bed the night before the match and whisk them away in secret for a last training session by moonlight. They traveled by truck to the outer reaches of Mongolia. They stopped in a silvery desert, got out and looked around. A hoop reared on the horizon, a hundred and twenty feet high. Facing it, on the opposite horizon, was another hoop, the pole half hidden by the curvature of the earth. A motorcycle that had been following them roared to a halt. They stared at the rider, who dismounted and removed his helmet. It was Gravity. The Chinese giants, who had seen him only on television, gaped in amazement. This is what happens with media celebrities: it's hard to accept that they really exist. Mr. Drop floated over to the motorbike, and together they undid the straps that were holding a large chest in place behind the seat. The Vatican's coat of arms was carved into the lid. Inside the chest was a golden seal's head, which weighed fifty kilos. This was what they were to use for the last training session, pushing their strength to the limit, and receiving the head's famous powers in return.

"Long passes," ordered Drop. They began. The crushing weight of the seal's head bent them double. Catching it, they staggered backward; their veins swelled and they grimaced in pain. Drop shouted himself hoarse, demanding more speed, more precision. And to Gravity, who was beside him, looking on worriedly, he said, "A few drops of height are no match for savagery." The players' falling sweat echoed throughout Mongolia.

With the movement and the handling, the seal's head warmed up. The gold began to shine; the fat in the seal's brain melted, running between the player's fingers, making the large projectile slippery, all the more difficult to catch and throw.

In the end, the group rose up, forming a kind of cone whose apex was the seal's head, exuding fat, shinier than the moon, with the five basketball players underneath, stretched like phylacteries. They took off, into the black, starless sky. Gravity was irresistibly drawn up in their wake, and the motorcycle followed him. Drop watched them shrink as they climbed, until they disappeared. The only thought that occurred to him was that the wedding would have to be put off again.

Later he was criticized for his extravagant and inappropriate training methods. He even wondered himself, for a moment, if he hadn't gone too far.

But for him it was a point of honor to maintain a superior indifference. The game of realism, by its very nature, neutralized everything. Even invention, to which the scattered drops had devoted themselves with a passion, had a retroactive effect on realism. It might have been said that in each of its avatars, invention was writing itself with a drop of ink and an obsessive attention to plausibility. Each drop was self-contained, thanks to the delicate balance of its surface tension. There was no context, just pure irradiation.

The drop had neither doors nor windows. History had countless generative tips. A certain drop, virginal and vaginal in equal parts, had, by a miracle of naptime surgery, undergone gender reassignment and adopted the name Aureole. Initially his name had been Dr. Aureole. Due to a suspension, Aureole was left hanging in the air ...

The suspension gave rise to a sublime romanticism: Aureole, in a nightgown, on the balcony of her little castle, overlooking a dark garden alive with the sounds of insects and fountains, lost in her reverie, her spidery weaving. The castle was in flames, but the fire was suspended too. The drop was in another dimension. It could only have happened to her: another display of indifference, made plausible by the devices of realism.

Suddenly, on a third level of the story, three cloaked figures dropped from the eaves and the drainpipes, landing all at once on the balcony. Torn from her reverie, Aureole began to spin, squealing in distress. She tried various falling movements to escape from the gloved hands of her attackers, but it was as if she were floating on mercury. All she succeeded in doing was to make them tear her nightgown and mess up her hair. Working as a team, the three figures thrust her, terrified and tearful, into a box, which closed with a resonant clack. The crowd that had gathered around the castle to watch the fire saw nothing of this maneuver, and the firemen busy extending their ladders like pirates boarding a ship saw even less. The kidnappers took advantage of the confusion to escape with their captive; a car was waiting for them on the other side of the moat. They traveled through the hills for a long time, and before the moon rose they came to the gardens of an abandoned country house. They entered the house through the back door and shut the prisoner in the cellar.

Only then did they relax and take off their hoods. They were a trio of dangerous criminals: Shower, Hose, and Faucet. For many years they had been plotting to kidnap a drop. Chubby, hoarse, chrome-plated, they danced about on the table like Maenads, making metallic noises, drank a bottle of cognac, and called Gravity on the telephone to demand a ransom.

Ring ... ring ... ring ...

The sound of the little bell reverberated throughout the mountains. The echo carried it from peak to peak, creating a kind of succession.

The documents relating to the case were published by Drop Press. Pocket museums had become a possibility, thanks to technical progress in photography and printing. Here a flashback to an earlier part of the story is needed to complete the "picture." The *Mona Lisa* is, as it happens, the emblem of the mechanical reproduction of the work of art (whether by photography, printing, or digital media). The merits of this splendid portrait are not to be denied, but it's important to recall some of the historical events that propelled it to the position of supremacy it occupies today. There are other portraits of women by Leonardo that could perfectly well have stolen the limelight. There's the portrait of Cecilia Galleriani, the *Lady with an Ermine*, which more than a few critics have praised as the most beautiful ever painted, the most perfect. Or the portrait of Ginevra de' Benci, that childlike woman with her severe, round face. Neither is lacking in the mystery that stimulates the imagination ... What, then, explains the incomparable popularity of the *Mona Lisa*? It so happened that throughout the nineteenth century, as tourism began to develop and the books that would establish the canon of Western art were being written, the *Mona Lisa* was on display in the Louvre for everyone to see, while Cecilia and Ginevra were languishing in obscure collections in Krakow and Lichtenstein.

The theft of the *Mona Lisa* in 1911 put the picture on the front pages of the newspapers, just when photography and printing were making it possible to reproduce works of art on a massive scale. The news story had natural flow-on effects, and the *Mona Lisa*, reproduced ad infinitum, became an indestructible icon.

But there was something more, another new development in civilization, which contributed to the process: the invention of the global news story. Just when journalism had reached its industrial maturity, two events occurred within a few months of each other that justified that maturity and brought it to fruition: the theft of the *Mona Lisa* and the wreck of the *Titanic*. Both events instituted a myth. Because these stories were the first of their kind, they were the biggest and the most productive. All the rest were condemned to operate within a system of substitutions. It was pure poetic justice that one of the *Mona Lisa*'s runaway drops should set up a news agency, and precisely in China, humanity's great neural puzzle.

The DropToday agency specialized in the hunt for the new Grail, the greasy golden seal's head that had begun to think for humans. There was a lead to follow: the spectacular melodrama of Gravity, who was wandering through the deserts of the world after leaving the Pope at the altar, dressed as a bride, holding a suppository. Gravity himself was impossible to follow, but his movements could be calculated using geographical logarithms. He also left a trail of slime. Laboratory tests revealed that this slime was principally composed of an organic substance, newtonia, whose cells could expand in response to sexual desire. The expansion was practically unlimited and the discovery of the cell membrane's flexibility and strength revolutionized the textile industry. From then on, the substance was used to make shirts for basketball players, who kept getting bigger and taller.

Sparky, the funny drop, became a humorist. He strung together a bunch of old jokes and got up every night in a bar in Baden Baden adjoining the casino to run through his routine. He was slotted in between a pair of sopranos and the Sensitive Steel Robot, and the master of ceremonies presented him as "the funniest drop in the world." The jokes were terrible, but the comic effect was produced by the contrast between his diminutive size and his stentorian voice, between his helpless condition as a drop, easily squashed by a fingertip, and the way he fancied himself as a Don Juan, eyeing off the fat ladies of the *nomenklatura*, who had come to the spa town to blow the rubles that their husbands had squeezed from the udder of Soviet corruption. Even before he opened his mouth, his look assured him of a certain indulgence: the top hat, the close-fitting dinner suit, the monocle, the cane, all adapted to his spherical form, without arms or legs. Quite a few members of the audience would gladly have bought a reproduction, to take home as a souvenir.

The season at the casino lasted three months. The rest of the year Sparky hibernated in a log cabin in the middle of a forest, leading the life of a hermit, without servants or neighbors. Like so many humorists, he was a melancholic and a misanthrope. The telling of jokes exhausted his humor and left him feeling bitter and empty. He would have liked to call himself Sparky, the Drop of Gall. He used the same jokes year after year, as if to see how long they'd go on getting a laugh, although they were tattered and shabby, falling apart from the wear. They appeared before his eyes at night, trying to scare him, floating over his canopied bed. And when they realized it was no use, they slipped away to the wasteland, sighing.

Melodious voice, voice of the woods.

Evenings of classic beauty in Buddhist lands. Men and women walking through poor neighborhoods carrying little silver pitchers full of water. Everlasting poverty resisted all the interventions of the permanently new. The only permanent thing was everlasting dailiness. And yet … suddenly everyone looked up into the sky. And in the sky there was a drop, the drop that decided to make itself visible. It was red, pink, greenish, saffron, orange, turquoise, slightly phosphorescent, velvety, tense, and it had a dimple. It was full of itself but hollow, empty, a little hole in the air. It descended slowly, reaching ground level before night fell. The impoverished Buddhists tried to grab it. In its fluid form, it served as a hinge between the public and the private. The existence of the poverty-stricken Asian masses had become a public issue, a social problem, to be measured statistically; privacy and secrets were limited to the lives of the rich. The silver pitchers, purchased with slowly accumulated savings and cherished as personal or family treasures, prefigured the public-private nexus. The drop made them anachronistic. In the end, no one dared touch the drop, and a delightful park sprang up around it, which by virtue of its sacred status served as a sanctuary for the little foxes that would otherwise have become extinct.

But the forest kept invading the Buddhist lands. And with the forest came snakes, which ventured into the villages and drank the goats' milk and the blood of the children. They coiled around the bare legs of the lotus worshippers and tripped them up. There was a historical solution to this legendary misadventure: as soon as the poor gave up carrying those pitchers, they had both hands free and were able to do battle with the slippery snakes.

The drop, enthroned at the center of the fox park, was named God Prospero Brilliantine. He didn't move or speak or gesture. But all thoughts converged on him. The anthropologists of tea studied his social effects and his composition. Was he made of gel? Cerebral matter? Nougat? They couldn't tell. From the smell, they thought he might be a lunar particle. They gave up on the effects, because they were always indirect, too indirect. The poor folk established a tradition of making silk caps for the foxes; each family had its particular color and pattern. As with the pitchers, they spared no expense, saving up to buy the best silks, even if it meant going hungry. The anthropologists were puzzled. They felt they were touching on the secret of poverty, but from a distance, by remote control.

A drop settled in a foggy country. He lived in a three-story, French-style house, an incongruous, stately edifice, built on top of a cliff. He withdrew to his study on the third floor, set up a camera with a telephoto lens on his desk, and, dressed in a tartan bathrobe, smoking three pipes as he watched the churning of the waves, managed his companies and investments all over the globe. None of his many employees in the world's great capitals ever suspected that the mastermind behind the operation was a drop. They knew he was eccentric and suspected that he was a misanthrope, perhaps even slightly mad. He had adopted a communication system based on images, which were decoded by computers. It was exceedingly inefficient: tens of thousand of images were required to translate a single word (and even so there was often confusion). The method could be justified as a security measure, given the confidential nature of his messages, but that was just an excuse; its real purpose was to cover up the supremely implausible fact that the great financier was a drop of Renaissance paint.

Not all the drops adopted such capricious ways of life, or were engaged in such memorable adventures and discoveries. Most of them, in fact, adapted to the usual ways of getting by: the skeptical conformism of the majority, the minor pleasures of home and work, a comfortable enough routine. They had the same dreams as everyone else; their opinions belonged to the common stock. And when they had to vote (since democracy was spreading around the world), they wondered, as we all do, about the ultimate meaning of life.

All the drops were the *Mona Lisa*, and none of them were. The submarine goddess of the Louvre no longer existed, in the Louvre or anywhere else, although millions of memory membranes preserved her reflection for a human race without illusions, but not without images. Déjà vu sprang from the heart of every being, smoke without fire, flower without fruit. There are no two people in the world (this calculation has been confirmed) separated by more than six common acquaintances. Both the living and the dead can serve as links. And the law of social entropy always ends up shortening the chain. The general, irreversible tendency is toward recognition. Demographic explosions are really implosions. The time will come when a single man, Anti-Adam, will run into himself and see that the two of him are exactly the same, like peas in a pod or two drops of water, or, rather, like a single drop.

One drop settled in Argentina, the land of representation. He took the very Argentine name Nélido and set about finding a girl to marry. A few hours would have been enough for anybody else. But he was shy, awkward, and conversationally handicapped. He tried for years, without any success. He seemed to be under a curse, or to be dogged by bad luck, but not even he could pretend not to know that luck, good or bad, was a thing of the past. He never turned down an invitation to a party or a gathering, went dancing, took yoga and painting classes, participated in demonstrations and marches, searching desperately, almost like a dog with his tongue hanging out. He knew that opportunities had to be seized as they arose, that it could all depend on an instant, so he sharpened his attention, cultivated his spontaneity, practiced his charm. It's not that he wasn't sincere; on the contrary. He wanted, he needed to find a soul mate, and at the end of each day that had passed without breaking the divine porcelain of his solitude, he could feel the bitterness of failure shriveling his tiny droplet's soul.

He even thought about turning queer. After all, a partner is a partner, love is love, and maybe it wouldn't be so noticeable in a drop. But he soon put the idea aside, not because of any moral or aesthetic scruples, but simply because it would have been more difficult. And anyway, he didn't want to do anything unusual; he wanted to have a wife to hug and kiss and cuddle on cold winter nights like everyone else ... You can't get more normal than that. It's the original urge of every living being, the motor of eternity that powers the car of time.

Perhaps that was the problem: he didn't have mortality to spur him on. After all, in his franker moments, he had to admit that there was a difference between a drop of oil paint and a young man, from a woman's point of view, at least. This was brought home to him every day, not only in his fruitless quest, but also in his work. And it was a mistake to think of those two aspects of his life as separate; he had read in a magazine that eighty percent of relationships begin in the workplace. He had a job in a factory that manufactured cardboard boxes, but there was no chance of starting a relationship there because he worked all on his own in the little printing unit, and anyway there were no women workers. (They had hired him to roll his tiny round body over the spring-loaded stamp that printed the words "MADE IN ARGENTINA" on the cardboard.) So the only possibility was at his other job, selling candy and cigarettes in a kiosk (he started at four after leaving the factory and worked till ten p.m.). Opportunities might have arisen there, and they did, but they weren't the right kind. Customers approach a kiosk from one side or the other, and they see the vendor at the last minute, suddenly, without any time to adjust. They've come to buy something completely banal like a chocolate bar or a pack of cigarettes, so they're not expecting anything beyond the kind of everyday interaction that people generally have with their fellow human beings. Encountering a colored drop a millimeter in diameter instead of a familiar human form, they were unpleasantly surprised. It was hard to establish, or maintain, any kind of rapport. As for the regulars, they simply stopped noticing him and conducted the transaction in an automatic, absent sort of way.

Eventually, Nélido came to believe that the disease contained its own remedy. A fairly obvious thought occurred to him. If he wasn't a man, if he was a drop, and a drop from the world's most famous artwork, he wasn't constrained by human laws, so he could do anything. In a picture, a drop of paint is powerless, entirely dependent on the matter surrounding it, the artist's intentions, the effect, and a thousand other things. But once the drop has become independent, and ventured into the world to discover the strange taste of freedom, everything changes.

And yet it hadn't worked like that. Nothing had changed.

How odd. Perhaps because the laws that apply to beings of any kind, from the most complex organism down to the atom, come into effect universally as soon as one crosses the threshold of reality. The fantastic drop's reality was the same as that of a human being.

This insight, which had emerged from the experience of a humble Argentine cigarette vendor, was confirmed at the cosmic level as well. There were drops that crossed the last frontier and left the planet behind. They realized that they had been going round and round the world of humans by force of habit, simply because it hadn't occurred to them to try the measureless expanses of the universe. One drop set off, then others followed. It wasn't hard at all for them. They didn't need to breathe, and they weren't affected by radiation or adverse conditions in the ether. At most they softened a bit in the proximity of suns and hardened when the temperature plummeted below zero. Distances were not a problem. They could cover three hundred thousand light years in a second, thanks to the partitioning of time that had occurred when they dispersed. So the galaxies saw them go whizzing past. Beneath the red skies of those dusks in the void, the drops took charge of organizing matter, leaving the atoms and particles gaping in surprise.

No one was bored in the cosmos. It was as if fierce races were being run in those vacant abysses: luminous, mechanically complex racing cars running on endless circuits. Darkness opened behind screens made of light painted on nothingness, a light without shadows but not without figures. And from a single point of darkness on the screens, new universes opened out, becoming The Universe. Roaring curves, the beams of the headlights sweeping through titanic basement spaces, nebulae for barriers.

Two drops met at one of those inconceivable intersections of parallel lines. On a distant planet, in a sphere of gas, in the midst of a density festival, a drop cast its shadow on a ground of rocky atoms. Because of the drop's perfectly spherical shape, its shadow was always the same, wherever the suns and moons happened to be. Another drop was approaching from the opposite direction in a rocket. They communicated via microphones. The shadow of the spacecraft expanded and contracted like bellows. The sky remained black, with ringlets of helium.

They got out to explore. The two drops, sealed in their space suits, floated in the fourteen thousand dense atmospheres of planet Carumba. On the horizon, Perspective appeared, perched on stilts, wearing pearl necklaces, carrying a yellow handbag, her white hair swirling in a cloud of quarks. She seemed indifferent. She never looked at anyone because she knew that all eyes were on her; and the enraptured drops were no exception. They had been missing that beautiful deity ever since they left the painting. They would have liked to shelter again under her invisible wings. But she didn't see them. Her eyes were fixed on the beyond. Was that abandonment the price they had to pay for the freedom that had allowed them to go so far? Unwittingly, the three of them had formed a perfectly symmetrical figure.

Then something happened. With a sound like thunder, the black concavity of the ether tore open, and Gravity appeared, in his crimson plastic cape and pointy shoes. The drops took fright, thinking he would fall and squash them. To their relief, he passed overhead and landed on the downward-curving line of the horizon. Perspective, who was on the same line, slid along it and fell into the arms of Gravity. He was waiting with open arms and an erection. She connected perfectly, like a heart impaling itself on a lance. When they made contact, there was a sound of kissing, and bright rays of light, on which the constellations would come to rest, went shooting out in all directions. What had happened? Simply that the meeting of two drops had brought the ever-remote Perspective into her own proximity. And Gravity, who had been anticipating this opportunity for countless thousands of years, didn't let it pass him by. In recognition of the favor, he turned, without letting go of Perspective, and gave them a knowing wink. The two drop-astronauts were amazed that their presence in a place that could have been Anywhere should have produced such an extraordinary effect. Since leaving the painting back in the Louvre, they had become accustomed to causing no effect at all. The embrace continued and worked a transformation. Gravity, formerly so serious and rotund, became slim and amusing. Perspective shed her customary air of decrepitude, taking on a compact and tangible form. Their nuptials were celebrated at an instant party; there was no need to send out invitations (they'd been on their way since the Big Bang).

The two drops looked at each other, as if to say: "How about that?" The same thought had occurred to them at the same moment: now they knew for sure that the Pope would remain a bachelor forever. They imagined him in the Vatican, jilted at the altar, standing there in his white dress, holding the suppositories, a tear rolling down his wrinkly old cheek. It was the last fantasy, and the most realistic.

The pair of newlyweds drove off in a car, trailing tin cans through the firmament. It was to be a combative honeymoon, for they were preparing the final assault on Evolution, the eternal spinster, and this time, now that the balance of power had been upset (divide and conquer), she would be defeated.

But the drops that were treading reality's fantastic limits ... remained within the real and succumbed to melancholy.

JUNE 19, 2003

The All That Plows through the Nothing

THERE ARE TWO LADIES AT THE GYM WHO TALK NON-stop, occasionally to other people, but always to each other. They seem to be lifelong friends, with everything in common: the same dyed-blond hair, the same clothes, the same reactions, and no doubt the same tastes. Even their voices are similar. They're the kind of ladies who, having turned fifty and reached middle age, feeling they should take care of their bodies, de-cide to start going to the gym together, because they wouldn't go on their own. Not that these two need much extra physical activity; they're slim and active and seem to be in good shape. They're local housewives, with nothing to set them apart ex-cept for their chattiness, which is hardly an exceptional qual-ity. It's not as if the gym's the only place they can talk, because they're already talking when they arrive. If I'm on one of the bikes near the entrance, I hear their voices as they come up the stairs; they talk in the dressing room while they're getting changed; then they work out together on the bikes, the tread-mills, and the various machines, without interrupting their conversation for a moment; and they're still talking when they

145

leave. I'm not the only one to have noticed. Once when they were in the women's dressing room and I was in the men's, I could hear them talking, talking, talking, and I said to the instructor: "They sure can talk, those two." He nodded and raised his eyebrows: "It's scary. And the things they say! Have you listened to them?" No, I hadn't, although it would have been easy, because they speak loudly and clearly, as people do when they have no secrets or concerns about privacy. They conform to a stereotype: housewives and mothers who are sure of themselves and their normality. Once, years ago, in a different gym, I came across a similar but different case: two girls who talked all the time, even when they were doing really demanding aerobic exercises; they were young and must have had tremendous lung capacity. One day when whey were on facing mats, doing the kind of sit-ups that take your breath away, talking all the while, I pointed them out to the instructor, who said, excusing them: "It's because they're good friends and they both work all day: this is the only time they get to spend together." But it's not like that for the two ladies, who are clearly together for a large part of the day: I've seen them shopping in the neighborhood, or looking in store windows, or sitting in a café, always talking, talking, talking.

I didn't really think about this until one day, by chance—they must have been on bikes near mine—I heard what they were saying. I can't remember what it was, but I do remember that it made a strange impression on me, and though I couldn't articulate that strangeness at the time, I resolved in a half-conscious and somewhat halfhearted way (after all, what was it to me?) to get to the bottom of it.

At this point there's something I should explain about myself, which is that I don't talk much, probably too little, and I think this has been detrimental to my social life. It's not that I have trouble expressing myself, or no more than people generally have when they're trying to put something complex into words. I'd even say I have less trouble than most because my long involvement with literature has given me a better-than-average capacity for handling language. But I have no gift for small talk, and there's no point trying to learn or pretend; it wouldn't be convincing. My conversational style is spasmodic (someone once described it as "hollowing"). Every sentence opens up gaps, which require new beginnings. I can't maintain any continuity. In short, I speak when I have something to say. My problem, I suppose—and this may be an effect of involvement with literature—is that I attribute too much importance to the subject. For me, it's never simply a question of "talking" but always a question of "what to talk about." And the effort of weighing up potential subjects kills the spontaneity of dialogue. In other words, when everything you say has to be "worth the effort," it's too much effort to go on talking. I envy people who can launch into a conversation with gusto and energy, and keep it going. I envy them that human contact, so full of promise, a living reality from which, in my mute isolation, I feel excluded. "But what do they talk about?" I wonder, which is obviously the wrong question to ask. The crabbed awkwardness of my social interactions is a result of this failing on my part. Looking back, I can see that it was responsible for most of my missed opportunities and almost all the woes of solitude. The older I get, the more convinced I am that this is a mutilation, for which my professional success cannot compensate, much less my "rich inner life." And I've never been able to resolve the conundrum that conversationalists pose for me: how do they keep coming up with things to talk about? I don't even wonder about it anymore, perhaps because I know there's no answer. I wasn't wondering how those women did it, and yet I was given an answer so unexpected and surprising that a terrifying abyss opened before me.

Suddenly, in the ceaseless flow of their dialogue, one said to the other: "They gave my husband the results of his analysis, and he has cancer; we asked for an appointment with the oncologist ..." I took that in and began to think. Naturally my first thought was that I'd misheard, but I hadn't. I don't know if I'm reproducing her words exactly, but that was the gist, and the other woman replied, in an appropriately sympathetic and worried manner, but she wasn't overly surprised; she didn't cry out or faint. And yet this was really big news. Too big to crop up casually in a conversation, as if it were just one among many other items. I was sure that the two of them had been in the gym for at least an hour, and they'd been talking all that time; also, they'd arrived together, which meant that their conversation had begun a fair while before ... So had they discussed ten, twenty, or thirty other topics before they got around to the husband's cancer? I considered a number of possibilities. Maybe the woman concerned had been keeping this momentous disclosure in reserve, in order to drop it "like a bombshell" at a particular moment; maybe she'd been gathering the strength to tell her friend; maybe she'd been inhibited by some kind of reticence, which had finally given way. Or it could have been that the news was not, in fact, all that important: suppose, for example, that the man she was calling "my husband" (for the sake of convenience) was an ex-husband, and they'd been separated for many years, and there was no longer any bond of affection between them. More daring or imaginative explanations were possible too. Perhaps they were talking about the plot of a novel or a play that the woman was writing (for a writing workshop they attended together, just as they exercised together at the gym); or it could have been a dream that she was recounting (although the verb tenses were wrong for that), or whatever. And there was a further hypothesis, which was barely less improbable: that the women had been dealing with more important and urgent matters since they'd met two or three hours earlier and had just got around to the cancer when I overheard them. Absurd as it might seem, this was in the end the most logical and realistic explanation, or at least the only one left standing.

In the course of these reflections, I remembered the previous occasion on which I'd heard them talking and the vaguely strange impression it had made on me. Now I could bring that impression into focus and understand the strangeness retrospectively. It was the same thing, but to enter fully into my consciousness, it had to be repeated. The first time (now I remembered) the news had been less amazing: one of the women was telling the other that, the previous day, the painters had started on the inside of her house, and all the furniture was covered with old sheets; it was utter chaos, the way it always is "when you have the painters in." The other woman sympathized and replied that, although it was terribly inconvenient, repainting was something that had to be done; you couldn't go on living in a flaky old ruin, and so on, and so on. The little puzzle that I hadn't been able to formulate was this: how could such an upheaval in the existence of a housewife simply crop up in the middle of a conversation, instead of being announced at the start or, indeed, discussed for days in advance? The matter of the husband's cancer had opened my eyes because it was much more shocking, but the same fundamental mechanism had been at work in both cases.

From then on, I began to pay attention. I have to say it wasn't all that easy, for physical as much as psychological reasons. The main physical difficulty was that the gym is a very noisy place: the machines clang when the iron weights are stacked, the pulleys squeak, there's a high-pitched beep every fifteen seconds to regulate the time spent at each station, the electric motors of the treadmills hum and moan, the chorus of exercise bikes can be deafening when several are being used at once, everyone talks and some people yell; and, of course, there are music videos on the TV all the time, with the volume up high, and usually, on top of that, there's the much louder music of the aerobics class in the back room (it makes the windows shake). The two women, as I said, speak loudly—they don't care who's listening—so it's easy to hear that they're talking, but it's not so easy to hear what they're saying unless you're very close. My exercise routine gave me plenty of opportunities to get close to them because it kept me on the move, but it also meant that I couldn't stay close for long without provoking suspicion.

Even so, what I heard was enough to nourish a growing perplexity. Whatever the time and whatever they were doing, whether they were coming or going, halfway through their routine or in the dressing room or on the roller massage tables, they were always reporting some important piece of news and discussing it with due zeal. And if, by stepping up my surveillance operation, I managed to hear them two or three or four times in a day, there was always something new and important, far too important to be coming up after hours of conversation—except that their conversation consisted of nothing else. "In the storm last night the tree behind our house fell down and crashed right into the kitchen." "Our car was stolen yesterday." "My son's getting married tomorrow." "Mom died."

That wasn't small talk, not at all. But I don't really know what small talk is. I thought I did, but now that I've begun to doubt its existence, I'm not sure anymore. If those two women are representative, maybe people always talk because they have something to say, something really worth saying. I'm starting to wonder if there's such a thing as "talking for the sake of talking," if it's not just a myth I invented to disguise my lack of life, that is, basically a lack of things to talk about.

Or is it the other way around? Maybe those two ladies are the myth I've invented. Except that they exist. And how! I see (and hear) them every day. And their existence is not confined to the "magnetic field" of the gymnasium. As I said, I've seen and heard them in the street as well. Just yesterday afternoon, as it happens. I'd gone out for a walk and I ran into them; they were coming out of a perfume store, in the midst of an animated conversation. I managed to catch a couple of sentences as I went by. One was telling the other that she and her daughter had argued the day before, and the argument had ended with the daughter declaring that she was moving out to live on her own … It was seven in the evening, and they'd been together and talking all day (I'd seen them at the gym that morning). I'm leaving aside the possibility that they say these things "for my benefit," not just because, as a practical joke, it would be too complicated, but also because they haven't even noticed I exist, nor is there any reason why they should.

One way to solve the problem would be to make a list of all the topics they cover in a day, and see if there's a basically plausible progression from more to less important. I would be better placed to undertake this task than almost anyone because I have access to them first thing in the morning, at the gym, for two long hours. But I haven't done it and I won't. I've mentioned the physical obstacles already, and I said that there were psychological difficulties too. These come down to one thing, in the end: fear. Fear of a certain kind of madness.

There's a bylaw in Buenos Aires that forbids the transportation of animals in taxis. Like all laws in Argentina, this one can be bent. In these hard times, if a lady wants to get in with her lapdog, ten out of ten taxi drivers are going to let her. But the law is still in force, exerting a pressure on the conscience, giving chimerical grounds for caution. According to one of those

tenacious urban legends, one day a woman got into a taxi carrying a capuchin monkey dressed up as a baby, with a little coat,
slippers, a nappy, and a pacifier, and the driver didn't notice the
ruse until the monkey bit off half his ear. Embittered and coars-
ened by a life chained to the wheel, he'd probably been thinking (if anything): "Gotta pity her, with an ugly kid like that!"

Someone once told me you can even take a goat in a taxi, as
long as you promise to hold it down on the floor and give the
driver a tip. That shows just how flexible the laws of our "au-
tonomous" province can be. And yet a taxi driver can turn away
a passenger who's carrying a plant. Amazing but true, as anyone
can verify. I'm not talking about a tree or a rhododendron with
a six-yard circumference: just a regular little plant, in a pot or a
plastic bag, an oregano seedling, an orchid growing on a piece
of old tree trunk, a bonsai.

And the drivers can be intransigent, if they feel like it. There's
no point objecting or trying to argue. Convinced that they're
acting as designated agents of the law, they'll leave a passenger standing there with his or her little plant, even if it's an old
man, or a mother with small children (and pregnant to boot),
or a disabled person, even if it's raining. The law, of course, says
nothing about plants; it mentions only animals, and extending
the prohibition to the vegetable realm is a clear and indefen-
sible abuse of power.

But that's the way it is. What is and what should be the case
are superimposed. Although they're contradictory, both continue to exist in reality at the same time. The same "simultane-
ous superimposition" is more clearly apparent in the following

attempt to answer the question: How many taxis are there in Buenos Aires?

The number is huge—as you can see just by stepping out into the street. If you really wanted to know how many there are, you could ask, or do some research, for example by checking the city's list of registered automobiles, which I guess would be in the public domain. But there's a way to work it out that doesn't involve any asking or talking or even getting up from your desk. All you have to do is apply your powers of deduction to something that's very widely known.

From time to time, remarkably often in fact, there's a story in the papers about an honest taxi driver who finds a briefcase on the backseat containing a hundred thousand dollars and returns it to the rightful owner, after a more or less difficult search. It's a classic news story. It might be a bigger or smaller sum of money, but it's always enough to solve all the problems a taxi driver might have (or an average, middle-class newspaper reader). That's what gives the story its impact: the exorbitant cost of honesty. Let's suppose—this is the first in a series of minimal estimates that will, I hope, enhance the credibility of the calculation—that such an event occurs in Buenos Aires only once a year.

So, if we consider the occupied taxis passing in the street, we can ask, for a start, how many are carrying passengers who have a briefcase containing a hundred thousand dollars in cash. There must be very few. As a result of the widespread use of checks, bank drafts, credit cards, and electronic transfers, handling large amounts of cash has become rather anachronistic. I've never gotten into a taxi (or gone anywhere) with that amount of money, nor do I know anyone who has, but there can be no question that such people do exist. Leaving aside illegal or criminal activities, there are people employed by large companies that pay wages in cash, or people doing property deals, trading on the stock market, or whatever. Let's say, and this too is a very conservative estimate, that one in a thousand passengers is carrying that much money.

Now, considering that limited set, how many of the passengers riding in taxis with a hundred thousand dollars would forget about their briefcases and leave them behind? I know I wouldn't, no matter whether the money was mine or someone else's (though I don't know which situation would make me more vigilant). It really is the height of absentmindedness. No one's indifferent to money these days, whatever they say, especially when large sums are involved. So we can reckon that of a thousand passengers who take a taxi carrying a hundred thousand dollars, not more than one will leave the money behind. (Though maybe there would be more than one, because a familiar psychological mechanism ensures that the more you worry, the more things go wrong.) And even if it's fewer than one, the overestimation will be offset by the cautiousness of my previous estimate.

So, given the very restricted set of taxis in which someone has left that enormous amount of money, we still have to work out how many of the drivers would demonstrate a superlative probity by finding the owner and returning it. This is trickier, and I suppose that estimates will vary according to people's ideas about human nature. Some will say no one's that honest, while others will consider such a claim to be abstract and theoretical, and prefer to think that, confronted with a real situation of this kind, most people would obey the voice of conscience. Personally, I'm not sure what to think. I've never had to make the choice; I've never faced the test.

I'm envisaging it as a statistical possibility, and if I really had to choose, I don't know what I'd do. It's important to remember that honesty is an abstract concept too (however much I like to think that my own is beyond doubt). No one chooses to be a taxi driver; not for a whole working life, anyway. It's hard work, and, these days, a hundred thousand dollars must be equivalent to twenty years of taxi driving. Weighing up the pros and cons, I'd say that, faced with a choice of this kind, one in a thousand taxi drivers, on average, would return the loot, and the other nine hundred and ninety-nine would hang on to it.

Having arrived at these estimates, we can reverse the process to work out how many taxis there would have to be for one honest taxi driver to return a hundred thousand dollars to a passenger who happened to leave that amount of cash behind, which is something that actually happens, and relatively often. The result is a thousand million (the product of multiplying a thousand by a thousand by a thousand).

So that's the answer to our initial question. In the city of Buenos Aires, there are a thousand million taxis. Or rather, there are (as demonstrated by the calculation, which is incontestable) and there aren't (how could there be a thousand million taxis in a city of ten million people?). It's simultaneously true and false.

With this apparently paradoxical result (the paradox is only apparent), I conclude the notes that I was intending to make during my trip to Tandil, where I arrived this afternoon. Before beginning the journal of my stay in this pretty hill town, I shall give a brief account of the circumstances that brought me here.

My grandmother turned eighty-five last week. She's in good health, happy, cheerful, affectionate, and mentally alert, although she has some minor memory lapses, which are normal at her age, and she's the first to laugh at them. She's the soul and center of the family, and when she tells us about her forgetfulness, we all have a good laugh, too. It's not just by telling funny stories that she has acquired and maintained her central position. Her strength gives us the reasons to live that we can't find within ourselves. We've often wondered how someone so full of life could have spawned such feeble progeny. The next two generations (her children and grandchildren) are lacking in vigor, and the same, I fear, will be true of the third, which is just coming into existence. What little energy we have, the meager hope that keeps us going, we draw it all from her, as from an inexhaustible source. We wonder apprehensively what will become of us when she's gone.

As you can imagine, there's an undercurrent of worry when we get together to celebrate her birthday. There was a big party for her eightieth, which gathered all the relatives for a kind of grand declaration of our dependence. From then on we began to feel that an ominous countdown had begun. We made a special fuss this year, too, for her eighty-fifth. Though none of us said anything, we were all privately counting and calculating. She looked so well, it wasn't overly optimistic to imagine that she'd live another ten years. Why not? Ninety-five is not unheard of. And even allowing for her inevitable decline, ten years is quite a long time, long enough perhaps for us to find our respective ways and discover happiness, without relying on her vitality to maintain a semblance of human life.

The day before her birthday, one of my aunts asked if my grandmother was going to use her new age when she played the lottery. My grandmother hesitated for a while, enjoying the attention. They had to insist: "It's not every day you turn eighty-five!" Which is true, and it's also true that my grandmother is an inveterate lottery player, who never lets a chance go by. Once, she was hit by a car, which broke her tibia, and in the midst of the commotion and the pain she had the presence of mind to notice the last two numbers of the car's license plate, and before she was taken into the operating theater, she sent one of her sons to play the numbers, and she won. She spent the next two months with her leg in plaster telling everyone the story.

So the day before her birthday, when she was doing her round of the neighborhood stores, she stopped by the agency to put in her coupon. She's well known there, a favorite customer; they're always having a laugh with her. In her usual chatty way, she announced that it was her birthday and said she wanted to play the two numbers corresponding to her age. The lottery man wished her a happy birthday, approved of her idea, took out a coupon and started filling it in as he usually did. So, the number was ... ?

"Fifty-eight," said my grandmother.

It wasn't a joke. A minor confusion: the numbers had changed places in her head. The man asked her a couple of times, to make sure that he'd heard correctly; at first he thought she was kidding, but she didn't respond to his complicit giggle. Imperturbably she repeated, "Fifty-eight," in all sincerity. She left with her coupon, and it was only when she was about to wedge it between two apples in the fruit bowl (that was the Kabbalistic site where she kept her gambling documents) and looked at the numbers again that she realized her mistake. The next day at the party she told us what had happened, with her usual humor. And while the party was still going on, she went to the kitchen for a moment to listen to the radio to find out how River (her team) was doing, and it turned out that 58 had won a big prize.

That's where the money for my trip to Tandil came from. My grandmother knew I'd been dreaming about it for years; she knew it was important to me. Was there anything she didn't know about me, and the rest of us? Deeply familiar as she was with the mechanisms of idleness and fear that ruled all her descendants, she knew I'd never make the trip without some kind of prompting, which only she could provide.

I have always felt that I was her favorite grandson. I have lived on that conviction—if evasively skirting around reality, which is what my experience comes down to, can really be called living. My grandmother didn't hesitate to give me half her winnings, "for your little trip," as she said. That was all she needed to say; we both knew what she was talking about. But there are many deferred projects of this kind in the family, and almost all of her children, grandchildren, and children-in-law could have benefited, as I did, from her generosity. Had she been obliged to make a choice? What would she do with the rest of the money? I didn't ask myself these questions at the time, perhaps because they might have led to uncomfortable conclusions. But after all, given my grandmother's function as our source of life, the fact that she had chosen me could only mean that my need was the greatest.

The trip was (and is) related to what I've been claiming as my "vocation" all these years: literature. I know that my grand-mother would prefer me to have a life. I'd prefer that too, of course. But I'm stubborn, as the weak-willed often are, and I cling to a profession that's really no such thing, even though I may not be cut out for it, and haven't yet shown the slightest sign that I am. I persist in asserting, precisely, that literature does not require proof of aptitude. In my heart of hearts I never felt called to literature, or saw myself doing the work that such a vocation would entail. If I were to reply sincerely to the ques-tion of which professions I would have liked to pursue, had I possessed enough vigor to lead a real life, I'd have to list, in this order: ladies' hairdresser, ice cream vendor, bird and reptile taxidermist. Why? I don't know. It's something deep, but at the same time I can feel it in my skin, in my hands. Sometimes, during the day, I find myself unintentionally gesturing as if I were doing those kinds of work and, in a sort of sensory daydream, experiencing the satisfaction of a job well done and the desire to excel myself; and then, as in a dream within a dream, I begin to hatch vague plans to market my skills, build up my client base, and modernize my premises.

What my three unrealized vocations have in common is a certain analogy with sculpture, of which they appear to be impermanent and degraded (or repressed) forms. My observations in this area have led me to conjecture that behind every frustrated vocation lies the desire to sculpt.

If that's the case, the frustration that I've felt with literature up till now must also be related to sculpture. In fact, now that I think of it, the idea of basing my literary project and my attempts to distinguish myself as a writer on the search for "new forms of asymmetry" (to cite the title of my only published book) must have arisen from a twisted analogy with shapes and arrangements in three-dimensional space.

The trip to Tandil has finally confronted me with experience in itself. Before leaving, I put a notebook in my pocket and all the way here on the bus I was writing these preliminary notes. Now, as I begin my journal, I would like to dedicate it to someone. The obvious person, for various reasons—loyalty, gratitude, good manners, simplicity—is my grandmother. But no. A dark urge impels me to write something else, namely this (as a dedication, it's pretty dull):

"To my beloved reproductive organs."

It's nearly midnight; I'm sitting at a little table against the wall in this hotel room in Tandil. The door is bolted, the shutters closed. For once, I don't have to look for a theme. Because today, as soon as I got here, something extraordinary happened to me, which has not only given me a theme to write about, but has also transformed my very person into a theme. Nothing like this has ever happened to anybody before. I'm the first, the one and only, which obliges me to bear witness, but also simplifies my task, since whatever I say and however I say it, my words will automatically constitute a testimony and a proof (by virtue of the fact that I am the person saying them).

This is what literature really is. Now I can see it. Everything that came before, everything that people, including writers, think of as literature, that is to say the laborious search for themes and the exhausting work of giving them shape, all of that collapses like a house of cards, a youthful illusion or an error. Literature begins when you become literature, and if there's such a thing as a literary vocation, it's simply the transubstantiation of experience that has taken place in me today. By pure chance. Because of a fortuitous encounter, and the revelation that followed.

I saw the back of a ghost. Today, a little while ago, shortly after arriving. I came to the hotel from the bus terminal, checked in, went up to my room to leave my bag, and went out for a walk almost straightaway to stretch my legs and get to know the city. Tandil's not much more than a big town built on the pampa, at the foot of some hills that are among the oldest in the world. It seemed to be livening up a bit at that time: kids were gathering on the street corners, people were leaving work and heading home, or going to cafés, but only in the small downtown area. I returned to the hotel via some streets a bit farther out (just a bit), and they were deserted: I didn't see a soul for quite a while. By then it should have been dark already. The day's afterglow was still hanging in the air. All the colors were shrouded in a uniform silver, and a deep silence reigned. The rectilinear streets ran away toward the horizon, and they looked so alike that on one corner I thought I'd lost my sense of direction. I hadn't, but when I set off again, sure that I knew which way to go, I walked a bit more quickly, paying more attention. To what? There was nothing to pay attention to.

Perhaps because of the pallid absence surrounding me, I noticed a little movement that I would have overlooked in the bustle of a busy street. Not so much a movement as its shadow, the shifting of a minuscule volume of air, or not even that. I was walking past an empty house, whose façade was hollowed out into a kind of loggia with columns: no doubt the whim of a traditional Italian builder, one of the many who left their mark on our provincial towns. Time had darkened the gray of the stucco, and, beyond the arch, the dim light of dusk gave out entirely. There at the back, floating halfway between floor and ceiling, in front of the walled-up door, was a ghost. The movement that had revealed his presence must have been a tic. It was followed by intense stillness. He looked at me, we looked at each other, for barely an instant, no more than the moment it took for fright to imprint itself on his weary features. Before I had time to be afraid, he had turned and gone back in. Clearly, it was a chance occurrence that he could not have foreseen. Decades of habit and boredom would have convinced him that no one went past at that time. But that "no one" didn't include me. I was a stranger who had just arrived in town, walking about idly with nowhere to go. My presence there took him by surprise, interrupting his "stepping out for a breath of fresh air," which was perhaps the repetition of an evening habit from the old days, when he was alive. And he reacted to the surprise by turning around and going back the way he had come (through the wall), without realizing that this instinctive movement would show me something no human being had ever seen: his back.

Humans have seen a great many things in the course of their long history; it might be said that, collectively, they have "seen it all." I thought I'd seen it all myself, even with my limited experience. The individual repeats the "alls" and the "nothings" of the species, but there is always "something" that is extra or missing. Only the unrepeatable is truly alive. That unrepeatable "something" is a single, unique entity, in which the worlds of life and death come together like the points of an inconceivable double vertex. And nobody, until today, had seen the back of a ghost.

I saw it for the very briefest moment, but I saw it. Then, suddenly, the scene vanished, and I continued on my way, quickening my pace, rushing to get back, to shut myself into the hotel room and start writing (the floor plan flashed vividly before my mind's eye, with the table and chair, and even the notebook open on the table). That was when I said to myself for the first time: Literature ... Or rather I shouted it, inwardly. But there was no need to articulate the word: I could feel it in every fiber of my body. Such was my excitement that I really did get lost this time. I had to summon all my orientation skills to find the way, walking faster and faster. I was almost running. Even so, every few steps I reached into my pockets, took out the ballpoint pen and the papers that I happened to have on me (the bus ticket, the hotel card, a few other scraps), and, barely stopping, scribbled a note, then set off again more quickly than before.

And here I am, at last, writing like a man possessed. As well I might: not even a whole lifetime of adventures and study could have given me more reason to write. And now I come, with a natural ease, to the climax: the description of that back, hidden from the eyes of humanity until now.

But ... I don't know if it's my impatience, or the excess of energy that has taken hold of me since the ghost turned around, but there's a sharp pain in the middle of my chest, and it keeps getting more and more intense, forcing me to grimace horribly. It's becoming unbearable, climbing to a spasmodic peak, and when it seems about to relent, it doesn't. I'm finding it hard to write. My vision is clouding over, my eyes are half closed, and I'm clamping my jaws so tightly to stop myself crying out that my molars feel like they're going to explode.

At this very moment, as I persist in the effort to trace these increasingly distorted letters and words, I'm assailed by the idea that I could die right here, bent over my notebook, before I can describe what I saw ...

Is it possible? Could anyone be so unlucky? Now the pain has eased a little, but it's worse: I can feel it tearing the chambers of my heart with "a sound of silk being slashed," and the blood's gushing inside me, getting all mixed up. My writing hand is shaking and starting to turn purple ... I don't know how I've managed to keep the pen moving ...

My sight is blurred, I'm staring desperately at the lines my hand keeps tracing ... At the darkening edge of my field of vision, I can see the crumpled papers on which I made notes when I was out walking ... But they're not even notes; they're no more than cryptic reminders that nobody will be able to understand (because of my pernicious habit of using abbreviations). My death will condemn them to indecipherability forever ... unless someone very clever comes along and by means of meticulous inductive and deductive reasoning (over years or decades) is able to arrive at a plausible reconstruction ... But no, that kind of treatment is reserved for the papers of a great writer; no one will bother with mine ...

Maybe I could leave some kind of key ... but no, it's impossible. I don't have time. I can't maintain the rhythm and the rigor of good prose, the kind of prose I would like to have written, the kind that would have made me a great writer, worthy of serious study. All I can do is use the last of my strength to scrawl a few disjointed, almost incoherent sentences ... I don't have time because I'm dying ... Death is the exorbitant price that a failure like me has to pay for becoming literature ... The hardest thing for me is that I did, in fact, have time (once), and I wasted it shamefully. The lesson, if a lesson can in some small way redeem my wasted life, is this: you have to get straight to the point ... I should have begun with the crucial thing, which no one but I knew about ... I wouldn't even have had to sacrifice the flow and the balance of a well-told story, because I could have written the introductory sections later and rearranged it all when preparing the final draft ... This stupid compulsion to narrate events in chronological order ...

DECEMBER 8, 2003

The Ovenbird

THE HYPOTHESIS UNDERLYING THIS STUDY IS THAT human beings act in strict accordance with an instinctive program, which governs all of our actions, however unpredictable or freely chosen they may seem, and that our "cultural" free will is consequently no more than a kindly illusion with which we dupe ourselves, as much a part of our innate heritage as the rest. On the face of it, this proposal is extremely bold or outright preposterous: the idea that everything could be foreordained would seem to be refuted by the wild variety of human lives, beginning with the extravagant iridescence of thought, the unpredictability of our least reactions, and the ideas that come to mind willy-nilly; and if it's unconvincing in an individual case, how could it explain the incalculable differences between one human being and another, no matter how closely related they are? But this impression of difference is precisely the illusion that the hypothesis aims to dispel, and all one has to do (I'm not saying this is easy) is accept that it is an illusion for the variations to become irrelevant and the veil that hid our essential instinctive uniformity to fall away. There's no need to give up those variations, or sacrifice one's "surface" differences to a "deep" essence, because, in fact, there's no such essence; it's all surface. And what's to stop all the countless minutiae of our acts, thoughts, desires, dreams, and creations, everything that happens second by second between birth and death, being inscribed a priori in our genes, in the form of a program that's identical for every member of the species? Science has accustomed us, by now, to greater wonders of computing. Humans have always been very sure that their actions are determined by a kind of causation that is free and superior, "cultural" rather than natural ... while the equally ancient hypothesis of instinctive programming has always been reserved for animals and applied to them with fanatical rigor.

I don't know if I'll be able to persuade anyone. The idea is too shocking and arbitrary; and in a way it's self-defeating because if it's not built into our program, how could we accept it? But maybe it *is* built into our program; after all it occurred to me (and I'm not the first). And it's true that persuasion is one of our instinctive gifts, along with fiction.

What humans have traditionally believed about animals owes a great deal to fiction. I'm not saying it isn't true. How could I? Let's take it at face value, and turn it around. Let's imagine, for the purposes of demonstration, how an animal of some kind might apply its reason to this issue. It might be objected that animals don't have reason to apply. Very well, I'm quite prepared to use another word; in any case, it's just a question of terminology (and I know I'm not expressing myself well). By the "reasoning" of an animal, then, I mean something different, for which we don't have a word, precisely because we have always stayed on this side of the line. Let's forget all the tales and the fables: the traveling ant, the grumbling bear, the fox and the crow ... Or, rather, let's take them to their ultimate conclusions. Instead of "fiction," let's call it "translation," and translate thoroughly. Now's the time to do it, because only translation can get to the bottom of this nature/culture dialectic. I think it will be clearer if I give an example, but I should point out that it's not an example in the conventional sense, that is, a particular extracted at random from the general by discursive means. What follows is all general, from start to finish, pure generality.

Let's imagine an ovenbird, in the year 1895, in the province of Buenos Aires. And let's stay with the human perspective for a moment, in order to make the contrast clearer.

The ovenbird begins to build in autumn ... while building its nest, the bird keeps an eye on its human neighbors ... when the construction has attained its spherical form ... the bird mates for life and gathers its food, which consists of larvae and worms, exclusively on the ground ... it struts around with a gravely serious air ... its strong, confident, clinking cry ...

That's enough. The reader will have recognized the tone. It's a human speaking, a naturalist. Like all styles, this one takes the eternal existence of its object for granted. We have turned the lives of the animals into a voyage through various styles, and in the process our lives have become a voyage through styles as well (which is what allows me to conduct this experiment).

The ovenbird was building his hut. Let's say it was autumn, so as not to offend against plausibility, or just for fun. Enormous country afternoons. A shower at five. The sixteenth of April 1895. Let's go back to a sentence from the naturalist's paragraph: While building its nest, the bird keeps an eye on its human neighbors (in context, the point of this observation is to explain why the entrance to the bird's hut always faces the nearest house or ranch, or the road). In his plentiful spare time, the ovenbird thought . . .

But is this possible? Is it possible to go this way without straying into the world of Disney? Isn't this taking translation too far? It might be acceptable to the use the verb "to think" as a translation, a way of communicating, when referring to what is going on in the animal's brain, or its nervous system, or, more precisely, in its life and history. But what about the content of this thought? Even if it's acceptable for me to say that the bird thinks, can I say *what* he thinks? I think I can. Because it's the same thing.

So, what was he thinking? Nothing. His mind was blank. Fatigue and anxiety (these words are translations too, like all the words that follow; I won't be pointing this out again) had left him in a daze.

Translating from "ovenbirdese": he felt overwhelmed by an accumulation of disasters, which is how he saw his life. So much work, so much suffering, so many obligations! And the constant uncertainty: always having to choose, without ever knowing if you were making the right choice . . . The only thing

he knew for certain, and this ruled out the only possible consolation, was that there *was* a right way, a manner of doing things
well, of being happy. And he would never follow that way, or he
would, but only as far as the first intersection, where he would
turn off. He knew this for certain because of the humans, always there right in front of him. Now, for example: the family
had come out onto the balcony, after the rain, and they were
drinking maté. He envied the automatic instincts that determined the behavior of humans and all the other animals, except for the ovenbird, that accursed species (so he thought).
He shivered as he watched them brewing the maté, passing the
gourd around, the whole complicated ceremony, involving the
use of implements and accompanied by words, gestures, movements ... Human instincts were so amazing! By instinct they
were able to perform this intricate ballet (and so many others:
he was always seeing them do something new) without hesitation or stopping to think, without wondering if it was the right
thing to do or not, without deliberation, just because that's
how it was written in the immemorial archives of their happy
species. While he ... Ovenbirds, he thought, had paid for the
skills that allowed them to survive with a drastic weakening of
the instinctive system. It was futile, and perhaps ungrateful, to
complain, but he felt that the price was too high. That's what
the example of the humans was telling him. Humans lived, and
they knew in advance how to do it. The ovenbird was subject to
the terrifying arbitrariness of ideas and thoughts and states of
mind, of will and its endless weaknesses, of climate and history.

How had they known it was time to drink maté? The rain and its stopping had nothing to do with it, because they often drank maté when it hadn't rained or stopped raining, and they didn't drink it every time the rain came to an end. The unfathomable wisdom of instinct! And the drink gave them so much pleasure, lucky bastards. To think that the same instinct had sent them to the store to buy the maté, to the kitchen to boil the water, to bed for their siesta ... They were perfect. Perfect machines for living. An object lesson for an anguished wretch like him. But what could he do if he belonged to the only species that nature had neglected to endow with an instinct worthy of the name? There was no point bemoaning that fateful moment in evolution when the species had strayed from the safe path of adaptation ... Maybe the solution was to keep forging ahead into maladaptation until things came good again ... But no, it was futile, and dangerous too; making things worse was not the way to go.

Meanwhile, he was feeling increasingly ill. He was dizzy, everything was spinning. What was he doing there, in the fork of a hackberry tree, six yards from the ground? He was a ground animal, heights disagreed with him. But he couldn't go down right then because there happened to be a hungry, bad-tempered rat prowling around under the tree. Every time it rained a few drops, that stupid rodent's burrow would flood, which made him crazy and vicious. It was true that the ovenbird could fly far away and land anywhere and walk for a bit, if only to find some relief from his worries. But it was a bother; afterward, he'd have to come back ... And where would he find a decent place for a walk, with all the puddles that had formed? It was better to stay where he was and try to control the dizziness. Also, he had to wait for his mate, who'd set out before the rain and ended up who knows where; she'd come back wet, muddy, grumbling, and they'd have to sleep in that ruin with damp feathers and empty stomachs ... he turned to look at the half-built nest. His indecision added a mental dizziness to the physical sensation, which almost made him lose his balance and fall like a stone. Sadistically, the rain had chosen the worst possible moment. By stopping just when he was normally getting ready to end his day's work, it confronted him with another one of those difficult decisions that made up the story of his wretched life: when the sun broke through the clouds, there were still at least two hours of daylight left. He couldn't start working instantaneously; he needed a while to set up the systems for transporting, mixing, and so on. Two hours was a fair stretch of time, enough to add an inch or two and maybe replace all of the new section he'd built that morning, which had been damaged by the rain. But he'd already wasted an hour watching the humans, lost in his melancholic daydreaming. So was it still worth the effort or not? The mud would have been too thin, but there was plenty of it ... He'd lost the will to work, but he knew he'd feel guilty if he didn't do something. What could he do, though, in the short time left before it got dark? If he didn't get to work, he'd just go on being depressed. Which is what happened. A wasted day.

The nest was half built. It didn't exist. Mud origami. All right: tomorrow, first thing, he'd get straight to work. Or should he do something now? There was more time left than it seemed, he felt sure; the daylight always lasts longer after rain. Oh, well … Tomorrow. At least he had the consolation that the weather would be fine. The clouds had gone away; there wasn't one left in the sky.

The ovenbird saw his constructive art as an accumulation of vague and useless forms, from which, by chance, something equivalent to a function ended up emerging. He told himself that he should follow the example of the humans, with their hyperfunctional houses, built automatically, always the same: vertical walls, a roof, openings, a system of ways in and out … At least they didn't have to bother with architecture! They did it the way they did it. They just did it, the same way every time, and the houses lasted forever. Take location. Guided by an infallible instinct (that is, by instinct itself), they always built on the ground, right on the ground, on the surface. They didn't have to choose; nature had chosen for them. An ovenbird, by contrast, was subject to the most unpredictable whims: a post, a tree, a roof, the eaves of a house, five yards from the ground, or six, or fifteen … And then there was the question of which kind of mud to use, and the proportion of straw or horsehair … There were practically no fixed standards to go by (or that, at least, was how he saw it). And the accidents! Like the rain today. He was at the mercy of circumstances: the slightest variation could change everything; the consequences of the most trivial events would ramify right to the end of his life, piling up to make it unlivably motley and baroque. Humans, by contrast, like all the other living beings on the planet, had a way of neutralizing the accidental: a healthy and well-structured instinct allowed them to cancel out randomness by improvising new circumstances. But not him! Every other creature but him! That was because the ovenbird was an individual, like all ovenbirds, while humans were a species. The species was firmly grounded in necessity; the individual was up in the air, suspended in dizziness and contingency.

But shouldn't that exceptional status have had some advantages too? Whenever you pay, thought the ovenbird, in the depths of his terrible wretchedness, you get something in return. And the "accursed race" to which he belonged had paid a substantial price: they had given up the peace of living without anxiety, generation after generation, in happy, trusting submission to the sweet mechanisms of nature. There had to be some compensation for such a great loss. There *must* have been some advantages. There were: they were great and definitive. A single word summed them up: freedom. He had freedom. All he had to do was enjoy it.

If only it were that simple! he silently exclaimed in the throes of a mental agony, and lifted his aching eyes to the sign that the world had used as an equivalent of "freedom": the sky. A rainbow had appeared in its empty dome. He was seeing it aslant, diagonally, and that made it look more monumental and impressive. For him, it was charged with "poetic," "philosophical," "moral," and "aesthetic" resonances (these are equivalents as well, but I trust they will serve to convey my meaning), while the humans, who were looking at it too, saw it for the simple meteorological phenomenon, the simple gift, that it was. Beyond: the pink splendor of the dusk.

Yes! (Now he was getting excited, poor thing.) Freedom! The immense freedom of flying over the world, over the various worlds. That was something humans didn't have! The rigid blind of instinct came down in infancy, and all they did for the rest of their lives was automatically obey the dictates of their nature. The ovenbird, on the other hand, was progressing on the path of infinite possibilities.

But that path was too much like the void. His current state, which felt like premature old age, an exhaustion caused by the constantly draining struggle simply to stay alive, proved that freedom was inherently excessive. Freedom really had to be defined anew, and in that definition he would come off badly. Beings who lived in strict accordance with an uncontaminated nature, like humans, were free in a superior sense of the word. Slaves of instinct? Granted, but "instinct" had to be redefined as well; and if instinct was equivalent to infallibility and happiness, what greater freedom could there be? All the rest was illusory. They weren't missing out on anything.

The humans there on the balcony were nearly finished with their maté because the water had gone cold, and the leaves had lost their flavor, and they'd had enough ... in short: because the magnificent Law that governed all the little causes had so decreed. The entire universe was manifest among the humble and the meek, and attended to them like a god, serving and obeying them. Time that destroys and dominates all things slowed to a standstill in the eternal present of simple existence. Calm and sensual, strangers to the torments of conscience and doubt, trusting to the gentle flow of life, mating, reproduction, and even death, they (unlike him) could truly say, "To die, to sleep—to sleep, perchance to dream." They had no fears ... And yet they too had "resonances." When, as now, they contemplated the pink and violet sky, the pristine countryside, and time frozen in the delicate whorls of the air, they too were sensitive to metaphysics, poetry, morality, and aesthetics—more sensitive than he was, because they saw reality without veils! Had he been tempted to imitate them, as he'd occasionally tried to do, it would have been futile: another whim of consciousness, another project doomed to fail, one of the many on which he wasted his energy over and over ...

Now they were talking. They had been talking the whole time, confidently, calmly, with their dry little words and whispers. That was another sore point for the ovenbird. Although it wasn't an important part of life for him (it is for us humans, but not for him; which shows that one shouldn't rush to translate back the other way: the equivalences, although complete, are not symmetrical), he found it especially galling. What came out of human throats was effective, simple, and practical; the ovenbird's songs and chirps were a dreamlike tangle in which function and frill, sense and nonsense, truth and beauty were chaotically mixed. Humans didn't have problems like that; Nature had made it easy for them: from birth, or shortly afterward (from the moment, in their first year of life, when the "blind" of instinct came down), they deposited all meaning in language, and whatever didn't fit was considered marginal or insignificant. But for the ovenbird, meaning was dispersed in a thousand different telepathies, while song was an aesthetic without precise limits, which could be used for just about anything, or be of no use at all. He sang for love, or because he had the hiccups, or felt like it, or just because of the time of day ... And his song, like everything he did, was subject to the unpredictable fluctuations of consciousness, to excess freedom or the excessiveness of freedom itself.

Night was falling over the sacred pampa. The little bird, still and quiet like a curl of mud in front of his unfinished dwelling, went on wallowing in anxiety and nostalgia for real life, which he saw as the life of others in an inaccessible elsewhere. I don't know if I've made myself clear, and even if I have, I might not have been convincing. The only aim of this piece is to offer some counterevidence, which I hope will be thought-provoking, although it's hardly conclusive. The method itself could be challenged: after all, this was written by a human. But what does that prove, except that humans are equipped with an instinct that enables them to write? How else could they do it? Why don't birds write? Precisely because they have too much freedom: they could write or not; there's nothing in them to trigger the activity in a failsafe way; unlike humans, they don't have a program that would allow them to write with perfect automatic facility. The action of writing these pages is itself written into the genetic endowment handed down to me from the dawn of time. That's why I can do it just like that, without hesitations or corrections, like breathing or sleeping. From the ovenbird's point of view, there's a gulf between this magic facility and the deliberations that make all of his tasks so laborious.

MAY 8, 1994

The Cart

A CART FROM A SUPERMARKET IN MY NEIGHBORHOOD was rolling along on its own, with no one pushing it. It was a cart just like all the others, made of thick wire, with four little rubber wheels (the front pair slightly closer together, which is what gives the vehicle its characteristic shape), and a bar coated with bright red plastic for steering it around. There was nothing to distinguish it from the two hundred other carts that belonged to that enormous supermarket, the biggest and busiest in the neighborhood. Except that the cart I'm referring to was the only one that moved on its own. It did this with infinite discretion: in the tumult that reigned on the premises from opening to closing time, to say nothing of the peak hours, its movement went unnoticed. It was used like all the other carts, filled with food, drink, and cleaning products, unloaded at the cash registers, pushed hurriedly from one aisle to the next, and if the shoppers let it go and saw it roll a fraction of an inch, they assumed that it was being carried along by momentum.

The wonder was only perceptible at night, when the frenzy gave way to an uncanny calm, but there was no one to admire it. Very occasionally, the shelf-stackers starting work at dawn would be surprised to find the cart astray down at the back, next to the deep-freeze cabinets, or between the dark shelves of wine. They naturally assumed that it had been left there by mistake the previous night. In such a large and labyrinthine establishment, oversights like that were only to be expected. If the cart was moving when they found it, and if they noticed the movement, which was as inconspicuous as the sweep of a watch's minute hand, they presumed that it must have been the result of a slope in the floor or a draft of air.

In fact, the cart had spent the whole night going around and around, up and down the aisles, slow and quiet as a star, without ever hesitating or coming to a stop. It did the rounds of its domain, mysterious, inexplicable, its miraculous essence concealed by the banal appearance of a shopping cart like any other. The employees and the customers were too busy to detect this secret phenomenon, which made no difference, after all, to anyone or anything. I was the only one to notice it, I think. Actually, I'm sure: attention is scarce among human beings, and a great deal of it was required in this case. I didn't tell anyone, because it was too much like the sort of fantasies I'm always coming up with, which have earned me a reputation for craziness. Over many years of shopping there, I learned to recognize my special cart by a little mark on the red bar; except that I didn't have to see the mark, because even from a distance something told me that it was the one. A wave of joy and confidence swept through me each time I identified it. I thought of it as a kind of friend, a friendly object, perhaps because in this case the inertness of a thing had been leavened with that minimal tremor of life that is the starting point for all fantasies. Perhaps, in a corner of my subconscious, I was grateful to it for being different from all the other carts in the civilized world, and for having revealed that difference to me and no one else.

I liked to imagine it in the solitude and silence of midnight, rolling very slowly through the dimness, like a little boat full of holes setting off in search of adventure, knowledge, and (why not?) love. But what could it find in that array of dairy products, vegetables, noodles, soft drinks, and canned peas, which was all it knew of the world? Nevertheless, it didn't lose hope, but resumed its navigations, or never interrupted them, like someone who knows that his efforts are futile but keeps trying all the same. Someone who keeps trying because he has pinned his hopes on the transformation of everyday banality into dream and portent. I think I identified with it, and that identification, I think, was how I discovered it in the first place. Paradoxically, for a writer who feels so distant and different from his colleagues, I felt close to that shopping cart. Even our respective techniques were similar: progressing by imperceptible increments, which add up to make a long journey; not looking too far ahead; urban themes.

Given all this, you can imagine my surprise when I heard it speak or, to be more precise, when I heard what it said. Its declaration was the last thing I was expecting to hear. Its words went through me like a spear of ice and forced me to reconsider the whole situation, beginning with the sympathy I felt for the cart, then the sympathy I felt for myself, and more generally my sympathy for miracles. I wasn't surprised by the fact of it speaking; I had been expecting that. Perhaps I felt that our relationship had matured to the point where linguistic signs were appropriate. I knew that the moment had come for it to say something to me (for example that it admired me and loved me and was on my side). I bent down next to it, pretending to tie my shoelaces, so that I could put my ear to the wire mesh on its side, and then I was able to hear its voice, a whisper from the underside of the world, and yet the words were perfectly clear and distinct:

"I am Evil."

MARCH 17, 2004

Poverty

I'M POORER THAN THE POOR, AND I'VE BEEN POOR FOR longer. An eternity of deprivation stretches out in my resentful fantasy, which is not confined to measuring the duration of the ill. It also gauges the magnitude of the catastrophe. There's so much I could have, if only I had the means! So many things, experiences, and comforts! Listing them, putting them in order, and calculating their potential contributions to my pleasure leaves me feeling exhausted and entitled to their possession, if only as a reward for that obsessive labor. But my real experience is taking me further and further away from the well-being that money could provide, while sharpening my appreciation of its advantages. I don't have to fantasize about this; I just have to look around me. I live among people who keep getting richer year by year. I haven't kept up with the poor friends I used to have, and to be frank I don't want to. We have nothing in common: no tastes, habits, or interests. Soccer bores me stiff. The people I can have a conversation with are sophisticates with money to spare, but of course the idea of sharing it with me never occurs to them. Why would they do that? In their frivolous innocence, they consider me a great writer, a figure from literary history living in the present. But in fact I'm destitute. I watch them orbiting in spheres that are more and more inaccessible to me, and my resentment grows. I become bitter and depressed; I accentuate my eccentricity—it's an understandable defense mechanism, and a way of hiding the truth. I'm ashamed of my leaky shoes, my unvarying and inadequate wardrobe, the scruffiness and poor personal hygiene that are symptoms of a repressed desperation. I hole up in my apartment, and I can't invite anyone over: the furniture's too rickety, there are too many damp patches on the walls, and our supplies of cheap noodles are too strictly rationed. From the window I see my neighbors in Barrio Rivadavia (a shantytown) and remark that they're not as poor as I am, because they always have something to spare, while I don't have enough of anything. I observe their feasts and drinking bouts, their Sundays in the sun; even when they go out towing their rickshaws to rummage through the trash, they're richer than I am because they find things. Meanwhile, I exhaust myself performing the most abject tasks, engaging in the most humiliating middle-class begging, barely earning enough to feed my children, who have to make heroic efforts to endure the inevitable comparisons with the lives of their friends, and justifiably regard me as a failure. How long is it since I bought a book or a record, or went to the cinema? My computer is obsolete; by some miracle it still works, but I can't even dream of upgrading. All around me people are buying, spending, adapting, changing, progressing. Crisis or no crisis, my country is subject to pe-

riodic rashes of consumerism that end up affecting everyone.
Everyone except me. How can I buy anything, even a pencil,
when my pockets are empty? I don't even have a credit card. I've
had to become a tax evader because I just don't have the means
to pay. And when all my friends and acquaintances get tired of
amassing new things and rewarding experiences, and go away
for vacations on tropical beaches or cultural visits to beautiful
cities, I'm left behind in my sty, chewing over my resentment.
Only a miracle could produce a windfall and light up my squalid
existence, but it's already miraculous that I've managed to get
what I need to survive, and you can't really ask for two miracles.

Why did it have to be like this? Why couldn't it have turned
out differently, if, in the end, it would have made no difference
to the universal scheme of things? Why did I have to be the object of your fierce persecution, Poverty, demanding and vexa-
tious goddess — or, rather, witch — that you are? Why me? For
some mysterious reason you noticed me back in Pringles, when
I was a kid; maybe you were drawn to my pretty eyes, which
you afflicted with myopia, adding physical to economic misery, making me neurotic as well as a pariah. Our close association dates back to those early days. My little house, echoing
with scarcity, was yours as well. That was where I got to know
you, listening to my parents' endless arguments over money,
in which I discovered language and a model for life. And if I
went out, you accompanied me, you took me by the hand and
pointed out the boxes of colored pencils that my school friends
had, their rustling pads of tracing paper, the ice creams they ate,

the Mexican magazines they bought ... Where did they get the money? Why didn't I have any? You never told me.

The truly remarkable thing is that when I left town you came with me, as if you couldn't bear my absence. My mother resigned herself to the separation, but not you. You came to Buenos Aires; you clung to me and settled in my lodgings, and all my ploys for eluding your relentless company failed. If I went to work, you accompanied me on the bus; if I lost my job, you stayed at home watching me read one sad volume after another. When I got married, you were the only wedding present I could offer my wife. You were the only fairy who bent over my children's cradles. You were the sinister Christmas tree, my psychic roulette, the confidante to whom I poured out the all-too-obvious contents of my heart. Tossing and turning in bed, tortured by insomnia, I hatched all manner of escape plans, shriveling my brain. You always let me choose my course of action freely, but at the last minute you'd come along too. It was like one of those obsessive cartoons: I could cross oceans and continents, and believe that I'd escaped from your persecution, for a while at least ... but then I'd find you in my room, calm as could be, busy with some mean little scheme. It was automatic. I ended up becoming the most sedentary of men. And the metaphoric forms of flight—new jobs, resolutions, self-hypnosis—were, predictably, even less effective: when the literal doesn't work, metaphors are worse than useless.

Enough! I've done my time. Not even a murderer gets a forty-six-year sentence, and I've never broken the law; on the contrary, I'm so well meaning and inoffensive, I sometimes feel I'm a saint. Can't you leave me in peace? Don't I deserve a break, at least? I know it's my fault, but it still seems unfair. I want to be left alone, to fend for myself, if I'm still up to it; I want to be subject to the laws of chance, like other men, and know that there's a possibility, however slim, that luck might smile on me. I'm fed up with your relentless presence, Poverty. Your homeopathy has made me sick; I wish I could have you eradicated ... If there was any chance you might listen, I'd threaten to kill myself, but that wouldn't be any use either ...

At this point in my soliloquy, the figure of Poverty appeared before me: gaunt, stiff, ragged, and—in her way—magnificent. My words must have had some effect, because her falsely submissive air had been replaced by a look of genuine fury: eyes aflame, fists clenched, lips opening and closing violently.

"Fool! Featherbrain! Moron! All these years I've kept quiet, putting up with your complaints, your immature whining, your maladjustment, your ingratitude for all the gifts I've showered on you since you were born, but I can't stand it anymore! Now you're going to listen to me, though it probably won't do you any good, because some people never learn.

"Who told you that my company was a disadvantage? The fact that you believed it just because that's what everyone says goes to show how incurably frivolous you are. And that's exactly the vice that I've been striving to save you from, with a perseverance that I now see was wasted. After all this time, do I have to spell out what I've done for you? I don't know where to start, because I gave you everything you have. And more than that: I gave you the framework to accommodate it all. I gave you the energy you'd never have been able to muster by yourself. Without me you'd have given up almost straightaway, devoid of ideas and the brainpower to come up with them. I put variation and color into what would have been a monotonous routine. I gave you the joy of always being able to hope for better times. If you'd possessed something, what would you have hoped for? (Except the loss of it, knowing you.) As it was, you were always expecting things to improve. Fearful and timid as you are, and always would have been, however much you'd had, you would have lived in constant fear of thieves and swindlers, who would always have been too clever for you. I gave you a reason to go on living, the only one you had. Do you think you'd have written a word if I hadn't been there all the time, peeking over your shoulder at your notebooks? Why else would you have written anything? And if you had, it would have been worse than what you've produced. Much worse! But I have to explain that too, don't I?

"Even with your limited intelligence, you must have noticed that the rich are different. And this is why: the rich man substitutes money for the making of things. Instead of buying wood and making a table, he buys a table ready-made. There's a progression: if he's not so rich, he buys the table and paints it himself; if he's richer, he buys it painted. If he's not rich at all, he doesn't even buy the wood; he goes to the forest and cuts down a tree, et cetera. Poverty (yours truly) provides a certain amount of process. The rich man gets everything ready-made, including goods and services. Which means that he loses reality, because reality is a process. Worse still: the availability of ready-made things waiting to be used comes to seem natural, and he begins to expect it in the world of thought as well. That's why the rich use ready-made ideas, copied opinions, tastes invented by others. They delegate the process. Even where their feelings are concerned, which is what makes them so stereotypical and superficial: the caricatures by which they're generally represented are actually far too complex and flattering. Would you have wanted to be like that? Do you have any idea what you're saying? Without me, your books would have lacked the one modest virtue that no one can deny them: realism. I gave you that, and you have the nerve to hold it against me!

"And how! With your first thought in the morning, you revile me; with your last thought when you go to bed as well. And in between it's nothing but protests, complaints, and whining. I'm aware that with the advance of technology and consumerism, the world is adopting the system of the rich, which will be generalized eventually. That must be what makes you feel marginal and old-fashioned, as if I were a burden holding you back in a past of pre-industrial labor. Maybe that's why you resent me, but it's the source of all your originality, and given your maladaptation, without originality, you're nothing.

"Anyhow, I'm not going to go on justifying your existence. I'm sick of being your bête noire; I'm fed up with your insults and rudeness. I can't stand you anymore. I'm moving out! If that's what you really wanted, you've got it: you won't see me again. I'm going to Arturito Carrera's place, where I know I'll get the appreciation I deserve."

And with that, she got up and headed for the door, offended, rigid with indignation. It was true! She was going! One more step and she'd be outside. Panic swelled in my chest, unbearable as a heart attack. Speeches always convince me, this one especially, because in a way it had sprung from my own heart and mind (that's how allegorical figures operate). I leaped up from my armchair and shouted:

"No! Don't go, Poverty! Forget everything I said, I beg you, and what I'll say in the future, too, because I know what I'm like; I won't be able to stop complaining. But I don't really want you to leave. After all, I'm used to you now. It would almost be like my wife leaving me. I couldn't bear the humiliation. I wasn't born to be an orphan. Stay with me, and I'll get by. Don't listen to what I say. I'm rude, I know, and I don't deserve you, but please, please, don't go."

She stood perfectly still with her hand on the doorknob for a moment of unbearable suspense, and then she turned very slowly. There was a serious smile on her lips, and I knew that she had forgiven me. She walked toward me with ceremonious steps, like a bride approaching the altar.

And Poverty has lived with me ever since. Not for one day has she left my home.

ROSARIO, NOVEMBER 29, 1995

The Topiary Bears of Parque Arauco

THE PHOTOS WILL BEAR ME OUT: ON EITHER SIDE OF
the entrance to the mall on Avenida Kennedy are topiary forms,
clipped from a plant with small, dark (perennial) leaves, which
represent:

On one side, a perfectly proportioned polar bear, thirty-five
feet high, holding a bottle of Coca-Cola in his right paw (the
bottle is to scale, i.e., huge). Some way off, there are two smaller
forms, clipped from the same plant, representing two bear cubs,
one standing and reaching out toward the full-grown bear, the
other sitting on the ground but also looking at the adult.

On the other side, at the opposite end of the mall's façade,
about a hundred yards away, another big bear, just like the first,
with the same bottle of Coca-Cola, and a single cub, but this
one is up against the adult with his front paws outstretched as if
he wants to be picked up or is trying to reach the bottle.

The sequence of figures sketches out a little story. In the first
scene, you might say that the bear is appearing before his cubs
and saying, "Look what I've brought." In the second, one of the
cubs has rushed up to him and is trying to scale his big body

of green leaves, reaching out for the bottle, which the father is holding aloft as if to say, "Not yet." The cub's little brother has disappeared.

It's a happy Laocoön, a living sculpture made from plants that grow and thrive and renew themselves. And since there are two sculptures, as opposed to the Laocoön, which is a single group, they suggest an outcome, a formula that divides the passion into installments. The formula of death has become the formula of life: the formula of Coca-Cola, which is at once secret and universal, a secret within everyone's reach.

The cars whiz past on the avenue, anonymous, indifferent. The bears are a fleeting vision, so fleeting there's hardly a fraction of a second between the two groups, as in a flip book. The drivers, concentrating on the hellish traffic in this part of the city, don't notice them. But the children do: it's a favorite scene; they press up against the windows to see it. If they regularly pass this way, they know when to start looking out: a bit before the mall so they can savor the anticipation and be sure not to miss anything. If not, they're taken by surprise, but even so they understand what it's about, they interpret, they get the message, even the youngest.

It's a universal language, and universal languages are aimed at children, not at adults. But in this case there is something more than a message, and something more than a language. The children passing by in cars or joyfully entering the mall, led by their parents, are not the only beneficiaries. There are others: the invisible, hidden children who are the protagonists of this fable, the fable of the topiary bears of Parque Arauco.

When the sun rises over the massive Andes looming beyond Las Condes, poor children from all the slums of Santiago come with empty plastic Coca-Cola bottles, one bottle each (no more than one: this is an unwritten rule). It's a daily pilgrimage; they come from near and far, some from very far away, with such humble little steps it seems they'll never get anywhere and yet they cover enormous distances. Some have to set out well before dawn. As day breaks, they converge on the mall opposite Parque Arauco, but not all together, not in groups; some delay their arrival, or hurry up, or stop and wait patiently, quietly, giving way to another child who got there first. One by one, they approach the bears ...

And there, in that dawn communion, a little miracle of charity is repeated over and over. A poor child approaches one of the bears (either one) and raises his or her old, dented, empty Coca-Cola bottle in both hands. With the slightest rustle of vegetation, the bear moves his head of green leaves, and fixes his gaze on the child. Without an expression, without a smile, perhaps without even what, in this world, we refer to as a gaze, he seems to gauge the child's poverty, to understand and love that need. And then, with movements of infinite precision, he tips his big bottle to fill the child's, mouth to mouth, without spilling a single drop. Clasping the treasure that refreshes, the child withdraws, and hurries home, making way for the next in line. And so they all have their turn, all the poor children of Santiago. Not one goes away empty-handed, because the big magic bottles of the topiary bears are never empty.

There are no bad dawns. There is no drought, neither in winter nor in summer. And when the day barges in and the big orange buses begin to discharge the multitudes who come to work in the mall's stores and restaurants, the last of the poor children is already far away, with his bottle full of bubbling Coca-Cola, and the bears resume their majestic stillness for the rest of the day.

Like a sundial, the giant tower of the Marriott throws its shadow, which falls like a friendly caress over one bear at a certain hour of the day, and then over the other. I'm in the Executive Lounge on the twenty-third floor, with nothing to do (I never have anything to do), drinking whiskey and thinking about the sublime reality of the world.

The Criminal and the Cartoonist

THE CRIMINAL WAS HOLDING A KNIFE TO THE CAR-
toonist's throat with one hand while furiously brandishing an
open comic book with the other, and, in a voice as full of men-
ace as his body language and the whole situation, subjecting
his victim to violent but also bitter and plaintive reproaches.

"You had to go and tell my story, didn't you, filthy snitch …
Rat, squealer, faggot! And you had to tell it in minute detail,
and give the police everything they need to catch me and get
a conviction."

He was trembling with indignation (but the blade of the
knife remained steady, gently pressed against the carotid ar-
tery), and the comic book, printed on the usual flimsy paper,
was shaking in front of the cartoonist's pale, terrified face.

"You even drew me! And it's a good likeness, too, son of a
bitch: the nose, the mustache, the expression … the clothes!
The black waistcoat, the belt buckle, the striped socks … You
really went to town, you rat. But now you're going to pay …"

The cartoonist, faced with what seemed to be the imminent
end of the scene, and of his life, drew strength from desperation,

and, in a barely audible voice, attempted to defend himself (he had a very strong argument).

"I never informed on you. I got all the information from the newspapers, down to the last detail, like you said! There are photos of you in the paper, hundreds of photos; that's what I copied your face from, how else could I have done it? This is the first time I've seen you in person! Everything was published already."

"Don't lie."

"I swear! You can check for yourself. You must know, but you won't admit it. You were in the papers every day until the public's morbid interest in your crimes began to wane, and that's all the documentation I used; I didn't put in anything that wasn't already in the public domain. I didn't have special sources or prior personal knowledge. I don't have any underworld contacts; I spend all my time bent over the drawing board, in a world of fantasy . . ."

"Don't lie. It's no fantasy. Everything you put in this comic happened exactly like you show it."

The cartoonist's voice was more natural now, not so shaky; he was taking heart from his irrefutable reasoning.

"But that's because I got it from the newspapers! It's all there, you can ask anyone. You weren't reading the papers in prison, so you don't know how much space they devoted to your story, how much information they gathered, how many photos of you they found, how meticulously they reconstructed each one of your exploits . . . The material was all there, ready and waiting, all I had to do was write the script … Well, I don't want to get too technical, but—"

"Don't lie."

The same hoarse refrain: the record was stuck. What more could the cartoonist say? His arguments having failed to persuade, the panic was returning and with it the pallor and the urgent desire not to die. He had placed too much faith in language and reason. He'd forgotten that he was at the mercy of a terrible criminal, who could not have become what he was had he not already been an insane monster, impermeable to humanity. Already, and still.

And yet, when the criminal spoke, which he promptly did (all this took place in a few fleeting instants of horror), he too resorted to the irrefutable.

"Look at the date."

These words introduced a new element, which, on the face of it, undermined the argument based on the newspapers, because if anything is dated, it's the daily press. A complex rearrangement took place in the cartoonist's mind, with the instantaneity that characterizes moments of high tension. He felt that he had settled the matter once and for all by appealing to the evidence of the newspapers; now the question of dates would oblige him to enter into the specific details of the proof. On the other hand, it was encouraging; by raising the question, his interlocutor was showing his willingness to rise to the level of a linguistic (and numerical) conversation, and that was a domain in which the cartoonist felt much more at home than in the world of action.

This relief, however, lasted only the few seconds it took him to focus (anxious sweat was running into his eyes, blurring his vision) and read the date in question, written by hand at the top of the cover. Those cheap comic books were almost never dated, and collectors like him had to determine the year of publication indirectly, by means of stubborn, laborious research. They calculated and triangulated, comparing the styles of the cartoonists and the themes of the scriptwriters, using providential references to current affairs that had found their way into the timeless extravagance of the adventures. A wealth of idle, playful erudition was mobilized, with no prestige or award to be won, but that only made it more enjoyable.

The date showed that the comic was forty years old, published when both of them had been children (the criminal and the cartoonist were roughly the same age). That explained the yellowish color of the paper, the neat grid of panels, the old-fashioned layout, and the dog-eared pages. It also explained, compellingly, why the cartoonist's syllogism had made no impression on the criminal. How could you argue that a comic published forty years ago was based on events reported by the press in the last few months?

Because of its age, this element was, paradoxically, too new for the cartoonist to absorb straightaway. He tried to step back and consider it from a distance, not only to see it in perspective, but also to put the exchange, if he could, on a more civilized footing, and above all to buy time, which, in the circumstances, was the only thing that really mattered:

"I'm a comic book collector ..."

The criminal interrupted him:

"Don't lie."

His leitmotif again! But this time the cartoonist had visible proof to back his claim.

"I've got lots of comic books, from the forties on, I've been collecting since I was a kid ... You can't say I'm lying, because you saw them and you took this one ... I don't know how you found it so easily, just like that, among the thousands of comics in my collection ... though they are well organized, it's true, by year, by publisher, by title ..."

"Shut up and explain—"

This time it was the cartoonist who interrupted:

"Creating and collecting are parallel activities for me. They're separate, but they nourish each other, inevitably. Most of my colleagues are collectors too."

"What do I care? Why are you lying? This"—the criminal shook the comic book violently, scrunching it up with no regard for its value as a collector's item— "didn't come out of the newspapers, son of a ... !"

"That comic, I swear ... I'd forgotten all about it. You saw yourself how many I've collected: thousands and thousands ... That's how it is with collectors, we can never have enough ... There must be lots I haven't even read ... All I take from the masters is the form, insofar as I can. For the plots, I use the newspapers, the crime reports ..."

The criminal exploded in fury (miraculously, his shouts

were not accompanied by a jerking of the wrist: the slightest movement could have been fatal).

"What the fuck do you mean? The police didn't know who I was, and the journalists had no idea! Now they know, thanks to you!"

"But I followed the cases in the newspapers!"

"Well, the papers are going to follow you now, smart-ass, bullshit artist! And they won't have any work to do, because you showed it all just like it happened, and it's obviously me in the drawings."

"No ... I don't know ... you're confusing me. Now you mention it, maybe I used the Identi-Kit pictures ..."

"Ha!"

The criminal laughed sardonically, full of contempt for those crude sketches patched together by the police. Although the cartoonist shared his opinion, he attempted a lukewarm defense:

"I don't know. Sometimes they get it right."

"Come on! Don't make me angrier than I already am ... No, do! Go on lying, so I lose control and get it over with, since I'm going to do it anyway."

"No."

It was a cry from the soul, and the vibration of the cartoonist's vocal cords perilously tensed the part of his neck on which the blade was pressing. The men were in an uncomfortable, strained position, both standing in the middle of the semidark studio, the criminal's massive body pressing against the cartoonist's back, his right arm bent, elbow out, so as to place the knife in exactly the right position for throat-slitting, the left arm around the other side, extended, holding up the comic book. It was almost like a sculptural group, except for the trembling of one figure, the other's expressive little jolts, and of course the moving lips of both. It was hard to see how the composition could remain stable, given the turbulent passions to which it was subject (revenge, terror). But it wasn't all that strange: statues hold still too, although they often represent, in a direct or allegorical way, volcanic passions, including, precisely, vindictiveness and fear.

"No," the cartoonist repeated. "Are you accusing me of plagiarism? No way … Not because I care about bourgeois morality or property rights … I'm not like that …" He was trying, crazily, to win over his attacker by taking the outlaw's side. "What I care about is innovation, invention, creation … Anyway, the world of comics is a kind of fan club; like I said, we're all collectors, we know our stuff, and we can tell a copy at a glance … You even have to watch out for unconscious memories!"

"What are you talking about? Why should I give a shit about any of that? My life is on the line here! Don't you understand? No, of course you don't: you're stuck in childhood; you know nothing about real life."

The cartoonist seized the opportunity to change the subject, and said with a stutter that came (like his earlier cry) from the soul:

"The ch-child is fa-father to the m-man."

"Don't I know it, jerk! I used to read this comic book when I was a kid; I bought it when it came out, at the stand on the corner of Lavalleja and Bulnes, where the tenement is. I used to wait for them to come out every week. I wasn't some stupid snobby collector; I bought it because it was the only way I could escape from the dismal reality of my life: we were poor, my father was in prison, and my mother had tuberculosis. And this comic, this one"—he shook it savagely, engrossed in the past—"I read it very carefully, I'm telling you. That's why I spotted it straightaway among the thousands of others, the tons of old paper you've piled up."

The cartoonist, who should have been comforted by the revelation of this common ground, this comic they had both read, because it was something he shared with a being who until then had seemed entirely other, jumped instead to a higher level of fear and alienation. Apart from fellow members of the trade, who had an artistic or professional investment in the medium, he wasn't used to dealing with people who actually read comics. People who read them for their content. He knew they existed, of course. But he had shut them out of his consciousness. And to find himself suddenly in the hands of such a person, literally in his hands and at his mercy, paralyzed him with terror. To make things worse, the terror was irrational, without a reason that he could identify and articulate. What happened next deepened the strangeness. Up until then, the criminal had been tight-lipped, but something must have pressed his talk button:

"Yes, I remembered it clearly, panel by panel, drawings and

text, every line, every word. Even though I read it when I was
… I don't know, ten or twelve, and I hadn't reread it until today. I remembered it so well because I didn't actually have to
remember. It wasn't just another comic for me, like it is for you,
with your thousands; for you, they're just a fetish, or at best a
source of 'inspiration.' " When he put the quotation marks into
his speech, a slow music began to play in the distance, a melody
made of detached notes, deep in pitch, plucked on some string
instrument, distant but curiously loud. "For me it had real importance. I don't know why God and the Devil set it up like that,
or why I read it just at the point in my psychophysical development when it was bound to have the biggest effect on me. And
what an effect! That comic strip has been my life, right up to this
day. Each one of its panels has become reality: each crime, each
flight, each abyss. My features have even come to resemble those
of the protagonist, and now no one could deny it's me …"

The cartoonist: "Sorry, but it's not true that this was just 'another comic' for me." (His use of spoken quotation marks made
the music stop.) "I don't know how you can say that, because
if you really meant it you wouldn't be here. That comic is my
masterpiece, at least in the eyes of the public; it's the one that
made me rich and famous."

"Come on, stop fooling yourself. They're all the same to you.
Evil, Cruelty, Blood, and Horror are just the morbid hooks you
use to make it sell, and if your marketing consultants told you
the fashion was over and something else was cool, you'd be
onto it."

"I don't have marketing consultants."

"You do it yourself, I know. You've got a fantastic nose for it."

"Artistic intuition is my only guide."

"Ha!" The blade pressed harder.

"But in that case," groaned the cartoonist, who hadn't lost the thread of the argument, in spite of the knife at his throat, "it's got nothing to do with me. I'm innocent! My only sin is having debased my art for commercial gain; you're responsible for the course your life has taken—you or the impressionable child you were."

"Don't lie. You know very well you're responsible ... not for the way my life turned out, true, but for the tip-off, the prison sentence ..." The thought of prison made his rage boil over, and he shouted: "You're going to pay! Right now!"

"Wait! Maybe we're misunderstanding each other, or I'm the one who doesn't understand. Didn't you say the comic predicted every detail of your life as an outlaw, and this was when I was in primary school and hadn't even dreamed of becoming a cartoonist? So what are you accusing me of?"

"Of denouncing me, what do you think?"

"But how could I, if it was all denounced already, a priori?"

"That's how you're going to die, 'a priori.' "

Music again, exactly as before: the same deep, resonant notes, very far apart, making up a superhuman melody.

"Hold on, explain. If I'm going to die"—it was the first time he'd acknowledged this, but no doubt just as a way to buy time—"at least I want to know why."

"There's nothing to explain."

The comic book was quivering; the criminal was still holding it in front of the cartoonist's face, although he'd clearly made his point. The rectangle of paper was yellowish, almost brown with age, but it stood out clearly in the steadily deepening dimness. The scene took on a posthumous, terminal air. The cartoonist felt this, and his heart, which had been clenched all along, contracted further still, becoming an iron ball. He was unable to stifle a sob:

"It was you, you and the comic ... not me ... It was the comic and you ..."

"But nobody knew."

The oral underlining of these words added an unrelated, subterranean tom-tom beat to the musical notes that had been playing since the last quotation marks.

Although his brain was clouded by anxiety, the cartoonist realized the utter irrefutability of the sentence he had just heard. He felt defeated and overwhelmed by the defeat, and yet he knew that irrefutability had been the norm, not the exception, throughout the dialogue. So there was still some hope, like a faraway light: maybe there would be another irrefutable argument, on his side. But then the criminal would produce another one in turn ... There would be no end to it. Only a difference of speed in coming up with these arguments could tell in favor of one or the other, and he had the impression that his killer was quicker. It wasn't just an impression, either; clearly the killer was always the first to come up with an irrefutable argument.

There was a reason for this: his wits had been sharpened by a lifetime of dodging the long arm of the law, while the cartoonist, perpetually bent over his drawing board, in the peace and quiet of his studio, had not undergone that training. In the comics he drew there were conflicts and miraculous last-minute escapes, but they were subject to corrections and revisions; sometimes it took him weeks to come up with a reply or work out an ending.

On this occasion, with the knife blade at his throat, he felt he'd never be able to find a reply, even in an eternity of searching. And to tell the truth (his truth, anyway), every second he spent in that forced, uncomfortable position felt like an eternity. Which must have been why he came out with the answer immediately:

"I didn't know either! How could I have known? You said it yourself: 'no one' knew."

The quotation marks, indicated orally, put a stop to the deep musical notes that had been playing since the last set; but the tom-tom beats continued, on their own now.

"Now everyone knows, thanks to you, you dirty snitch."

It was useless. There was no point talking. The irrefutable and the indisputable would go on intervening. Although it wasn't exactly the case that talking was pointless. There was always a point to talk, because it was the only way to know what was happening. But it was pointless to *go on* talking, because by the time you knew what was happening, time had spun around, turned back on itself, applying its obverse to its reverse, and the contact between past and future events had created a mass of irresolvable paradoxes.

So there was a silence, punctuated by the monotonous tom-tom. And the silence confirmed the immobility of the characters. Which wasn't absolute: they had not been petrified or frozen in a still image. Little tremors ran through their bodies; there were imperceptible changes of position, which didn't alter the overall postures: weight was shifted from one leg to the other, shoulders moved forward or back a fraction of an inch, eyes blinked, breath went in and out between slightly parted lips, occasionally moistened by a tongue. The criminal's right hand went on holding the knife, with the blade pressed against the cartoonist's throat, while his outstretched left hand held the old comic book in front of his victim's face. No one else would have been able to hold up his arms for so long, but living like a hunted animal had given him the strength it took. Each arm performed its function: the knife arm made the threat serious; the comic arm explained it and gave it meaning. One without the other would not have been enough to create the scene, which was a product of their coordination. As for the cartoonist, he kept still for obvious reasons, neck tense and stretched, eyes on the comic.

At a certain point, the light stopped fading, it too froze, in an ambiguous dimness. It had not changed markedly from the beginning of the scene to what appeared to be its end. The effect might have been psychological, the natural illusion of darkening produced by our habitual experience of dusk. But who's to say that this episode was taking place in the evening? The source of that ambiguous light could have been the morning sun, its radiance dimmed by clouds, or filtered through shutters or venetian blinds, or it could just as well have been the moon, a full moon in a clear midnight sky ... And the lighting could also have resulted from a combination or succession of various hours of the day, or all of them. (Artificial light sources were out of the question, because of the blackout affecting the city.)

Apart from the men, the studio was lifeless. It would have been futile to look for a fly buzzing, or an ant crossing the floor, or a piece of paper stirring in a breeze, or a drop falling from a faucet, or a speck of dust dancing in the air. It was as if even the electrons had frozen in their orbits. Everything that had the capacity to move was concentrated in the two standing fig-ures intertwined at the center. They really were at the geomet-rical center of that square room, and the empty space around them made it all the more obvious; the drawing board and the ergonomic stool had been knocked over in the struggle and fallen apart. The four walls, equidistant from the human fig-ures, were entirely covered with shelves, and these were chock-full with comic books, of which only the slender spines were visible, pressed up against one another from wall to wall and from floor to ceiling.

How had two such different beings come to be present in the same place at the same time?

Given the stillness of their deadlock, it would have been pos-sible to cut them out (in three dimensions, of course), breaking their potentially violent embrace, and place the separate figures in other scenes: the criminal slitting or about to slit the throat of one of his many victims, a defenseless woman, for example; the cartoonist horrified to see that a bad printing job had spoiled a work that he had spent months bringing to perfection. No changes or adjustments would have been necessary: the same posture and gestures, the same facial expression, could work in any number of different situations, and work so well that nobody would ever know.

Eventually, the top halves of both figures, from the waist up, began to lean forward simultaneously. The relative positions of the arms and heads remained the same, although the faces took on a gray luminosity. The leaning slowed to the point where it was imperceptible to the eye; but after a certain lapse of time it was clear that their faces were now a little closer to the floor. It was as if they were leaning down to look for something at their feet, both at the same time. But it was also as if they were suffering from material fatigue, and the hinges or joints in their waists were loosening.

SEPTEMBER 25, 2009

The Infinite

AS A KID I PLAYED SOME EXTREMELY STRANGE GAMES. They sound made up when I explain them, and I did, in fact, make them up myself, but many years ago, when I was still in the process of becoming the self that I am today. I made them up, or else my friends at the time did: it comes to the same thing because those kids contributed to the accumulation that resulted in me. The reason I've set out to describe the games and give a written account of them is that people have told me on more than one occasion that they really should be recorded, so that if I die tomorrow, the ideas won't be lost forever. I'm not so sure of their uniqueness. Children are always coming up with the craziest things, but the repertoire is not infinite. Relying on my intuition and the law of probabilities, I'd be prepared to bet that the same or similar ideas have occurred to other children, at some point, somewhere. If that is the case, and a copy of this publication falls into the hands of a reader who was one of those children, these descriptions will serve as a reminder, and perhaps a resurrection, of a forgotten past. It will, I think, be necessary to go into some fairly complicated details, and this may lead to excessive technicality, but I'm undertaking this task in the hope of discovering what my childhood had in common with other distant, unknown childhoods, and since the shared element is bound to be something small, a fine point, and I don't know which small thing it is, which detail in particular, I have no choice but to set them all out. There's also a more practical reason, which relates to comprehensibility: even the most insignificant details are important for the complete explanation of mechanisms that might, at first glance, seem absurd. One has to work through the list of senseless oddities so as not to miss the one that has the magic power to make sense of everything.

I will begin with a mathematical or pseudomathematical game for two players, which consisted simply of naming a bigger number than the one just named by your opponent. If one player said "four" the other had to say "five" (or more: he could also say "a thousand") in order to stay ahead, and so it went. Basically, that was the essence of the game; as you can see, it was extremely simple. Obviously, given the ordered sequence of numbers, to win you had to avoid the mistake of naming a number smaller than the one that had just been named ... But it's also obvious that victory by default would be accidental in such a game and would not affect its essence. The winner was, essentially, the one who came up with a number so big that the other player couldn't find a bigger one. We respected this principle: we never made mistakes, and if one of us had slipped up, the other would have been more than prepared to ignore it and keep going. So it's hard to imagine how the game could ever have played itself out fully. There seems to be a contradiction in the fundamental idea. But I think all the difficulty springs from adopting an adult perspective, trying to understand the theory of the game and reconstruct a session of play. For us it wasn't hard to understand; on the contrary, it was almost too easy (that's why we complicated it a bit). The difficulties, which in any case we found amusing and absorbing, were on another level, as I will try to show. The game itself seemed perfectly natural to us.

Before getting down to details, however, some clarifications are necessary. First: age. We would have been ten and eleven years old (or eleven and twelve: Omar was a year older than me; we were at primary school but in the final grades). Which is to say that we were no longer little children learning how to count, fascinated and amazed by the miracle of arithmetic. Not at all. Also, back then, thirty-five years ago, learning was no game: it was straight down to business; not a minute was wasted. Even in our semirural school (School Number 2 in Coronel Pringles: it still exists), the academic level was remarkably high; these days it would seem too much to ask. And all the children, though most of them came from farms and had illiterate parents, kept up with the pace, no two ways about it. The "hump" was sixth grade, and many stopped there, but if you were in that class you marched with the rest, and it was no dawdle.

The characters: Omar and myself. I never played this game with other people. I can't remember if I ever tried, but if I did, it didn't work. It was the kind of game that has to find its players, and does so only by a modest miracle. It had found the two of us, and we had adapted so well to its intricate, crystalline recesses that we had become a part of it, and it a part of us, and everyone else was necessarily excluded. Not so much because we would have had to explain the rules, or allow for idiosyncrasies (it was a mathematical game), but because the two of us had already played so much—all afternoon, hundreds of times—and we couldn't start over; other players could, but not Omar and I.

Omar Berruet was not my oldest friend; his family had moved to the neighborhood a couple of years earlier, from Greater Buenos Aires (Berazategui), but his parents were from Pringles. His mother and mine had been childhood friends; one of his father's sisters lived around the corner and had two sons, the Moraña boys, whom I'd known for much longer; the older one was in my grade all through primary school. The Berruets rented the house next door to ours. Omar was an only child, a year older than me, so we weren't in the same class at school, but being neighbors we got to be friends. We'd spend the whole day together. He was tall and thin with straight blond hair, pale-skinned and lymphatic, unlike me in every way: the attraction of opposites brought us together. I suspect that I tended to boss him around and subject him to my erratic and fanciful moods.

He was happy to go along with my whims, but he also had a hidden strength that a number of painful experiences taught me to respect. Omar wasn't lacking in intelligence, but when it came to demonstrating it, he was, again, my opposite: while I was all boasting, noise, and display, he responded quietly, with irony and realism. (This is as good a place as any to mention that he stayed in Pringles, became a bank teller, and had eight children, one of whom died.)

And finally, the scene. Back then, the town of Coronel Pringles was more or less like it is today, but a bit smaller, not so built up, with more dirt roads. Calle Alvear, where we lived, was the last paved road; another hundred yards and there were vacant lots (whole empty blocks), farmhouses, the country. On our block there were five houses, all on the same side: Uruñuela's place on the corner, the house where my aunts Alicia and María lived, our place, Gonzalo Barba's house (he was my dad's nephew and business partner), and the Berruets. On the other corner: my dad's business Aira & Barba, with its yard and offices. The houses rented by Gonzalo and the Berruets belonged to Padelli, and their backyards adjoined his place, which was just around the corner. On the other side of the street, behind a long wall, was the land belonging to the corner houses, Astutti's on the left and Perrier's on the right. The most interesting things in those wild tracts were, in Astutti's yard, a supermodern mobile home that the owner's brother (I think) was building or cobbling together (this hobby outlasted my childhood), and in Perrier's yard, a tree, which was in fact a pair of twin trees, with intertwined branches, a gigantic conifer, the biggest tree in Pringles, as high as a ten-story building and perfectly conical in shape.

Nothing ever happened in the street: a car went by every half hour. We had vast amounts of free time: we went to school in the mornings, and the afternoons lasted entire lifetimes. We didn't have extracurricular activities the way kids do today; there was no television; the doors of our houses stood open. To play the number game we climbed into the cabin of the little red truck that belonged to Omar's father and was almost always parked just outside the front door ...

Right. Now, the game.

Who came up with it? It must have been one of us. I can't imagine us taking it from somewhere else, ready-made. Thinking back, I've always seen the game as a blend of invention and practice. Or rather, I see the practice of it as permanent invention, without any kind of prior idea. And if I try to work out which of us was behind it, I have to conclude that I was the inventor. There's something about the thrust of it, a kind of fantasy or exuberance, something elusive but utterly typical of me as I was at that age. Omar was at the opposite extreme. But, strangely, those vertiginous tunnels could be entered from the opposite extreme as well.

There were no rules. Although we spent our lives inventing rules for all our games, as kids always do, this game had none, perhaps because we realized that they were inadequate, bound to fall short, or just too easy to make up.

Now that I think of it, there was a rule, but it was transient and could be revoked at our convenience. We applied it once and forgot it the next time, but for some reason it has remained in my memory, and it must have remained in the game as well. It was pretty inoffensive: all it did was specify that the biggest possible number, the upper limit, would be eight. Not the number eight itself, but any number containing eight: eight tenths, eight hundred thousand, eight billion. It was really an extra accelerator (as if we needed one!) to take the game to another level.

It's not that there were levels in the game, or series within the series, or if there were such things, we didn't bother with them. But there were differences in speed, alternations between "step by step" and "leap," and we could take them to extremes that are not to be found among the mobile, spatiotemporal sculptures of physical reality. These differences were always rushes, even our lapses into the hyperslow. But it never got out of control; even the all-encompassing acceleration was a kind of slowness. Which meant that within the game's austere monomania, we could use speed to keep changing the subject of the conversation (since subjects are speeds).

"Three."

"A hundred."

"A hundred and one."

"A hundred and one point zero one."

"Eight hundred and ninety-nine thousand nine hundred and ninety-nine."

"Four million."

"Four million and one."

"Four million and two."

"Four million and three."

"Four million and four."

"Four million and four point four four four."

"Four million and four point four four."

"Four million and four point four."

"Four million and four point three."

"Four million and four point one."

"Half a trillion."

We never bothered to find out what a trillion was (or a quadrillion, a quintillion, a sextillion, although we used the terms). Whatever it was, we stuck with it.

"Half a trillion and one."

"A trillion."

"Eight trillions."

"Eight trillions and eight."

We did the same with "billion," although in that case we knew that it meant a thousand millions. So if a million was "one," a billion was a thousand of those "ones." But we never went as far as counting how many zeros it contained and using that to calculate (there should be nine, I think). It would have been tedious, a drag, no fun. And we were playing a game. We were impatient, like all kids, and we had invented a game ideally suited to impatience: the leaping game. Although we spent hours and whole afternoons sitting still in the cabin of the little red truck that belonged to Omar's dad, we were exercising our impatience. Otherwise, it would have been a sort of numerological craftwork, and I would describe our game as art, not craft.

We didn't even know if a billion was bigger than a trillion. What did it matter? It was better not to know. We both hid our ignorance, and never put each other to the test. And in spite of this, the game remained very easy to play.

We were attracted by big numbers, inevitably: it followed from the nature of the game. They were the gravitational force accelerating our fall. But at the same time we held them in contempt, as indicated by the fact that we didn't bother to find out exactly how big they were. Numbers were one thing and big numbers were another: with numbers we were in the domain of intuition (eight could be eight things or eight points; the same with eighty, or even eight hundred million); but when it came to really big numbers we were thinking blind; the game became purely verbal, a matter of combining words, not numbers.

"A billion."

"A trillion billions."

"Half a billion trillion billions."

"A billion billion trillion billion trillions."

It's true that numbers reappeared on the far side of these accumulations.

"A billion billions."

"A billion billions and six."

"Six billion billions and six point zero zero zero zero zero zero six."

These were luxuries, embellishments that we allowed ourselves, as if to stave off a boredom that we didn't feel and couldn't have felt, but could nevertheless imagine. On the other hand, we both agreed not to accept things like "six billion six billions": that wasn't a number but a multiplication. We had more than enough to do with numbers pure and simple. Why make life complicated?

I don't know how long this game lasted. Months, years. It never bored us, never ceased to surprise and stimulate us. It was one of the high points of our childhood, and when we finally stopped, it wasn't because we'd exhausted the game, or tired of it, but because we had grown up and gone our separate ways. I should add that we didn't play it all the time, and it wasn't our only game. Not at all. We had dozens of different games, some more extravagant and fantastic than others. I have resolved to describe them one by one, and this is the one I happened to begin with, but I wouldn't want the rather artificial way in which I've isolated the number game to give a false impression. We weren't a pair of obsessives permanently shut up in the cabin of an old truck spouting numbers. A new fantasy would excite us and we could forget about the numbers for weeks at a time. Then we'd start over, exactly like before ... On reflection, the way I've presented the game in isolation is not so artificial after all, because various features did set it apart: its immutable simplicity, its naturalness, its secrecy. I think we kept it secret, but not for any special reason, not because it *was* a secret: just because we forgot to tell anyone, or the opportunity never arose.

The game was very simple and austere, and that's why it was inexhaustible. By definition, it couldn't be boring. And anyway, how could we have been bored? It was pure freedom. In the playing, the game revealed itself as part of life, and life was vast, elastic, endless. We knew that prior to any experience. We were austere, like our parents, the neighborhood, the town, and life in Pringles. Today it's almost impossible to imagine just how simple that life was. Having lived it myself doesn't help. I'm trying to imagine it, to give some form to that idea of simplicity, putting memories aside, avoiding them as much as possible.

Sometimes, in the plenitude that followed an especially satisfactory session of play, we did something that seemed to depart from simplicity, but in fact confirmed it. We played the same game as a joke, out of pure exuberance, as if we hadn't understood, as if we were savages, or stupid.

"One."

"Zero."

"Minus a thousand."

"Zero point zero nine nine nine."

"Minus three."

"A hundred and fifteen."

"A million billion quadrillions."

"Two."

"Two."

This didn't last very long, because it was too dizzying, too horizontal. A minute of it gave us a totally different perspective on what we'd been doing for hours before, as if we'd jumped down off a horse, descended from the world of mental numbers to that of real numbers, to the earth where the numbers lived. If we had known what surrealism was, we would have cried: Surrealism is so beautiful! It changes everything! Then we went back to the normal game like someone going back to sleep, back to efficiency and representation.

All the same, a certain nostalgia crept in, a vague feeling of dissatisfaction. It didn't happen at a particular moment, after a day or a month or a year ... I'm not writing a chronological history of this game, from invention and development to decadence and neglect. I couldn't, because it didn't happen like that. The successiveness of this narration is an unavoidable defect; I don't see how I could avoid it while still giving an account of the game. The dissatisfaction had to do with the difference between numbers and words. We had made the very austere decision to limit ourselves to real, "classical" numbers. Positive or negative, but everyday numbers, of the kind that are used for counting things. And numbers are not words. Words are used to name numbers, but they're not the same.

This, of course, had been a choice, a pact that we renewed each time we started playing, and we didn't complain. The game made thought mobile and porous, loosened it like a kind of relaxing yoga, allowing us to see the kingdom of the sayable in all its amplitude while preventing us from entering it. Words were more than numbers; they were everything. Numbers were a little subset of the universe of words, a marginal, faraway planetary system where it was always night. We hid there, sheltered from the excesses of the unknown, and tended our garden.

From our hiding place we could see words as we'd never seen them before. We'd distanced ourselves from them so that we could see how beautiful, funny, and amazingly effective they were. Words were magical jewels with unlimited powers, and all we had to do, we felt, was reach out and take them. But that feeling was an effect of the distance, and if we crossed the gap, the game dissolved like a mirage. We knew that, and yet some strange perversion, or the lure of danger, sustained our crazy longing to try...

We were testing the power of words every day. I never missed an opportunity: I'd see one coming, feel that I was grasping the mirage, taking control of its unerring death ray, and

I wouldn't rest until I'd fired it. My favorite victim, needless to say, was Omar:

"Let's play who can tell the biggest lie."

Omar shrugged:

"I just saw Miguel go past on his bike."

"No, not like that... Let's pretend we're two fishermen and we're lying about what we've caught. The one who says the biggest lie wins."

I emphasized "biggest," to suggest that it had something to do with the number game. Omar, who could be diabolically clever when he wanted, made it hard for me:

"I caught a whale."

"Listen, Omar. Let's make it simpler. The only thing you can say is the weight of the fish, its length in yards, or its age. And let's set some upper limits: eight tons, eighty yards, and eight hundred years. No! Let's make it really simple! Just the age. Let's suppose fish go on growing until they die. So by saying the age you're saying the length, the width, the weight, and all that. And let's suppose they can live any number of years but the highest number we can say is eight hundred. You start."

Omar would have had to be really stupid not to realize by this stage that I had something up my sleeve, something very specific. And he wasn't stupid at all; he was very intelligent. He had to be, supremely: he was the measure of my intelligence. In the end, he resigned himself:

"I caught an eight-hundred-year-old fish."

"I caught its grandfather."

Omar clicked his tongue with infinite scorn. I wasn't especially proud of the idea myself: it was an unfortunate attempt to play a practical joke on my friend by recycling a gag I'd read in a magazine, which must have gone something like this: "Two fishermen, inveterate liars, are talking about the day's catch: 'I caught a marlin *this* big.' 'Yeah, yeah, that was the newborn baby. I caught its mother.' " What a flat joke! I worked so hard to set it up, and for such a paltry result! What did I ever see in it? Nothing but the power of the word. The joke contained, in a nutshell, both our number game (the lying fishermen could go on increasing the dimensions of the fish *ad libitum*) and that which transcended it: a word (like "mom," or "dad," or "grandfather") triumphed over the whole series of numbers by placing itself on a different level.

So that's what I was referring to. That was the game's limit, its splendor and its misery.

Until we discovered the existence of *that word*. This, I repeat, did not occur at a particular moment in the game's history. It happened at the beginning—it was the beginning.

The word was "infinity." Logical, isn't it? Perhaps even blindingly obvious? In fact, it has been a strain for me to call it the "number game," when it was really the "infinity game," which is how I've always thought of it. If I had to transcribe the archetypal session, the original, the matrix, it would be simply this:

"One."

"Infinity."

Everything else sprang from that. How could it have been otherwise? Why would we have denied ourselves that leap when every other kind of leap was allowed? In fact, it was the other way around: all the leaps that we allowed ourselves were based on the leap into the heterogeneous world of words.

From this point on, we can, I think, begin to glimpse an answer to the question that has been building subliminally since I began to describe the game: when did the sessions come to an end? Who was the winner? It's not enough to say: Never, no one. I've given the impression that neither of us ever fell into the traps that we were continually laying for each other. That's true in the abstract, in the myth that was ritually expressed by the various series, but it can't always have been the case in the actual playing of the game. To be honest, I can't remember.

I *feel* I can remember it all, as if I were hallucinating (otherwise, I wouldn't be writing this), but I have to admit that there are things I don't remember. And if I were to be absolutely frank, I would have to say I don't remember anything. An escalation, once again. But there's no contradiction. In fact, the only thing I remember with the real microscopic clarity you need in order to write is the forgetting.

So:

"Infinity."

Infinity is the limit of all numbers, the invisible limit. As I said, with the big numbers we were thinking blind, beyond intuition; but infinity is the transition to the blindness of blindness, something like the negation of negation. And that's where the real visibility of my forgotten memory begins. Do I actually know what infinity means? It's all I can know, but I can't know it.

There's something wonderfully practical about leaping to the infinite, the sooner the better. It thwarts every kind of patience. There's no point waiting for it. I loved it blindly. It was the sunny day of our childhood. That's why we never wondered what it meant, not once. Because it was the infinite, the leap had already happened.

Our refusal to think it through had a number of consequences. We knew that it didn't make sense to talk about "half an infinity," because in the realm of the infinite the parts are equal to the whole (half of infinity, the series of even numbers, say, is just as infinite as the other half, or the whole). But, returning surreptitiously to healthy common sense, we accepted that two infinities were bigger than one.

"Two infinities."

"Two hundred and thirty million infinities."

"Seven quintillion infinities."

"Seven thousand billion billion quintillion infinities."

"A hundred thousand billion billion trillion quintillion infinities."

And so we continued until the word made its triumphant return:

"Infinity infinities."

This formula could, in turn, be included in a series of the same kind:

"Ten billion infinity infinities."

"Eight thousand billion trillion quadrillion quintillion infinity infinities."

We didn't pronounce these words, of course. I should make it clear that in general we didn't actually articulate all the little series that I've been transcribing here; neither these particular ones nor others of the same kind. I've set it out in this long-winded way to make myself clear, but it wasn't our intention to labor the obvious; on the contrary. All these series, and in fact all the series that might have occurred to us, were virtual. It would have been boring to say them. We weren't prepared to waste our precious childhood hours on bureaucratic tasks like that; and, above all, it would have been pointless, because each term was surpassed and annihilated by the next. Numbers have that banal quality, like examples: they're interchangeable. What matters is something else. Stripping away all the stupid and bothersome foliage of examples, what we should have said was:

"A number."

"A number bigger than that."

"A number bigger than that."

"A number bigger than that."

Although, of course, if we'd done that, it wouldn't have been a game.

The word returned once more:

"Infinity infinity infinities."

Only one number was bigger than that:

"Infinity infinity infinity infinities."

I mean: that was the smallest bigger number, not the only one, because the series of infinities could be extended indefinitely. And so we ended up repeating the word over and over in a typically childish way, at the top of our voices, as if it were a tongue-twister.

"Infinity infinity infinity infinity infinity infinity infinity infinity infinity infinity infinity infinities."

There was, believe it or not, an even bigger number: the number that one of us would say next. It was pure virtuality, the state in relation to which the game deployed all its marvelous possibilities.

Amazingly, given our greediness, it never occurred to us to add the name of a thing to the numbers. Bare like that, the numbers were nothing, and we wanted everything. There's no real contradiction between the two half-wild children I've been describing, in a society that seems archaic and primitive today, and the fact that we were greedy. We wanted everything, including Rolls-Royces and objects that would have been no use to us, like diamonds and subatomic particle accelerators. We wanted them so badly! With an almost anguished longing. But there's no contradiction. The supernatural frugality of our parents' lives had apparently achieved its goal, and perhaps that goal was us. They were still using the furniture they'd bought when they got married; the rent was fixed; cars lasted forever; and the mania for household appliances would take decades to reach Pringles ...

What's more, we always had enough money to buy the few things on sale that interested us: picture cards, comic books, marbles, chewing gum. I don't know where we got it from, but it never ran out. And yet we were insatiable, greedy, supremely avid. We wanted a schooner with a solid-gold figurehead and silken sails, and in our fantasies about discovering a treasure— doubloons and ingots and emeralds—we weren't so rash as to spend it at once on this or that; we converted it into cash, placed the sum in a bank and, as the compound interest mounted, bought ourselves Easter Island statues, the Taj Mahal, racing cars, and slaves. Even then we weren't satisfied. We wanted the philosopher's stone or, better, Aladdin's lamp. We weren't deterred by the fate of Midas: we were planning to wear gloves.

The numbers were numbers and nothing more. Especially the big numbers. Eight could still be eight cars; one for each day of the week, and one extra with swamper tires for rainy days. But a billion? An infinity? Infinity infinities? That could only be money. Why we never talked about this is a mystery to me. Maybe it went without saying.

The tree, a giant dark-green triangle hiding half the sky, kept watch over the little red truck, with the two of us inside, tireless and happy. The day was a stillness of sunlight.

Among the many daydreams prompted by the natural world, an especially frequent variety explores the perfection of the mechanisms by means of which living beings function. Gills, for example. A fish, as it swims, lets water pass through what I presume is a sort of hydrodynamic valve, and extracts from that water the oxygen it needs. How it does this doesn't matter. Somehow. To simplify and conceptualize, as I did in the two previous sentences, it's relatively straightforward: you can imagine an apparatus, an alembic, in which water is broken down and oxygen retained while the hydrogen is allowed to escape. Daydreaming retains something, too, and lets something else escape. What it retains in this case is the size of the fish: some fish are tiny, no bigger than a match, and in a fish so small the apparatus becomes a marvel ... Or does it? To put it together and take it apart, we'd have to use magnifying glasses and microscopes, screwdrivers and tweezers and tiny hammers the size of needle points; it would be a feat of patience and dexterity. A feat that might be pulled off once, at a very optimistic estimate; but there are billions of those fish in the sea ... At this point we should bow to the evidence and admit that the reasoning behind the daydream contains an error. Two errors, actually. The first is having overlooked the difference between doing something and finding it done. No one has ever set about making gills for little fish. They are ready-made. Constructivism is an empty illusion. The second has to do with size. Here the error lies in taking our human size as a fixed standard. In fact, the demiurge chooses a scale appropriate to each case, or rather he chose it at the outset, in the process of creating all the sizes. It's a fluid, elastic studio, where it's always a pleasure and a joy to work, in comfortable conditions, by hand. I think that's why concepts are so attractive, why humans cling to them so stubbornly, from childhood on, scorning all reality checks. It's examples that are cumbersome and unwieldy; for them, we're never well proportioned, we're always giants or dwarfs.

Daydreams are always about concepts, not examples. I wouldn't want anything I've written to be taken as an example.

MARCH 21, 1993

No Witnesses

CIRCUMSTANCES HAD REDUCED ME TO BEGGING IN THE street. Since direct and sincere requests were ineffective, I had to resort to fraud and trickery, always on a small scale, pretending, for example, to be paralyzed, blind, or afflicted with some terrible disease. It wasn't something I enjoyed at all. One day it occurred to me that I could try a subtler, more ingenious strategy, which, even if it worked only once and wasn't very lucrative, would at least give me the satisfaction of having carried out a well considered, and, as I saw it, almost artistic plan. I needed someone gullible to come along, preferably in a place where there would be no witnesses. I walked for a while, on my aching feet (they really were aching), through alleys that were all too familiar to me, since I lived and slept in them, until I found a corner that was, I felt sure, well out of the way. That was where I settled down to wait for my prey. I leaned against the wall, half hidden by a Dumpster, holding a shallow box I'd found, which someone must have thrown away: this box was what had given me the idea of trying a trick to get some money. I should explain that at this point I still didn't know what the trick would be. I was going to improvise it at the last moment. Suddenly it was night. The corner was very dark, but accustomed as I was to gloomy places, I could see fairly well. And just as I had predicted, no one passed by. It was what I needed: a quiet place with no witnesses. But I also needed a victim, and after some hours had elapsed I became convinced that no one would come along. I must have fallen asleep and woken up again several times. The silence was deep. I'm guessing that it would have been midnight when I heard steps: someone was approaching. I didn't move. It was a man, that's all I knew; there wasn't enough light to see details. And before I could move, or call out, or get his attention, I saw him go to the Dumpster and start to rummage in it. I couldn't really make him the target of my clever scam. All the same, I would have given it a try, if only to get a coin out of him so I wouldn't feel I'd wasted the night. But before I could even begin to move, the stranger lifted something heavy out of the Dumpster and stifled a cry. I exercised my penetrating night vision. It was a bag full of gold coins. I was overcome at once by the most bitter regret I have ever experienced: it was a fortune, and it had been there, within arm's reach, for hours—hours I'd wasted waiting for some innocent to come along so I could trick him out of a tiny sum of money. And now that innocent had come and snatched the treasure from under my nose. He looked both ways to make sure that no one had seen him, and started running. He hadn't noticed me down on the ground. I've never had quick reflexes, but on this occasion, which was, I felt, momentous and unique, something like desperation impelled me to act. I simply stretched out my leg and tripped him. Just as he was speeding up, his foot caught on my leg and he fell flat on his face. As I'd predicted, the bag fell with him, and the coins scattered over the uneven paving stones of the alley with a loud jangling noise, shining auspiciously. I thought he'd rush to pick up as many as he could before running away, and that I'd be able to gather coins too, unchallenged, his fall and the scattering of the booty having put us on an equal footing as misappropriators. But that was not what happened, to my surprise and horror. Agile as a cat, the man picked himself up and hurled himself at me from a crouching position, pulling a huge knife from his pocket. In spite of living rough on the streets, I hadn't toughened up. I was still timid and would run away from any kind of violence. But there was not the slightest hope of running away this time. He was already on top of me, raising the knife, then plunging it into my chest with tremendous force. It almost came out the other side and must have gone very close to my heart. I could feel death coming, with utter certainty. But imagine my surprise when I saw that the wound he'd inflicted on me had appeared in his chest, in just the same place, and was beginning to bleed. His heart had been wounded too. He looked down, baffled. He didn't understand, and it was no wonder. He had stabbed me, and the wound had appeared in his body as well. He pulled the knife from my chest, and, with death beginning to cloud his vision, as it was clouding mine, stabbed again, next to the first wound, as if to test the strange phenomenon. And sure enough, the second wound appeared in his chest. It, too, began to bleed. It was the last thing I (or he) saw.

NOVEMBER 1, 2010

The Spy

IF I WERE A CHARACTER IN A PLAY, THE LACK OF REAL privacy would make me feel wary, anxious, and suspicious. One way or another I'd sense the quiet, attentive presence of the public. I'd always be conscious that my words were being heard by others, and while that might be appropriate for some of my lines (certain clever remarks are made to impress as many people as possible, and in fact there are times when one regrets not having a public to appreciate them), other lines would, I'm sure, require a real, not a fictitious, intimacy. And they would be crucially important for understanding the plot: all the interest and value of the play would hinge on them. But their importance would not loosen my tongue. On the contrary, I would scrupulously observe the rule of secrecy, as I've always done. I would simply choose not to speak. I'd say: "Let's go to another room; there's something important I need to tell you that no one else should hear." But then the curtain would fall, and in the next scene, we'd be in the other room, that is, the same stage with different props. I'd glance around and sense something indefinable ... I know that in the fictional world of the play there are no rows of seats out there, and, as a character, I'd know it better still, because it would be the basis of my existence, but even so ... "No, I can't talk here either ..." I'd lead my interlocutor to another room, and from that one to yet another ... Realizing eventually that the stage would follow me to the ends of the earth, I would, of course, be able to stay out of trouble by making banal remarks that gave nothing away, which would mean sacrificing the interest of the play. But that's precisely what I would never be able to sacrifice, because my existence as a character would depend on it. So there would come a moment when I would have no choice but to speak. Even so, I'd hold out, gagged by an overpowering distrust. My lips would be sealed; the keys to the plot (the ones in my possession, at least) would not be revealed, no, never! As in a nightmare, I would look on helplessly as a large or small, but significant and perhaps even crucial, portion of the work's aesthetic value disappeared. And it would be my fault. The other characters would start to move and act like lost or mutilated puppets, with no life or sense of destiny, as they do in those botched plays where nothing ever happens ...

Then, and only then, would I grasp at my last hope: maybe the audience would guess what it was I had to say, in spite of my refusal to come out and say it. Hardly a realistic hope, because I'd be hiding facts, not just comments or opinions. If what I have to reveal, to someone in particular, with the utmost discretion and for very specific reasons, is that I'm a secret agent working undercover, and if that piece of information has, logically, been kept hidden in everything I've said so far and will say in the future (a competent author would see to that), how are the people in the audience supposed to guess? It's preposterous to hope that they could deduce it from my silence or my scruples about privacy, because, after all, I could be hiding any number of secrets: rather than a spy, I might be the illegitimate son of the master of the house, or a fugitive who has adopted the identity of the man he murdered ...

Crazy as it is, banking like this on the spectator's superhuman intelligence is the flip side of a fear that is also fairly absurd, but often turns out to be justified: the fear of being found out in spite of everything. The reason I refuse to speak, and behave so circumspectly, to the point of taking precautions based on a superstitious hunch (the feeling that one of the four walls really is missing and that there are people sitting in rows of seats listening to what I say), is that I have secrets to keep, dark secrets.

But isn't this exactly the wrong thing to be doing: harboring the hope that my secret will be guessed? How could it even occur to me to call this a "hope," in real life? The cause of this wild aberration is art, the world of art into which I have ventured by becoming a character. In art, there's a condition that takes precedence over all others: it has to be well done. Which is why I have to be a good actor, in a good play; if I don't act well, the play will not produce the desired effect, and the performance will collapse. In this field, more than in any other, "doing it well" and simply "doing it" are synonymous. So if I dissociate them, because of my hypersensitive wariness, all I have left is hope:

a ruinous hope, equivalent to death. Because my secrets are so terrible that I couldn't survive their revelation. This is something I hadn't realized until now, until I found myself in this fix, and I'm tempted to say that I entered the fatal game of art in order to come to this realization.

Up until now I have lived in the certainty that my secrets are safe; they're in the past, and the past is inviolable. I'm the only one who has a key to that chest. Or so I believe, at least: the past has been shut off definitively, and its secrets, my secrets, will never be revealed to anyone, unless I start divulging them, which is something I have no intention of doing. Sometimes, however, I'm not so sure that the chest is closed forever. Time might turn back on itself somehow, in a way that my imagination is unable to foresee—even though (or because) it's precisely my imagination that is generating these wild conjectures—making the hidden visible. But then I always come around to thinking that the past really is secure, inviolable, sealed, and that if worrying is what I really want to do, there are better things to worry about. So many, in fact, that if I started counting them, I could go on forever, because there'd always be something new. But they all converge on the center, the spot to which I'm rooted at the center of the floodlit stage, in my restless paralysis, quivering, bathed in a cold sweat ...

There's an actor joined to me. I can't separate him from myself, except by means of negative statements: I don't know what he wants; I don't know what he can do. I don't know what he's thinking, either ... He's a statue of fear, an automaton of apprehension, a fiber-for-fiber replica of me. The author has written him into the play, as a doppelgänger. The idea has been done to death: one actor playing two characters, who turn out to be twins or doubles. Given the limitations of the theater, the two characters have to operate in distinct spaces if they are to be played by the same actor. In between, there's always a door, an entrance or an exit, a mistake or a change of scenery. The staging dislocates the spaces, but also, insofar as it builds up the fiction, establishes a continuity between them, creating the horrific prospect of a face-to-face encounter with the double. And it's possible to go a little further, approaching Grand Guignol, and actually represent the encounter, with the help of makeup, costumes, and lighting, as long as the audience is not too close. (Note, however that this applies only to modern theater, because in ancient times, masks made physical distance unnecessary.) In cinema, montage solves the problem perfectly. In the theater, unless you resort to dubious tricks (or you have a pair of actors who are really twins), the process of making the double a theme has to become a theme in turn, so that the two identical characters turn out to be one in the end.

Looking back at what I've written, it all seems rather muddled, and if I want to be understood, I need to say it differently (not by means of examples, but, once again, by making it the theme). Sooner or later there comes a time when being correctly understood is vitally important. The hidden cannot endure without that transparency, against which it becomes visible. The hidden: that is, secrets. I have secrets, like everyone else; I don't know if mine are especially shameful, but I take all sorts of precautions to prevent them from coming to light. It's natural for people to feel that their own affairs are important; the self is a natural amplifier. When the person concerned is a character in a dramatic performance, at the very center of the plot, the amplification reaches deafening extremes. The whirl-wind of the action forbids any kind of detachment.

But if my best-kept secret is what I did in the past, perhaps that secret is revealing itself in what is happening now, since, logically, the present must be the result of the past, a result that, for an analytic mind, displays the traces of all the events that played a part in producing it. But any attempt to unmask me with the classic "by their fruit shall ye know them" would back-fire, because what I'm trying to hide is precisely the fact that in my case the process operated in reverse: the fruits remained in the past, and no one could deduce their nature from observa-tions of the flower that is open in the present. This curious ab-erration could be due to the nature of my original action, which was a separation, a "distancing" with respect to my own person. I thought that I was seriously ill (I'm not going to go into de-tails) and I did something disgraceful: I abandoned my wife and young children … The years went by, I adopted a new per-sonality, I lived. I realized the dream of living. As a young man I knew nothing of life, and as an older man too. All I knew was that life existed, and love, and adventure; that there was some-thing beyond the world of books. And since I'd always been an optimist and trusted my intelligence, I reached the alarming conclusion that I, too, could come to know what life was and how it should be lived.

So, in desperation, I broke with my past, before it was too late. When the curtain rises, I am the double of the man I was, a duplicate of myself, my identical twin. Twenty years have gone by, but I'm still at the same point (I can't fool myself), in spite of being an other, my own other. I have learned computing, and channeled the intellectual brilliance that characterized my writing into politics and betrayal, and now it turns out that I am a double agent working undercover for both the high command of the forces occupying Argentina and the secret Committee of the Resistance. The action takes place in the palatial salons of the Quinta de Olivos, around midnight, during a reception for the ambassadors of Atlantis. I'm wearing a dinner jacket, looking very stylish: cool, competent, and hypocritical as ever. The most amazing thing is that I haven't aged; the mirrors show me as I was at thirty, but I know that old age is just a step away, behind a door. I've always thought that my youthful appearance (which, even at thirty, was very marked) is a symptom of my failure to live. The sentence has only been suspended—for how long? The biological process follows its inexorable course, but if the suspension continues after a change of name, personality, and occupation, I really don't know what I should do.

I'm a leading man, the finest flower of humanity, open in the present, in the theater of the world. "By my fruits" I shall not be known, because I left them in another life. And yet those fruits are coming back, in the most unexpected way. They are coming back tonight, at this very moment, so punctually that the timing seems too good to be true; but such is the law that governs the theater of the world. If a man lives happily and peacefully with his family for decades, and one day a psychopath bursts into his house and takes them all hostage, and rapes and kills them, when will the film that tells the story be set? The day before?

There's an extra guest at the reception, the most surprising of all for me: Liliana, my wife (or I should say: my ex-wife, the wife of the man I was). She doesn't know I'm here, of course, or that I'm the gray eminence of the High Command; everyone thinks I'm dead, or that I've disappeared. My break with the past was so clean that I've had no news of Liliana in twenty years: she could have been dead and buried, but no, she's alive, and here she is . . . I see her by chance, in the distance, on the far side of the gilded salon, but she doesn't see me. I send a secretary to investigate, and slip away to other salons in that labyrinthine palace. Pretexts are easy enough to find: during the "real time" of the reception, meetings are underway behind closed doors. The situation is explosive; imminent upheavals are expected; the atmosphere is charged with anxiety.

Liliana has snuck in to make an appeal to the ambassadors of Atlantis. She won't have another opportunity because they will only be in the country for a few hours; they have come to sign off on a bridging loan and will leave at midnight. The motors of the limousines that will take them from the party straight to the airport are already running. Liliana's plan is to plead for the safe return of her son, who (I now discover) has been arrested. Her son is my son too: Tomasito, my firstborn, whom I haven't seen since I walked out, when he was still a child; I'd forgotten all about him. A simple calculation reveals that he must be twenty-two by now. Hmm ... so he became a dissident and joined the resistance and got caught. That kind of involvement in politics must have been a result of his mother's influence; and now I remember Liliana's aversion to Menem, Neustadt, Cavallo, and Zulemita. And I see how she was able to get into the villa to-night: the Resistance Command, to which I belong, must have organized it. I sent them a pair of invitations myself, as I always do, in case they want to plant a bomb or kidnap someone. And she hasn't come on her own (they've used both the invitations I sent): she's accompanied by a lawyer from the local branch of Amnesty International, whose presence is considered inoffensive; but I know that he has been, and still is, in contact with the Coordinating Committee of the Resistance.

There's something else, something that defies imagination, which I have discovered by eavesdropping on conversations from behind doors and curtains: Liliana has gone crazy. I have good reason to be amazed. Liliana, of all people! She's so sensible, so logical! When we were together, she counterbalanced my follies. But the most organized minds are the first to collapse in a major crisis, and hers must have given way under the stress caused by the disappearance of her son. My eavesdropping soon yields irrefutable proof of her madness, when I hear her say that she has been assisted in this mission by her lawyer ... and her husband! Maybe she has remarried? But no, because she mentions me by name: César Aira, the famous writer (she's exaggerating). She says I got held up in the salon, talking to someone who asked for an autograph, that I'll be coming soon ... She's crazy, she's hallucinating, poor thing. On the spur of the moment I make a bold decision: to realize her illusion, to resume my old identity and go with her to meet the ambassadors. This is not just a sympathetic gesture; it has a practical objective, too: I know exactly what to say to make the ambassadors of Atlantis take action and exert pressure on the occupying forces to return Tomasito: without me the mission is doomed to fail. And this is the least I can do, because although I've abandoned and disowned my family, he's still my son, my blood.

I have a room in the Quinta de Olivos, for use during the frequent crises that require me to be on call twenty-four hours a day. I hurry to my room and change, choosing casual clothes to re-create the way I remember dressing in my former life; then I mess up my hair and put on a pair of glasses, and I'm done! I make my appearance: "Good evening, my apologies for the delay, I'm César Aira, the father of the young man who has disappeared." The crazy woman doesn't bat an eyelid, which is proof of her craziness: twenty years of absence mean nothing to her deranged mind. She scolds me out of the corner of her mouth for not changing my sweater: You have another one, that one's all stained ... people will think I make no effort ... you could have put on your other pants, they're ironed ... The same as ever! My whole marriage comes back in waves; a marriage is a sum of little details, and any one of them can represent all the others.

It's tricky. In the middle of the explanation I have to find a pretext to slip away, put on my dinner suit, comb my hair, and attend to the senior officials of the occupying forces, who need my advice on questions of the utmost urgency: the internal strife within their high command is threatening to explode this very night, although it's actually a coup planned by the command itself (they're offering me the chairmanship of the Central Bank). The shootings and slaughter in their ranks will be hidden from the public.

In an intermediate room (all this is happening very quickly) I become "the writer" César Aira again, accompanying Liliana ... And then back into the tuxedo ... It's all entrances and exits, vaudeville style, further complicated by another mission that I've taken on: to inform the Amnesty lawyer about the sham coup, and transmit a plan that I've hatched, with instructions for the resistance so that they can take advantage of this internal turmoil and mobilize the people just when the occupying forces are virtually leaderless. It has to be tonight ... Speed and secrecy are crucial to the palace coup: they reckon it will all be over in a couple of hours (they're using the widely reported visit of the ambassadors of Atlantis as a cover and this reception as a way of gathering all the conspirators and their victims without awakening suspicion). It would never occur to them that the resistance might be in the know and poised to strike like lightning … And strike it will! At least if I can talk to this so-called lawyer, who is, I know, in contact with the Committee of the Resistance … I made sure he was kept busy during my previous maneuvers, so that he wouldn't be surprised by the unexpected appearance of "César Aira." Now, playing my other role, with my tuxedo and slicked-back hair, I take him aside … and it has to be "really" aside. I'm well aware, more keenly aware than anyone, that "walls have ears," especially here, but I also know that there are many little salons and offices where I can take him to make my disclosure … I supervised the installation of the microphones myself; I know where they are and how to place myself in a "cone of silence" … And yet I'm suddenly seized by a suspicion that is quite irrational, from the point of view of my current identity as a technocrat: I have the feeling that we are being listened to … as if the fourth wall were suddenly missing, and there were people sitting in the dark, intently following everything I say. It's just the kind of fantasy that would have occurred to the writer I was, who is returning now. I find it hard to believe, but I dare not disregard the possibility altogether: there is too much at stake. So I say to the lawyer: "No, wait a moment, we can't talk here, come into the office next door …" But when we're there, it's the same thing, and if we move again, the suspicion comes along with us. These useless sets are costing a fortune, and the cost could only be justified by record-breaking audiences, but this gives rise to a vicious circle, because the more spectators there are, the stronger my suspicion that I'm being spied on, and the more imperious my need to move in search of an elusive privacy ... Also, the minutes are passing, and the action's going nowhere ... It's a disaster, the play is collapsing. I don't know how to solve the problem: deep down I know it's too late for solutions now. My mistake was to forget, in the heat of the action, that this is a play ... Or rather, not to "forget" but "never to have known," because for me, as a character, all this is reality. I should make it clear that this scene, aborted by my infinite delays and relocations, was fundamental, because up till now the spectators (whether hypothetical or real—I can't tell anymore) had no way of knowing why one actor was playing two such different roles, and the conversation with the lawyer was supposed to be a major revelation that would function as an overall explanation of the plot.

The whole thing is falling apart ... Which is no great loss, because the play is absurd, farfetched, based on facile devices. Maybe it was a project without merit from the start, as well as being flawed in its execution. In my previous life I used to think of myself as a good writer, but neither success nor personal satisfaction could really count as proof. The isolated admirers who kept popping up didn't prove anything; they could have been as mistaken as I was. I used to think death would provide an answer; I thought it would cut the Gordian knot, but since my disappearance twenty years ago, nothing has changed: a few readers, always academics or students, writing theses on my work, and that's it. I never had a real public. A public would have made me rich, and then I could have forgotten about literature. Was I a misunderstood genius or some barely half-talented writer lost in the ambiguous meanders of the avant-garde? Impossible to say. The suspicion that gags and paralyzes me in the theater, with its layering of real and virtual spaces, also suspends the question of my life or death as a writer.

JULY 3, 1995

The Two Men

I WAS THE ONLY PERSON WHO VISITED THE HOUSE where the two men lived in seclusion; I used to wonder if anyone else knew of their existence. Once, in the early days, I resorted to a trick I'd learned as a kid, playing at spies: I stuck a hair to the front door and the frame, and the next day it was still there, unbroken. I think I did it again, to make sure, but later, as the years went by, those suspicions came to seem absurd. By then I was sure that the secret was safe, not because anyone was trying to protect it, but because of indifference, or incredulity, or the desertion of the surrounding area. I never saw any neighbors; it was a street of run-down little houses that looked as if they must have been inhabited by old people, but if that was the case, those people can't have gone on living through all the years of my visits. Maybe the houses were empty.

It seemed that the men had always been living there, just the two of them, all on their own. If they hadn't been born in the house (which seemed unlikely), they must have grown up there, behind closed doors, never going out, so as not to reveal their deformities. Merciful guardians had shielded them from the gazes of the world, so that they wouldn't be treated like monsters. They weren't monsters. Except for their hands and feet they were just like other men, and even well proportioned: athletic and strong, with something savage about them, something of the animal perfection that we like to attribute to savages; but this might have been a result of their circumstances. I estimated their age at somewhere between thirty and forty: the prime of life. Their features, gestures, and reactions were vaguely similar, but this too may have been an illusion created by the very special circumstances that had brought them together. I never knew if they were related; at first it seemed almost self-evident that they were brothers, but the simplest reasoning obliged me to abandon that idea, which persisted nevertheless, the term "brothers" taking on a broader or more figurative meaning. The more likely scenario was that they were unrelated, and had been brought together by their corresponding deformities, which were so strange that they must have been unique to that pair.

One of them had giant feet, the other, giant hands. The proportions were more or less the same in both cases. The feet of "the one with the feet" and the hands of "the one with the hands" were as big as the rest of their bodies, or even slightly bigger. The hands of the one with giant feet were, like the rest of him, normal in size. The "one with the hands" had normal feet. The oversize extremities were truly amazing: huge masses of flesh, bone, muscle, and nails, almost always resting on the floor. They didn't quite have the standard form: as well as being gigantic, they were swollen, and somewhat misshapen; perhaps the forms of feet and hands are gradually determined by use, and these were never used, or hardly ever.

That was all: the hands of one, the feet of the other. The two men couldn't have been more different, and yet, in a way, they were the same. It must have been because of the opposition, or a kind of asymmetrical symmetry, as if putting them together would have made a man with giant hands and feet, or as if they had resulted from the division of a man like that ... But putting them together the other way would have produced a perfectly normal man. You had to assemble and disassemble their images mentally, because there was something inherently illusory or inconceivable about those men, something that made it impossible to believe your eyes when faced with what, believe it or not, was real. It must have been their complementary opposition that made them seem alike.

They dominated the space they occupied, invincibly. They filled it right up, as far as perception was concerned, at least ... I couldn't take my eyes off them. The way they were was simple enough and yet I always felt that I still hadn't quite understood. Physically, they had plenty of room to move; after all, apart from the hands and feet, they were the size of ordinary men. The house in which they lived wasn't big, but nor was it especially small. It looked as if it had been uninhabited for many years before they came. In a way, it still seemed empty: the few pieces of furniture had been pushed into the corners, and stood there unused, covered with dust. The power sockets were encrusted with saltpeter and rust, and the wires were exposed. There were abandoned spiderwebs in the corners of the ceiling, hanging down in shreds. I didn't know if the house belonged to the men, if one of them had inherited it, or if they were squatters. That was just one of the many things I never found out. It surprises me how little I knew about a situation that was such an important part of my life. It's true that I didn't have anyone to ask. All I could do was speculate, invent a story on the basis of what I could see; but I didn't even invent much: an irresistible lethargy came over me as soon as I tried to think about it, a visceral aversion that may have resulted from the intuition that my brain was in danger. It was as if the vision they afforded, always the same yet always changing, was somehow meant to remain wordless.

They occupied what seemed to be the biggest room; I don't know if it really was because I never explored the whole house. It was the biggest of the rooms I went into when I visited, and strangely it wasn't the front room, which in that house (built back to front, apparently) was a little living room with a door straight onto the street, but a room right at the back, which must have been a bedroom. That back room had a window that looked onto a patio, but whether the patio was big or small, I really can't say, because I never went over to look, and even if I had, it wouldn't have been much use because the glass was frosted. I assumed there was a patio there because of the light coming in. I don't know if the electricity was connected. I never went to the house at night. My "visiting time" was midafternoon, and if I made two visits, the other one was just before midday.

I saw them against the background of that window, which filtered the light and, depending on the weather and the season, made them opaque or radiant, contrasting with their silhouettes or suffusing their bodies with a glow that seemed to emanate from within. The faded ochre of the walls gave that light an artificial, yellowish tinge that was slightly disturbing.

They were naked. At first, I think, it seemed natural to me. After all, how could you put on trousers if your feet had a girth of two yards? How could you get hands the size of sheep through the sleeves of a shirt? But thinking it over, I realized that explanation didn't stand up. The one whose feet prevented him from wearing trousers could still have put on a shirt, a jacket, or a tunic. And the other one, whose hands couldn't fit through any kind of sleeve, could perfectly well have worn trousers, even socks and shoes, had he wished, and covered his upper body with something like a poncho or a toga. The only thing they couldn't have done was dress in the same way; but they could have worn clothes, if they'd wanted to. Why didn't they? Was it that they didn't want to draw attention to the difference between them? Or were they renouncing human ways? They didn't need clothes for warmth. Oddly, in a house that must have gone for decades without repairs or maintenance, the room was well insulated. There was a series of very cold winters, but even then the house was always peculiarly warm, as if heated (although I never saw any kind of heater, and in fact I'm sure there wasn't one). I always saw them in that room, as I said, but that doesn't mean they were always there. What I know for sure is that it's where they received my visits or waited for them, like actors before a performance. They probably spent the greater part of their time in that room, and if they happened to be somewhere else when I arrived, they rushed back as soon as they heard me come in through the front door. I say this because, very occasionally, only one of them was there when I entered the room, and the other appeared just a few seconds later.

Maybe they generated that puzzling, constant warmth themselves ... why not? It might have come from their bodies, or from the huge hands and feet. No one had studied those unprecedented malformations; who could say what powers and properties they might have possessed?

Leaving aside the men's feet and hands, their preference for nudism could be explained by the movement of their bodies, which would have been sufficient to keep the surroundings warm. The one with the enormous feet moved his torso and arms, shook himself, quivered, raised his hands to the sky in a gesture somewhere between supplication and stretching, clasped his head, turned it, tilted it forward, bowed down, bent himself double, and waved his arms in all directions as if he were multiplying them, with the fingers wiggling around like worms. The other man, with his gigantic hands resting on the floor on either side of him, thrashed his legs and feet about, tapping, stamping, pedaling. Meanwhile, the enormous extremities were not entirely still; with movements of submarine slowness, they accompanied the nervous jittering of the other body parts, like whales among schools of fish.

They can't always have been so agitated; perhaps what I saw was exceptional, or a show they put on specially for me, but if so there was nothing systematic about it, because there were days when I would find them languid, or rigid like statues, sometimes not even blinking, seemingly void of life. Maybe they were alternating, or competing with each other, or playing. I really had no way of knowing what their routine might be: I couldn't extrapolate from my limited observations or speculate on the psychology of individuals so radically unique. There was never any real communication between myself and them, in spite of all those years of daily contact. But not because they couldn't speak. As for me, I'd say I'm fairly talkative, when I'm with people I know and trust, which is how I felt about them in the end, or maybe even from the start, although there was always an unbridgeable gap. The reason we didn't talk was that we had nothing to say. The difference that separated them from me was somehow too extreme. No, not too extreme. I take that back. In the end, it was just a question of sizes, a purely quantitative difference, if you like. But it had been applied improperly, differentially, to parts instead of the whole. I understood perfectly well that with hands like that, or feet, in the case of the other man, they couldn't manage their lives like everybody else. If life was a puzzle in which each piece had to fit into its place to recompose the landscape, what could you do with a piece a thousand times bigger than all the rest? That was what condemned me to silence. Only someone who could provide an answer to the question, a solution to the problem, would have been able to speak to them. And I had no answer, no solution. For a reason I never fully understood, I'd convinced myself that I was the last person who'd be able to come up with a solution, perhaps the only person who couldn't.

This lack of communication was also due to the brevity of my visits. "House calls" was how I thought of them, remembering a colloquial expression for the popping in and out that leaves no time for relaxed conversation, the dutiful visits typically paid by the young to the old, or the healthy to the ill, or the busy and successful to the idle and lonely ... But I was not a doctor, nor was I especially young or healthy, much less successful. Visiting the men had consumed my youth. I had withered. I wasn't much younger than they were; a little, perhaps, but they had a supernatural self-possession, an indefinable vigor, that rendered age irrelevant. I said that they gave an impression of strength and health, in spite of their complementary deformities. I had always been fairly healthy, but anxious too, in a vague sort of way, about illness and death. Of course I had normal-size hands and feet, and could get dressed and go out into the street, and live a normal life with my family, and take the men their food. Sometimes I'd think: I have the hands of one, and the feet of the other. What if it had been the other way around? What a nightmare! Together, with their well-formed limbs, they made up a normal man, and with the malformed ones, a complete invalid. As they were, they could only nourish my infinite perplexity.

I never stayed long, because I wasn't paying social calls: I was there to help and meet a need; I was their only point of contact with the outside world. But basically, the visits were brief because I didn't want my family to find out. Although that reason didn't always apply. There were times when I was alone at home and could have spent hours or whole afternoons with the men. Maybe the habit of not lingering (or not finding a reason to linger) had already been established. Of course I didn't keep a record of how much time I spent in the house, and for a fair while before and after the visits, I was too tense to look at my watch, so I couldn't work it out, but I estimate that on average it would have been three, four, or five minutes; maybe more, or less, I don't know. I was aware that it wasn't long, and a kind of automatic politeness or tact, which was entirely out of place in the circumstances, made me worry that I might offend them by giving the impression that I was running away from a disgusting sight.

There's a simpler and more concrete explanation for the brevity of my visits: in the room where they received me, as opposed to the rooms I passed through on the way, there was no furniture. That bare room had the air of a cage at the zoo, or an exhibition space, and accentuated the impression of inhumanity. As with the clothing, one might have thought at first that the physical peculiarities of the two men ruled out furniture; but, again, thinking it over sufficed to reveal that there was no fundamental impossibility. Chairs, armchairs, carpets, sideboards, pictures, tables . . . why not? Perhaps it would have been necessary to take certain precautions when moving around, but that was all. And if they could have worn clothes and had furniture, why did they prefer to remain naked in an empty space? This didn't puzzle me at the time. All through those years I simply accepted that things were as they were. That numbing of curiosity was psychologically justifiable: given the prodigious monstrosity of one man's hands and the other man's feet, details of clothing and furniture receded into the background. That enormous mystery (enormity itself) repelled any kind of explanation, while its gravitational force attracted and swallowed up everything else.

I shouldn't have felt guilty about my flying visits; no one else came to see them, so they had no point of comparison. Anyway, the notion of courtesy was completely alien to them. They were only interested in what I brought, which they accepted without a word of thanks or any particular signs of pleasure. This makes it sound like feeding stray cats in a square or a derelict house, or, to return to an earlier comparison, stepping into an animal enclosure at the zoo. Nothing could be further from the truth. The two men were utterly and terribly human; in that regard, there was, if anything, an excess, not a deficiency: they were all too human. There was no reason why the unfortunate deformities that isolated them should diminish their humanity; on they contrary, they accentuated it. And if the men treated me with something like disdain, or irony, or a hurtful indifference, how in the name of humanity, precisely, could I fail to forgive them? I had to be grateful that resentment hadn't made them hate me (although more than once, as I left the house, dismayed by their rude behavior, I suspected that they did). They had good reason to see me as privileged by fate: free as a bird, I could come and go unnoticed among my fellow men.

I had to make an effort to adopt their point of view. From where I was standing, my situation didn't seem privileged at all, and I didn't feel so free. My freedom was punctuated by the daily visits to their house, as if by the pecking of an implacable vulture. Sometimes I reproached myself for "taking it so seriously," but deep down I knew I had no choice; there were no intermediate degrees of seriousness. Although the commitment I'd taken on was entirely personal and had remained secret, I couldn't abandon the men. And I had to accept the consequences, which were so far-reaching that they shaped my whole life. Having to be on duty every day, without fail, meant that I couldn't envisage travel abroad, or vacations by the sea, or weekends in the country, or even long visits to museums or the houses of friends and family members. In order to maintain the routine, I had to pretend to be a man of obsessively sedentary habits, who went out for supposedly constitutional walks at certain times of the day, rain or shine, and kept to himself, which was terribly hard for me, as by nature I'm drawn to travel, adventure, and change. I didn't complain to anyone, because I would have had to explain, and I tried not to grumble to myself either, so as not to become embittered. When I heard other people complaining about some small or large but essentially solvable problem, I felt the full weight of my predicament. There was a kind of symmetry in this predominantly asymmetrical picture: the two men, prisoners indoors, had made me a prisoner outside.

I couldn't take on jobs that involved serious responsibilities and long hours of work, and I had to stagnate at a mediocre level that didn't reflect my capacities. Since I wasn't at liberty to reveal my real reasons for saying no, it was universally assumed that I was eccentric, neurotic, or disabled in some way. Me! I've always been rational and practical, almost to excess. The limitations sharpened my skills, and the little I was able to accomplish, though fragmented and impaired by my alienated way of living, was of remarkable quality, and resulted in an abundance of offers and invitations. But gradually they became less frequent, and then stopped altogether when everyone came to the conclusion that I would always decline. All those missed opportunities left me with a feeling of dissatisfaction, which turned into melancholy, discouragement, and despair. My youth was vanishing, it had gone by in a changeless twilight, leaving me with nothing. My projects and talents had promised so much, and in exchange for all that I had nothing; I felt dispossessed. Daily exposure to something tragic and irreparable, in an atmosphere of unreality, had cast a veil of misfortune, tinged with horror, over my life. After so many years, the secret had become definitive, cutting me off from the rest of the world, and even from my hopes.

But it wasn't all bad. It never is. When a whole life is affected, as it was in my case because of the way the two men had contaminated everything, the totality itself arranges certain displacements in order to reestablish a sustainable balance. Creative energy always finds some way to break through, even when cir-

cumstances conspire to smother it. And my circumstances did
not have an entirely negative effect. The negative, of course,
contains its own negation. Along with all the drawbacks of my
unfortunate situation, there was a decisive advantage: I was
the only one who knew about the two men, the only person
in the world aware of an extraordinary phenomenon. Though
sometimes I wasn't sure of that dubious privilege, and felt that
someone else must have known. Before I came along, someone
must have visited and fed them. Someone had brought them
together and taken them to that house. And before all that,
they'd had parents, grandparents, brothers and sisters perhaps,
a childhood, a history—and there's no history without people.
But as the years and the decades went by, I gradually became
convinced that the secret was safe with me and that I was its
sole guardian. I was standing in for the father, the grandfather,
and all the others. Dubious as it was, the privilege was mine.

From that point on, I couldn't help wondering how I might
derive some benefit from my position. Not that I imagined for
a moment preying on the misfortune of others. If I'd gone public, if I'd "sold" or exhibited them, I wouldn't have been able to
live with the guilt. Anyway, I wouldn't have known how to do
it. But it didn't seem immoral to hope for some material gain to
compensate for everything I'd been obliged to sacrifice.

I would have liked to photograph or film them, but of course
that wasn't possible. I wouldn't have dared to go there with a
camera. I would have had to explain, and I couldn't predict how
they would react. Although they had never behaved aggressively

with me (except for their haughty indifference), or with each other, their naked bodies had always seemed to harbor a potential for violence. Their mobility was not as limited as the colossal burden of their extremities might have suggested. They could move quickly. This had been confirmed on those rare occasions when I entered to find that one of them was absent from the room: very soon, and moving very quickly, the missing man would come in through a side door. Once in the room, where I almost always found them, they hardly shifted, even when they were seized by the Saint Vitus's dance that I described earlier. But their fixedness seemed to be a choreographic choice, rather than a limitation imposed by the law of gravity. Presumably, the giant hands and feet were equipped with muscles in proportion to their size; they can't have been dead weights. And the rest of the men's bodies, which, as I said, were well formed, must have become exceptionally strong. I never saw a demonstration of that strength; like so many other things about them, it was a mystery, a secret chamber that might have contained anything.

I couldn't predict how they would have reacted if they'd seen me taking photographs. They might have shut themselves up like that because they wanted to remain hidden, but their isolation might also have been a consequence of their limited mobility, or just the way things had turned out. Perhaps it was one of those confinements that result from inertia or procrastination. After all, there are plenty of people who never go out, not because they have something to hide but simply because they don't enjoy it, or they're happy staying home, or whatever. The case of the two men was special, but, precisely because they were so isolated, whether or not they knew it was special was open to doubt. If each of them had only the other as a model of normality, one man might have looked at his own giant hands, and at the normal-size hands of his companion, and then at his own feet and the giant feet of the other man ... There was really no way for them to know what the normal proportions were. How could they tell? It's true that they also had me to consider, and I didn't have giant hands or feet, but I might just have been a third case. When I had discovered them, many years earlier, they hadn't tried to hide themselves. Had they made an exception for me? And, if so, why? Why me? Or was it that they didn't mind being seen, and that the only reason no one else had seen them was that no one else had come? Maybe they'd only accepted me out of necessity or convenience, or because they knew, somehow, that with me their secret would be safe.

In any case, the photos that I didn't take would not have been used for revelations or publicity. Although I was motivated by a desire for material gain, my aim would have been different.

That aim, to express it in a rough and ready way, was "artistic." Art, too, could produce material gains, and I wasn't just thinking about money; the material realm is broader than that. Even if the "earnings" of a work of art are purely spiritual, the concrete nature of the work itself is enduring and effective, and capable of transforming life.

It's not that I had a clear and worked-out plan, but I felt that I could do something original with the vision they afforded me. Photos and video were out of the question, which left the possibility of drawing. Obviously I wasn't an artist, and I had no special training. Lacking the slightest talent for the visual arts, I never would have thought to venture into that field (or at least approach its edges) if I hadn't been led to do so by certain incidental circumstances for which the two men were responsible. So there was a kind of poetic justice in my use of them as models.

By "incidental circumstances" I mean simply the conditions imposed on my life by the work of visiting them daily. The two men came into my life just when it was liable to be thrown off course. I had completed my desultory studies in the humanities and was about to settle on a vocation. That, in a way, was what they provided. I don't mean that I devoted myself entirely to serving them, and neglected everything else. It might have been like that at the start (for the first few years, that is), but then I managed to confine them to a small compartment of my existence, partly, perhaps, by keeping them secret. And yet, although that compartment was small, it irradiated all the rest; the men were never far from my thoughts. How could they have been? Because of the daily routine, the unavoidable midafternoon appointment, every day without fail, they were always on my mind. The way the visits interrupted the day, and the strangeness of the interruption, its monstrous, almost supernatural character, prevented me from applying myself to other tasks in a concentrated way. I've already said how much I had to sacrifice in financial and professional terms. There was also a sacrifice of attention. In my youth I'd sometimes dreamed of pursuing advanced studies, which might have satisfied my taste for scholarship, but I had to give up that idea. As time went by, it became increasingly difficult for me to read a whole book, let alone undertake any serious and focused research.

I found myself reduced to reading magazine articles. But which magazines was I to read? My studies in the humanities had given me an appetite that news and political magazines could never satisfy, but I found the abstraction of academic journals exhausting, and although I went through phases of reading popular science and history magazines, they never really captured my interest. So in the end, the most satisfactory source of intellectual nourishment for me, almost the only source in fact, turned out to be art magazines. What began as a way to pass the time—not chosen but arrived at by elimination—became a kind of need. Reorganizing my meager budget, I took out a number of subscriptions, and rationed my reading so I'd never run out. Beyond a certain point, I didn't have to worry: since I kept the magazines carefully in boxes, my collection eventually ran to thousands, and the back issues (they didn't have to be twenty years old: one or two years was enough) became new again for me, given the distracted state of mind in which I read them. Though to call it reading might be a stretch; I really just leafed through them. I'd look at the illustrations, read the beginning of an article, or skim it to see how the author explained or justified the works that were reproduced, then keep flicking ...

This contact with art, though it might seem superficial from what I just said, gradually shaped my interests, my tastes, and even my vision of the world. In fact, a deep connection developed between my practical "job" of going to feed the two men and my amateur interest in the most extreme forms of so-called "contemporary art." I should make it clear that the magazines I'm talking about were not for antiquarians or historians; they focused on art in its current state, which since the 1970s has been a perpetual search for difference and originality, an endless escalation. From outside, it might have seemed like a meaningless eccentricity contest. But when one entered into the game, the meaning became apparent, and dominated everything else. It was, in fact, a game of meaning, and without meaning, it was nothing. The artists could exhibit whatever they chose: a glass of water with a few dead flies floating in it, old newspapers, a machine, a hairstyle, a diamond; or they could choose not to exhibit anything at all and go running after a car instead, or kill a chicken, or leave a room empty. Freedom was taken to its limits, and beyond. It was easy to criticize, or mock, these new developments in art, so easy that criticism and mockery lost their force and hardly seemed worthwhile. The perplexity and disapproval expressed by the enemies of contemporary art resulted from their way of viewing the work in isolation, taking no account of the history behind it. I sometimes felt rather weary myself, leafing through a new issue of one of the magazines, seeing nothing but photos of rubble, wheelchairs, blurry television screens, messy rooms, expressionless faces, or embalmed animals. But a reading of the texts that accompanied the photos, even a fragmentary and interrupted reading, showed that there was always a justification; sometimes it was disappointing, but sometimes, often (or was I fooling myself?), it struck me as acceptable, intelligent, even dazzling. I had my collection of favorite artists, to which I was always adding. Human creativity, on this set of premises at least, was inexhaustible.

One of the things that appealed to me about this new system, and prevented me from rejecting it out of hand, was that its multiform proliferation did away with the need for traditional talents and their cultivation, which had been seen as the substance of art. It was no longer necessary to be a born artist, or to undergo special training; the days of masters and apprentices, virtuosos and botchers, were over. Anyone could do it; there was only one condition: it had to be something that had never occurred to anyone before. Year after year I was amazed by the ideas that kept occurring to the new artists appearing on the scene. And often, almost always, those ideas were perfectly simple; their only merit was originality. The reaction they elicited was invariably the question: Why didn't I think of that?

It was this line of reasoning that led me to see the two men, with their strange deformities, as an artistic idea. An idea that might have prompted me to wonder, somewhat ruefully: Why didn't I think of that? And indeed, never in a thousand years would I have come up with it on my own. But there it was: given to me, to me and nobody else. In practical terms, I might as well have thought of it. In a sense, in every sense, it was typical of the "artworks" that I kept seeing in the magazines, the kind that got noticed at biennales and documentas, the kind that won prizes and were discoursed upon in articles. In a sense, too, I had a right, after all I'd done for that "idea," to say that "it had occurred to me." Admittedly, if that had really been the case, if I'd been choosing an idea for an artwork, I would have chosen something else. Morbid and monstrous subjects didn't appeal to me, although they were fashionable in the art world. But I had to make the best of it, because, left to my own devices, nothing at all would have occurred to me.

At least, nothing that good. Because although the subject wasn't to my taste, I had to admit that the "idea" was excellent. Two men, one with enormous hands, the other with enormous feet, symmetrical, asymmetrical, inexplicable: they had everything it takes to work as art. No one would believe they really existed; they were too much like the inventions of a mind intoxicated by contemporary art magazines. As to keeping the secret and not betraying the trust that had been placed in me, I could set my mind at rest because labeling something as art dispels all suspicion of reality forever.

But how was I to proceed? The medium didn't matter, I knew that much. All the medium had to do was record the idea. In these new forms of art, recording and documentation are everything. My initial plan of photographing the men might seem to be at odds with my artistic project. But although they might have thought I was intending to reveal their reality, no one else would have seen it that way. These days, in the art world, thanks to digital editing tools, which are widely accessible, photography is just another medium for documenting fiction. And apart from the fact that it's used extensively by avant-garde experimenters (though not as much as video), photography would have been ideal for me, mainly because I wouldn't have had to manipulate the images (I couldn't have, anyhow, given my technological ignorance), but everyone would think I had, and very well at that.

However, as I said, I had to give up on the idea of taking photos. Which left the perfectly adequate alternative of drawing. A series of drawings, a folio, and maybe a book eventually, with texts to explain or justify the idea—but not too much because the value of the idea depended on its mystery, its inexplicability, its openness to any kind of suggestion. It would be an open series, but not too extensive, twenty drawings at most, enough to show the men in all their positions and from every angle, at rest and in movement. I set only one constraint for myself: both men had to figure in every drawing; there would be no drawing that showed only one of them. That would unify the project, and supply its enigmatic meaning.

But the problem was that I didn't know how to draw. I'd never learned. Or, granting that everyone knows how to draw (badly, at least), I should say that I'd never actually sat down and done it: I'd never practiced. This wasn't an insuperable obstacle, because the quality of the draftsmanship wasn't crucial; the drawing was just a means of documentation, so all I had to do was make sure the viewer understood that it was a picture of two naked men, of normal size and shape, except that one had the feet of a giant sixty feet tall, and the other's hands were correspondingly huge. It can't have been that hard. The scene might have been made to be drawn.

It's easy to say, "All I had to do . . . ," but in order to achieve that effect, some effort and a certain degree of skill were required. Especially to make sure that the viewer understood *exactly*. Because if the drawing was clumsy, as mine would have been, the disproportionately large hands and feet might have come across as just another clumsiness, or a bad imitation of Picasso. And even if the drawing were adequate, there were still dangers: for example, the hugeness of the extremities might have seemed to be an effect of perspective.

But I'm getting ahead of myself. There was a prior difficulty, which I noticed when I started thinking about it in practical terms. I realized that substituting drawing for photography didn't get me very far. One way or another, you have to draw from life, and just as I couldn't take photos, I couldn't pull out pencil and paper and proceed to draw the two men. Or I might have been able to, but I wasn't planning to try.

Drawing in the absence of the model means working from memory, which would have required me to retain visual detail, and that was a capacity I didn't possess. Or maybe I did, but unwittingly, because it wasn't something I'd ever tried to do. So I began to try, without taking any precautions, not suspecting that the trial, even if it never went beyond the planning stage, could alter my relationship with the men. I tried to imprint them on my retinas: their lines, their shapes, their volumes. It was a new way of looking at them: in all those years, those decades, which made up the greater part of my life, I'd never looked at them like that. The difference was that now I was bringing memory into play, anticipating its operation, trying to turn time to my advantage. I'd never done this before. Why would I have bothered, when the one thing I knew for sure was that I'd be seeing them again the next day? Now my presence in the room, and theirs, was charged with memory in the form of an intensely physical, palpable, almost sensual attention. "I'd never looked at them like that." I wanted to take them away with me, and that intention, though I never came close to realizing it, disturbed me, stirred dark impulses, and left me feeling guilty. It didn't produce the desired effect. My visual memory, which had never been exercised, wasn't about to spring into action just because I told it to.

There were other ways of going about it. A drawing without a model was a caricature, a scribble, a diagram. But I didn't have to use a live model: life drawing was for students, and I wasn't studying to become a painter. Those jointed dolls that graphic artists use presented the same problem: too didactic. My very specific and pressing requirements could have been satisfied by photographs, or good drawings, of naked men. I could have copied them or used tracing paper (an invaluable crutch for novices like me). I would have been able to find satisfactory specimens in any pornographic magazine; but of course I would never have dared go to a newsstand and buy one, which made me curse my fearfulness, because that would have been

the ideal solution. There was another possibility: those drawing manuals with anatomical plates. I could trace the outlines
of two men, leaving the hands off one and the feet off the other,
and then use a photocopier to magnify the original drawing by
a factor of fifty, and trace the hands and feet off that. But what
would they think at the copy center if I asked them to blow up
drawings of naked men? The best thing would be to make a
good tracing of the hands and feet, without bodies, and take
that to be enlarged.

All this ingenious and detailed planning got me nowhere. It
might have been different if I'd done it at the start. But earlier,
when I was planning to draw the men from memory, I'd developed that new way of looking, the gaze with built-in memory,
which, although I'd since given up the idea of using it, discour-
aged me from copying or tracing photographs or drawings, and
even from looking for them. There was a vast, yawning gulf between the two approaches. Seeing the men in that new way, I
discovered how inexhaustibly rich the form of a body is, and
how drastically it is simplified by drawing, which intellectual-
izes it and turns it into a game. Perhaps if I had gone for a long
time without seeing the men, memory would have worked naturally and accomplished the process of simplification. But since
I was seeing them anew every day, memory adhered to vision,
and was loaded with subjective and objective reality; this en-
riched it, admittedly, but with a sterile richness, which paralyzed
me. My artistic dreams dissolved and left me with nothing.

I don't know if the men noticed these subtle machinations.

I had momentarily taken on the role of hunter and attempted to make them my trophies. It was a short-lived fantasy, soon swallowed up by a broader and darker confirmation of our relationship's immutability. Though it wasn't a real relationship, or not what we normally think of as a relationship between human beings. But that only made it more intimate. Again and again I wondered how it had all begun. I had ceased to wonder if it would ever end.

In the course of writing the above and trying to reconstruct my abortive artistic adventure, I realized that its failure was only part of a larger defeat. It wasn't just that I hadn't produced my folio or book of drawings; I'd never even tried to draw the men, not even in the sort of idle doodling that you do while chatting on the phone. More than that: I hadn't even drawn them mentally. It was as if some kind of taboo had been operating. It wouldn't surprise me: the whole thing seemed to have been placed under the sign of taboo. "Art" had come into in the story more as a means of deep explanation than as an actual project. The men themselves were the "artwork," such as it was, and they resisted transposition into any medium apart from the harsh reality in which they existed.

If art had been, and was, an unrealizable daydream for me, perhaps it had served to lighten the crushing load of reality waiting for me every day when I had to face that scene in the back room of the house. Which wouldn't have been all that hard, because there was already something unreal about the scene itself. Yet it was on the side of reality, and probably all the more real for being near the limit. I would have given anything to escape. But I didn't have anything to give, and I suspected that the limit would follow me: I was myself that blurry line separating the real from the unreal. The flight was within me already, crucifying me.

I don't think the descriptions I've given so far fully convey how desperate I felt. I'm not going to try to remedy that; my means of expression have wasted away under the effects of solitude and secrecy—they're means of isolation now. I couldn't even express it to myself. I felt only emptiness as I set off on that route I knew so well, there and back, the mute emptiness so typical of anxiety, an empty feeling that wasn't opening but closing, enclosing me, forever. I ended up trying not to think at all (which is impossible). I would have liked to be a machine, an automaton; and in a way that's what I became, at least in part. I brutally repressed all calculations of the time that had passed (the most distressing thing for me). But the calculations performed themselves, using various reference points, the handiest being the ages of my children. I had been visiting the two men in their house since before my children were born (though how long before, I refused to work out), and my children had grown up, they were no longer children, or teenagers, they had turned twenty, then thirty … I could see the signs of aging in my wife's face, as she could no doubt in mine. My family, my loved ones, the only ones with whom I could have shared a human destiny, had always been separate from me, leading separate lives. I had lived in the hope that my isolation would come to an end, as a blind man dreams of seeing or a paraplegic longs to walk again. These are not gratuitous comparisons. In some ways, if not in all, I seemed to be a normal man, one of the many who assuage their pervasive ill-being or psychological distress by reminding themselves that they're healthy, they have money, and that others are worse off. It's true that I could see and walk. Every day I walked to the house where the two men lived, and I saw them ... The miracle that the blind man and the paraplegic hoped for in vain had been bestowed on me, but only to engender a secret. There *was* something miraculous about the situation; but it was the worst kind of miracle, the kind that occurs only in real life.

That was what weighed most heavily: the reality of the secret. Not so much its substance as its defiant persistence. That was what I found so mortifying, such an unfair punishment; the secret had given real existence to the most unreal aspect of the world: time. The content of the secret, on the other hand, was not so problematic, because it bordered on hallucination, literature, cinema, and "special effects," any of which might have provided a justification. It was not a mere coincidence that I had looked for a way out via "art," whose function would have been to cover reality with a veneer of fantasy, and give me the illusory impression, at least, of having regained control.

But it didn't work. It backfired. Reality persisted, and the contrast with my artistic daydream made it all the more real and cruel. I began to long for another kind of secret: the kind that is kept in the mind and stops being a secret as soon as it is expressed. Mine was an external fact, with all the willful independence of facts out there in the world. And it wasn't one of those accidental facts, some fleeting, inoffensive conjunction in time and space. For my benefit and mine alone, it had revoked that temporariness in which the rest of humanity lulled itself to sleep with a beatific smile. I had to go to that room every day and see the men; I had to "believe my eyes," as novelists used to say in the old days (but the men were saying just the opposite). The golden light coming in through the large window, in mysterious gradations of transparency, was like an oil that made the men's movements fluid and silent. There was something animal about them; they had the poise and indifference of wild beasts. It seemed as if they could destroy the world from within, at the atomic level, just by being there ... But these are digressions, disconnected ideas, the only kind I ever had when I thought about the two men. Humans have no way to construct the perception of beings like them. That was the source of my solitude, and also, perhaps, of their human inhumanity.

I had intended to scrutinize their faces, in search of an expression, since no one can maintain a perfect neutrality forever. But it was futile. Their faces were irrelevant and inexpressive. They were smooth, regular faces, which seemed to predate the birth of expression, manly but with something feminine or childlike about them, too. They gave the men an archaic, doubly concrete character, making them undeniable. They were a small part of the world, a tiny part, and hidden, but it was a center that moved mountains and seas, all the while remaining a sordid little detail, a regrettable accident that had befallen me.

Yet I couldn't even be certain that it *had* befallen me. What happens hasn't really happened unless it can be told, and the two men didn't fit into any tellable story. It wasn't just the need for secrecy, or my shame, that stopped me from telling anyone. There was a kind of obliteration or hollowing in them that made it impossible. The story wasn't theirs but mine, the story of my failure and helplessness, of something vaguely monstrous slowly growing. In the end, the spiderweb of my lies and miserable stratagems—those flimsy strings of spittle with which I kept provisionally tying one moment to another—solidified, becoming impenetrable, rock-hard. But even rocks wear away with time.

Reason, or logic, the mechanical logic that blindly governs the events of this world, indicated that eventually, at some point, the conditions for my liberation would be fulfilled. There would be no need for a cataclysm or a revolution or a titanic effort of the will: everyday permutations would suffice. Which meant that the conditions could be fulfilled at any moment, perhaps very soon. Perhaps it had happened already, and all I had to do was open my eyes and see it.

But first I would have had to know what I was supposed to be seeing. I had no idea what those conditions might have been; I couldn't conceive of them, although this shouldn't have been inherently difficult. Again, as always, it was a matter of "seeing": that was the key. But seeing wasn't as simple as keeping your eyes open. A mental operation was involved. Thought had to blaze a path through the dense jungle of the visible ...

And then one day it struck me that the giant feet of one man and the giant hands of the other had begun to shrink. I'd been so distracted or blind that I hadn't noticed them reverting to almost normal, or completely normal, dimensions. I found the idea strangely confusing. Only time could have provided a confirmation of what was happening, but it was the action of time, precisely, that obliterated the traces, or scrambled them, tying them into a knot. It wasn't impossible. Every impossibility has a basis in the possible. After all, one of the men had always had normal-size feet, and the other, normal-size hands. This alternation, or distribution, or asymmetrical symmetry, might have been the source of my confusion. There was something in them that had always resisted clarification: for me they had always been an inseparable pair. I mentioned that they tried to avoid being seen singly; so my memory or perception of them (my "idea" of them) was double; but at the same time the difference between the members of the pair could not have been greater. I could only recognize them by means of that difference: one of them was "the one with the feet"; the other, "the one with the hands." The prodigious enlargement of those extremities was so striking that it made any other characterization impossible or superfluous. So if the monstrous element had disappeared, would I have been able to say which was which, or, more precisely, which had been which? Through all those years, maybe ever since I'd first seen them or (this comes to the same thing) grasped what made them special, I must have been under the unconscious impression that they were a single man. One man in two manifestations. First impressions, of course, are crucial. That's why I never considered the question of individuality. It wouldn't arise until the hypothetical moment, on time's farthest horizon, when the hands of one man and the feet of the other had shrunk to normal dimensions, when both, that is, had the same size feet and hands. In that scenario there was at once a possibility and something impossible.

By transporting myself in imagination to that far horizon of time, I could ask how the change might have come about. In such cases, the question is typically whether it took place in a gradual, continuous, and imperceptible way, or occurred by leaps from one stage to the next, or happened all at once. They say that habit has a blinding effect. The brain, which is always looking for ways to save energy, cancels or dulls the perceptions that are most frequently repeated in everyday life, skipping over them, taking them for granted, the better to concentrate on what's new, which might be important for survival, whereas familiar features of the environment have been ruled out as potential threats.

The misplaced tact that had always governed my relationship with the two men prevented me from fixing my gaze, in an obvious way at least, on the enormous hands and feet, but I was also inhibited by the very common reluctance (which, in my case, was particularly strong, almost a taboo) to look in detail at anything monstrous, deformed or horrible, for fear it might become an obsession, or prove to be unforgettable (when everything beautiful is forgotten). Perhaps this is a remnant of ancestral superstitions. Attention skirts around whatever might "leave an impression." To shut my eyes would have been impolite, as well as impractical. Which left me with only one option: peripheral vision.

This might seem a contrived and twisted solution, but it can be exemplified by a situation from everyday life that's familiar to all of us (or at least to all men): finding yourself face-to-face with a naked man, in the locker room of a gym, for example. You don't fix your gaze on his genitals, do you? But I should add that what I'm offering as an example, that is, as a rhetorical device to convey my meaning, is actually no such thing. Because it was incontrovertibly the case that the two men were naked, and their genitals exposed.

These associations of ideas might have led me to suspect that the two men got dressed and went out to work, or even that each of them lived with his family, and that the house was their secret place, to which they went in the afternoon, just in time to strip off and be there waiting for me when I arrived. An absurd and impossible fantasy, but it did cross my mind, like so many others. Fantasies I tried, in vain, to use as arms against the mental void into which the hopelessness of my life had cast me. It was enough to make me hate the human race and turn me into a misanthrope, if I wasn't one already. At certain moments, trapped in the circles of my partial, peripheral vision, I felt a fierce irritation, a stifled, suffocating fury. Why were they enslaving me? What did they need me for? They were younger and stronger than I was, more resolute and free. If they'd been real invalids, they would have aroused pity, and I would have had a good reason for taking care of them. But as they were— athletic, statuesque, proud—what I felt for them, rather than pity, was admiration: in them I saw the beauty of the savage and the terrible.

AUGUST 22, 2007

Acts of Charity

WHEN A PRIEST IS SENT TO EXERCISE HIS MINISTRY IN an economically depressed area, his first duty is to alleviate the poverty of his flock through acts of charity. Those acts will earn the gratitude of his beneficiaries, and, in due course, open the gates of heaven for him. He should remember, however, that poverty will not (alas!) be eradicated by the donations that his conscience, his vocation, and the directives of his superiors oblige him to make. Although charity may effectively address a temporary crisis or a specific case of need, it is not a long-term solution. Its provisional nature means that it has to be renewed over time, in the form of a continuous flow of material goods, for which a source must be found. The clergy, backed up by an institution that has, over the course of its millenary history, accumulated ample resources, is more than capable of meeting the demands of charity. But it should also be kept in mind that the minister of divine consolation has to live as well, with the dignity appropriate to his office, and the comforts that his upbringing and habits have rendered indispensable. These arrangements cost money, money that could, and really should, be used for charity. There has to be a balance, and common sense, combined with the priest's good judgment and sense of propriety, will find that balance and maintain it. And yet it remains the case that the less a priest spends on himself and his relatives, the greater the means at his disposal for helping the needy, and the closer he will be to obtaining the corresponding heavenly reward. And this, on reflection, may prompt a suspicion: isn't the exercise of charity shadowed by self-interest, pride, and vanity? Aren't the poor being used as stepping-stones to sainthood? The suspicion is justified, and easy to confirm, but dangerously corrosive like all doubts, and finally paralyzing, because the alternative would be an egotistical indifference to the suffering of others. Here again, prudence, tempered in this case with trust in divine providence, will determine the right course of action.

The aforementioned problems—how to balance personal expenses against charity, and how to avoid the vanity of the self-admiring benefactor—can be avoided by following the example set out below.

The priest begins by recognizing that he is a visitor passing through a world in which poverty and need are permanent fixtures. He will be replaced by another priest, who will be faced with the same dilemmas. And he realizes that a good way to practice charity is to ensure that it will not be discontinued in the future. This is not only a precaution but an act of humility as well, if the person acting charitably in the present deliberately gives up piety points in favor of his successor. In other words, and to be more specific, it's a matter of taking the money that might have been given to the poor today and investing it in amenities that will be enjoyed by the next priest assigned to the parish, so that he will be able to use his whole budget to protect the needy against hunger and cold.

Motivated by this reasoning, which might seem rather unusual, but has a solid logical base, the priest arranges for a house to be built as soon as he arrives to take up his new position. The existing house, which is his to live in, is old, small, uncomfortable, and dark. The roof leaks, the floors are bare gray cement, and there are no shutters on the little windows. It's surrounded by a patio full of weeds, a ruined chicken coop, and swampy scrubland. For him, it would be fine. He doesn't need luxuries, not even modest ones. His vow of poverty implicitly or explicitly enjoins him to share life's hardships with the least fortunate of his fellow men. And the money at his disposal would make a difference to many of those who live nearby: doing his initial rounds, getting to know the flock that has fallen to his care, he can see for himself the terrible poverty afflicting those helpless families, victims of unemployment, ignorance, and distance from major cities. It would be easy for him to play the role of benefactor, beginning, for example, with the most desperate situation (although it would be hard to choose among so many pitiful cases) and providing a remedy that would seem nothing short of miraculous. So acute is the deprivation that what he and his relatives would consider a trifle—literally: the price of a dessert—might keep those poor people in food for weeks.

Then he could move on to other families, and others, his action spreading like a drop of oil, finally earning the love and respect of everyone in the area ... But he would leave a minefield for his successor, who'd be tempted to look after himself rather than his neighbors, especially since he'd be able to say: My predecessor did so much for others, he was so self-abnegating; he left the priest's house in such a ruinous state, it's only reasonable for me to do something for myself, and for my successor. The poor, meanwhile, as well as having been spoiled by the largesse of the first priest, would find themselves without food, shelter, or medication.

So, although his heart is bleeding for the pitiful condition of his flock, he pays no heed, but hires architects and builders, buys bricks, cement, marble, and wood. And he embarks on the construction of a large modern house, equipped with all the latest conveniences, built to last, with the finest materials.

Under the innocent, admiring gazes of barefoot children, teams of builders brought in by a developer work in shifts to erect a worthy abode. The priest has discussed the plans at length with the architect. Every step of the way he thinks of his faceless, nameless successor, who may still be unborn, but is already foremost in his thoughts. The house is for that future priest, after all; it has been designed so that he will find it splendid and welcoming, so well suited to his taste that there will be nothing for him to do, besides devoting his days to the exercise of charity. But with a stranger, there's a lot to cover, if you're trying to cover it all; where there's a choice between two possibilities, you have to allow for both rather than choosing one. So the priest finds himself obliged to opt for a magnificence to which he is not accustomed, and yet he forges on without fear of excess, regardless of the cost.

In matters of taste, of course ... And alterations are costly, sometimes even more costly than building. So he has to figure it out as carefully as possible at every step. But tastes don't differ all that much, and in this case the differences are limited because he's designing the house for a priest like him, a pious man, devoted to his pastoral duties. So all he has to do is identify with his successor, imagine a version of himself transported into the future, for whom the previous incumbent has smoothed the way by leaving him a fully prepared and furnished dwelling, so that he won't have to worry about setting up house and will be able to focus entirely on spiritual matters and helping his neighbors. He is guided by his own taste, stretching it here and there to accommodate any unexpected idiosyncrasies. When in doubt, he opts for a Solomonic solution, but instead of dividing, he duplicates. With the bathrooms, for example: he knows that some owners prefer en suites, while others find them repugnant and hold that bathrooms should give on to a hallway. So he decides to have two main bedrooms, one with an en suite bathroom, the other with the bathroom next door, but opening off a hall. This problem solves itself as the plans are worked out and the bedrooms and bathrooms multiply: they can be disposed in a variety of ways to satisfy not only the eventual owner of the house but all his guests and visitors as well. When it comes to the kitchen,

however, there's a choice that can't be avoided by multiplication: should it be an "open" kitchen, giving on to the everyday
dining room, or a "closed" one, with a separating wall? It's hard
to know, because, really, it's up to the woman of the house, who
will be the main user of the kitchen, so all the priest can do is
speculate. Some women, he thinks, might want more privacy,
less interference when they're cooking, while others would
prefer not to be cut off from the other members of the family,
who might be chatting or enjoying some game at the table in
the dining room. A sliding door would seem to be the synthesis
that overcomes this problem, but, on due reflection, there's no
need for a synthesis: all one has to do is make the kitchen large
enough to include a dining area, should one be required, and
have a separate dining room as well.

The house has two floors, three including the attic rooms.
Or four, including the basement, where the laundry is, and
which is only half underground because the ground floor, the
piano nobile, is elevated. That's where the salons are, arranged
in a kind of circuit, so that, whatever the time of day, the ample windows of one, at least, can capture the sunlight. Having
climbed the twelve steps of the grand stairway to enter the
house and walked down a long hallway, one reaches a central
lobby, which is the only large space on the ground floor that
does not give on to the outside. Yet it is not deprived of daylight, because a spacious arcade connects it with another lobby,
of the same dimensions, which opens on to the rear gallery and
receives the rays of the sun. These twin spaces cater to differ-

ent tastes: for light or shade, for gatherings (or solitary medi-
tation) in the cool of the back lobby during summer, with the
doors open to the gallery, or in the snug warmth of the central
lobby with its fireplace in winter time. The design also allows
for choice between large and small spaces, between the majestic and the intimate. To the right of the lobbies, a maze of little
rooms, arranged in an arc around the lateral façade, satisfies
the taste for intimacy. They could be used as studies or waiting
rooms, for storing documents or accommodating extra guests
and residents who might prefer to be away from the main bedrooms on the first floor. A large bathroom and two smaller ones
service this area. Tucked away among these little rooms are two
without any windows, which offer the possibility of complete
isolation, should anyone need to withdraw in order to concentrate, or for any another reason. Preferences for large or small
spaces are not mutually exclusive: the same person might opt
for one or the other in different circumstances and at different
hours or moments of the day.

On the other side, to the left of the lobbies, is the grand
dining room, twenty yards long, then a little octagonal Chinese room for smaller but still formal meals, and a third dining room, for daily use, with a dumbwaiter going down to the
kitchens; but another kitchen is planned for the ground floor,
to allow the future owner to choose between two domestic arrangements: one that would suit the relaxed style of a lady who
likes to do the cooking herself, and another for the mistress of
the house who is happy to let her qualified staff take care of

everything. In the first case, the downstairs kitchens could be adapted for some other use, and joined up with the rest of the basement, accessed by a larger staircase: that's where the billiard room is, along with spaces that could be used as recording studios, darkrooms, or workshops for various hobbies.

The main library, in a prime location—one of the corners on the ground floor—is complemented by a smaller one upstairs, which provides a store of reading material handy to the bedrooms. These range in size from large to small, have views in all directions, and among them, as well as the library, are little salons, galleries, and two small dining rooms, one at either end. There are bedrooms with and without dressing rooms, private sitting rooms, and connecting doors, but each one has a balcony, and those at the ends of each wing have terraces as well.

On the next floor up, a long row of small but comfortable bedrooms, with good ventilation and natural light, for the staff, should they be required to live in, plus little sitting rooms, hallways, bathrooms, and ample storage space. The house is crowned by a circular cupola with a dome and glass walls. The various levels, from the basement to the cupola, are connected by stairways, the grander of which are made of marble with wrought iron and bronze railings, while the humbler are of timber or granite, but all are elaborately designed. Disabilities and weariness must be taken into account, so the priest reserves an empty space for an elevator shaft going right to the top of the building. He wouldn't hesitate to foot the bill for a state-of-the-art model, but he has second thoughts: the newer the mechanism, the greater the likelihood that a specialized technician would have to be called in if it broke down, which, in a remote region like that, would take time and cost a considerable amount of money. So he opts for an old design, so old it's almost anachronistic to call it an elevator at all, with a hydraulic mechanism (just like the ones built for Frederick the Great's palaces in Potsdam in the eighteenth century): it's primitive but, precisely because of that, ingenious and perfectly functional. The degree of mechanical skill that might be expected of any gardener or chauffeur is quite sufficient to puzzle out its system of pulleys, sheaves, and counterweights. Since it has to be built specially, it turns out to be far more expensive — five times more, in fact — than the latest model; but like all the other expenses, this one is balanced by a future saving.

There's no need to go into more detail. But that's what the priest does, plunging into the depths of detail, spending long days in research, reflection, and conversations with the architects. In those sessions, a doubt begins to surface, or not so much a doubt as the intimation of a danger: that of creating a monster. Reality consists of beings and things in which all possibilities but one have already been set aside. In reality, alternatives do not coexist. And what is he doing if not attempting to bring them into coexistence? There are many ways of defining monstrosity, he thinks, but their common feature is the coexistence of possibilities among which a choice should have been made. And the house that he is building conforms to that description frighteningly well. Or it will if he gets his way, if he realizes his project to its full extent and depth, and makes a house that is at once big and small, grand and modest, melancholic and joyful, eastern and western, this and that … The supposedly ideal house could end up inspiring horror, like some diabolical invention. Satan employs the same weapons, after all, subtly introducing possibilities into the real …

After a few sleepless nights of fretting over this problem, the priest reassures himself. His doubt becomes transparent and dissolves, like the memory of a nightmare yielding to the onslaught of day. After all, the house will be real, very real (that's the idea), it will manifest the possibilities he has chosen, and be beautiful and harmonious, insofar as his good taste allows. His doubts will be buried, or rather walled up, by the obduracy of matter.

So the construction of the house begins, and its reality shines like an authentic wonder, or the promise of a wonder, in that poor district where nine out of ten families live crammed in one-room tin shacks, shared not only by the numerous offspring of promiscuity and ignorance, but also by dogs, chickens, and pigs. The locals come to admire, although they don't really understand, nor do they criticize. Criticism would exceed their intellectual capacities, which have atrophied through lack of use, like their understanding. But even if the purely intellectual distance were overcome, understanding would still be beyond their reach because the project is an act of charity performed for their benefit (although with a delayed effect), so it includes them, it's a part of them, and understanding it would mean understanding themselves, and, in a way, ceasing to be poor.

The teams of builders, technicians, and craftsmen come from the city. The priest refrains from employing local workers, even though it would be beneficial for the region, because he's worried about the delays and imperfections that might result from their lack of expertise. Although he's working for the future, and, in a sense, for eternity, there is a certain urgency. It's a paradox worthy of Oscar Wilde (and worthier still of Thomas Aquinas): eternity has to be secured not in the short term but immediately. And the job has to be done well.

It's a lightning operation, reminiscent of prestidigitation or magic. But, of course, that's not how it actually works, because walls don't go up by themselves or by the power of a spell; they are subject to the step-by-step progression of reality. So, between the morning's discussions of logistical problems and the evening's review and forward planning, in the middle of the day the priest has quite a lot of time on his hands, which he spends exploring the town and its environs, an activity in which he has hardly engaged until now, what with the hectic demands of planning and supervising the early stages of the building. The task of getting to know his flock and assessing their material and spiritual condition is an essential part of his ministry, which he has been relinquishing for the sake of the future. He only takes it up now because he has time to spare; he wouldn't have done so otherwise, secure in the knowledge that he is working to ensure that his successor (indeed the whole series of his successors, since the house is intended to serve for a long time) will not have to defer that task.

He's saddened by what he sees: at close quarters, the poverty is more shocking than he'd imagined. Perhaps, he thinks at first, it's because of the contrast between the visions that have occupied his mind these last weeks—architectural visions of beauty and comfort—and the incredible deprivation in which those poor people live. But it's not just that, although the difference may have heightened the impression. What it means to live without a bathroom, without furniture, crammed into a tiny space, sleeping on bug-infested straw mattresses, under roofs of damp thatch that smell of rot is something that can be grasped without recourse to any kind of contrast. Hunger, malnutrition, and illness are the currency of the exchange between children and adults, young and old, men and women. As the priest approaches the doorways of the dark shacks, nauseating odors check his steps; in a paroxysm of horror and pity, his fantasy fills in what he can't see. The visible is barely half the problem. The other half is ignorance, resulting from an intricate knot of causes and effects: innocent, animal vice; the lack of long-term prospects; the stunned incapacity to see beyond day-by-day survival; the death of hope. His heart bleeds. The domain of charity opens out before him, a wasteland bathed by the angelic light of religion. He's ready and waiting for the sharp plowshare of compassion to open a deep furrow in him.

But that furrow will not be opened for some time yet, so much time that he will not be the one to receive the wound. At the mere thought of this, he is seized by a doubt. He knows that the reasoning on which he has based his enterprise is sound, and not only sound but just, and yet the heart has its reasons ... His heart bled to see the distressing deprivation that surrounds him, and, bloodless now, it contracts in a spasm of anxiety as he realizes that with the money he is spending on the building of the house he could relieve much of that suffering. He could, for example, build a complex of small houses equipped with all the basic amenities necessary for a hygienic, civilized existence; half the population of the area, or more, would be well housed, and there'd be money left over for a school, a clinic ... But then the priest's house would remain a depressing, dilapidated pile; at best, he'd be able to do a few repairs, with scraps of money pilfered from charity.

And in that case (here the priest, like someone who has reached the top of a slope and begun the easier descent, resumes his well-rehearsed argument), in that case, his successor might come to shirk the holy duties of charity, invoking the satanic proverb: "Charity begins at home." Or, even if he wasn't quite so bold, he could still consider the complex of neat little houses built by his predecessor and say: "It's all done." That would be a prodigious error, because the work of charity is never all done, not to mention the fact that to satisfy the housing needs of so many people with a fixed budget, one would have to use cheap materials and unskilled workers, and as a result the little houses in question would already be starting to need repairs by then. No, it certainly wouldn't be all done;

those ignorant people, raised amid filth and neglect, without a sense of civic virtue, would actively contribute to the deterioration of their homes. So it is essential to ensure that the charitable work of supporting, educating, and civilizing will continue. And the best way to do that is to leave a perfectly appointed residence for many priests to come. Once that task is accomplished, the priest will be able to give away all that he has, because he won't need anything for himself. And the only reason he can't do it straightaway is that he's already giving—in secret, which is the best way to give.

This self-granted consolation allows him to return to work on the splendid house, the house of the future, with fresh energy. And in the days that follow, he has no time to fret over the conditions of the needy, because, as the structure nears completion, his tasks have multiplied; in a sense, they're just beginning, because the walls and the roof are barely a skeleton and must be covered with all the things that make a house habitable. He has already decided which rooms will have marble floors (all those on the *piano nobile* except the main library and the rooms in the western wing), and where the floors will be wooden or tiled. Bluish-gray tiles of nonslip volcanic rock for the service areas, the kitchens, and the laundries; Slavonian oak, in boards of various widths and parquetry, for the first floor and the attic rooms. For the grand ceremonial staircase, pink Iranian marble, which will also cover the columns in the salons. White Carrara marble for the steps up to the main entrance and down from the rear gallery. The use of marble requires a certain sensitivity and tact: it's a material that can have an inhibiting effect because of its associations with solemnity or courtly grandeur, but that is precisely why some people like it: because it makes them feel important, as if they'd entered a world in which momentous decisions are being made. The priest attempts to reconcile these opposite reactions by choosing restful forms for the bases of the columns and the sweep of the staircase, in order to impress without intimidating.

For the private bathrooms he has towel racks made to measure from a light, warm wood. The shared bathrooms, which are scattered around the house, away from the bedrooms, are floored with black and white tiles, which create an atmosphere of childlike innocence. He supervises the polishing, tests the waxes, and already he's considering carpets.

The next step, although it has been under way for some time, is finishing the walls, in one of the three classic fashions: wood paneling, wallpaper (or hangings), and paint. In choosing the woods for the paneling from catalogs and samples, he runs the gamut from humble peteribi to precious cedar. The carvings of flowers, vegetables, animals, fish, scrolls, and capricious geometrical figures, which correspond over large distances so that instead of clearly echoing one another they seem vaguely, unplaceably familiar, are copied from old models and produced by craftsmen in various cities. They begin to arrive along with the wallpaper and hangings, some of which have been ordered from catalogs, while others have been custom-made. The salon walls begin to take on color as they are hung with damasks, brocades, and silks; the hexagonal coffers of the ceilings are covered with old gold leaf so as to hold the light. For the walls of certain bedrooms, floral wallpapers are suitable, while for others a uniform color is best: the pinkish bister of parchment or the midnight blue of Bengal cotton. On the rare occasions when the effect of the wallpaper (not in isolation but in conjunction and contrast with the other papers) is deemed unsatisfactory, it is removed and replaced. Harmony and variety must be reconciled, and monotony avoided without yielding to distracting excesses. The difference that the pictures and furniture will make must also be borne in mind. For the walls of the ancillary spaces, the paint selected is a creamy latex blend in neutral tones, but not so neutral as to exclude the hint of a metallic or watery sheen.

From a certain point on, once the boring installation of the plumbing, heating, wiring, and sewage is completed to the priest's satisfaction, and the floors, ceilings, walls, doors, and windows have been duly covered and adorned, he feels that one phase is finished, and he can now begin to concentrate on the next. His focus has always been, and always will be, his successor in the parish, in accordance with the plan that moved him to act in the first place. Not for an instant does he lose sight of his objective: to build a house that will satisfy all the needs of its inhabitant, who as a result will not have to spare a moment or a thought for himself, and will be able to dedicate his energies entirely to the welfare of others. In a way, he is building a monument to Charity. But he is also building a house, and must, unavoidably, apply himself to the practical questions that keep arising. For the moment, he is moderately satisfied to have finished what might be called the "shell"; now he can move on to the contents. What he has achieved is no mean feat, because that "shell" has two surfaces: the outer surface made up of façades, roofs, slates, awnings, balconies, shutters, cornices, chimneys, window frames, and moldings; and the inner surface: paintings, paneling, coffered ceilings, floors ... Inside the shell, there will be further layers, each with its inner and outer surface, even if he considers all the spaces as forming a whole, which is what he plans to do; layers that will gradually bring him closer (while also taking him farther away), closer to a center that still seems very remote. And that center—it strikes him now with the force of a revelation—is Charity, devotion to others. That's why any approach to it will also be a distancing: because what he has staked on this enterprise, with supreme generosity, is his own death.

In any case, the phase that is now beginning comprises innumerable complications and seems, at the outset, infinite. Since he's intending to have the house fully furnished and equipped, with every last teacup and towel in place, ready to be lived in as soon as it's finished (although he's not actually preparing it for himself but for an unknown successor, who won't arrive until some time after his death, possibly years later), he will have to get the whole thing finished and attend to every part, great or small, of that whole. It would be an exaggeration to speak of "infinity," because there's a limit to what can fit in a house; the house itself is that limit. But, in accordance with his previous reasoning, the asymptotic approach to the center, to the smallest and most central item (the coffee spoon, the adaptor plug), seems never-ending. The furniture in each of the many rooms, the decoration, the useful objects provided for every occasion in daily life ... And yet that proliferation has an advantage over the design and building of the structure: it facilitates more flexible variations with which to satisfy the needs of the future inhabitant who is the constant focus of his thoughts.

Now is the time to pat himself on the back for having multiplied the interior spaces: their number allows for the satisfaction of different, even incompatible, tastes and proclivities: thus a penchant for modern, comfortable design, and even for avant-garde experiments (in moderation), need not preclude stateliness in the French or English manner, or medieval austerity, or the rustic simplicity of straw-seated chairs and camp beds ... All this is easier to say than to do, of course; but it's a spur to ingenuity and inventiveness in furnishing.

The catalogs of the finest suppliers pile up on the priest's desk, but he is not satisfied. Thonet, Chippendale, Jean-Michel Frank, and Boulle, launched on their elliptical orbits, converge and coincide, pursuing harmony in diversity. Antique dealers on three continents pack and dispatch their treasures. From the far end of a room, an Empire bed with golden lion's feet responds to a heavy curtain of green velvet with crimson tassels. Wreathed in his tiny aura, a decorative, almost comic Ganesh in an Indian plaster relief presides over a large rug with blue djinns against a cream ground. The little Louis XV chairs and pedestal tables, so fragile, as if held up by a puppeteer's invisible threads, welcome the florid morning light pouring in through the picture windows ... Gradually the house fills up, like a puzzle patiently assembled. There is a danger of ending up with something like a bazaar or a showroom. The priest is aware that he is subject to forces pulling in opposite directions: one toward diversity, to ensure that the future occupant, of whom nothing can be known since he doesn't yet exist, will find some point or line to his taste; the other toward coherence, which is what will make the house an attractive whole. His best efforts are devoted to reconciling these demands, which is why he adopts a timeless design frame, somewhere between Victorian and art deco, within which striking or exotic touches will function as details: noticeable, pleasing, but also discreet.

Although he directs and oversees all of the work, and has the last word, he listens to his many helpers and takes their advice into account. Throughout the long days, he is accompanied by architects and designers, who stay on into the evening, chatting after dinner. He confides particularly in the cabinet-makers: rough tradesmen, and clearly very strong, but capable of an almost feminine delicacy and attention to detail in the exercise of their skills. He feels a secret affinity with them because, in his way, he too is creating a work, which although invisible for the moment will one day be as real and tangible as theirs: a man, a priest like himself, the long-anticipated one whose sanctity he is fashioning. He has come to love that man, almost to regard him as the son he will never have. He prefers not to think about the personal sacrifice he's making for him, declining to do the good works required by his ministry, which would be such a balm to his soul: in a way he is doing them, although the effects are displaced and delayed.

The priest is disheartened to discover that the tradesmen and professionals working on the house have little regard for charity (although this opposition also spurs him on and reaffirms his convictions). For them it's normal, and indeed entirely just, that he should build a luxurious mansion while neglecting to come to the aid of the needy. The way they see it, the poor deserve the conditions they live in, because they're lazy or don't even want to improve themselves; whatever you give them will only prolong their poverty. They've never known anything else, and they're satisfied with what they know. In merely practical terms, without having to go into moral, historical, or sociological considerations, it's obvious that poverty, especially in its extreme forms, is a phase that societies have to go through, and can't simply be eliminated. Why even try? The poor live happily with their lacks, and don't even see them as such.

The priest is strongly opposed to such an attitude: not only because of church policy, but also out of deep personal conviction. It's his duty, he says, and the duty of all the fortunate, to do something to improve the lot of the dispossessed. They have to be saved from destitution in order to develop a sense of dignity and decency, which will serve as a basis on which to build the other virtues. His defense of this position is implacable; he's not trying to impress his interlocutors, but he does, or at least reduces them to silence. Far from being a flight or a distraction from charity, his house is a monument to that queen and crown of divine virtues. It is designed to make charity perfect. In a way, it's a practical, active monument, a silent, efficient machine for producing charity.

But these theoretical reflections become less frequent as the work of filling the house intensifies. As the pieces of furniture arrive, they occupy a provisional place before being shifted to another; their arrangements keep altering in a game of trial and error that resembles the evolution of species. The interior landscape is gradually stabilized. When the curtains are hung, it is as if light were being installed as well, in the form of weightless receptacles of air. Now the work continues into the night, with the hanging of chandeliers, the placement of candlesticks and lamps, the dance of the shadows renewing and transforming the beauties of the day.

The priest feels that the voyage to the center is accelerating when the household items, which he refers to humorously as the "party decorations," begin to arrive in crates and containers, piling up like new pharaonic pyramids. Vases, tablecloths, paintings, tableware, ornaments. The systematic provision of wide variety continues. China and crystal alternate with rustic crockery, silver cutlery with dark bronze. There is a suitable cup or glass on a shelf somewhere for every conceivable hot or cold drink; there is a vase, Ming or other, to show every kind of flower to its best effect. Ostentation is, of course, to be avoided. But that's tricky, because concealing it only magnifies the effect. The money spent so far, though it comes to a very large sum, is a trifle compared to what is yet to be spent on works of art: paintings by old masters, hung in elegant isolation, given places of honor, or almost hidden, as if the visitor were being invited to search them out; watercolors in certain bedrooms, delicate representations of plants, or seascapes, or mountains, or little household scenes from days gone by; old engravings; and the silent presence of sculptures, half hidden behind armchairs, illuminating a corner or setting off a view through open doors. The folding panels of the decorative screens, their movement stilled, burst with flowers, stags, or flying bodhisattvas.

The aesthetic aspect is no more than that: an aspect. And there are others to attend to: mattresses, bedclothes, heaters, cleaning equipment, supplies for the kitchens and the bathrooms. When the priest takes possession of a consignment of Brazilian soap, and runs his fingers along the edge of a cake, appreciating its verdant Amazonian smoothness, he feels that he is very close to that center where life is happening already. And he comes even closer when he puts bouquets of fresh flowers in the vases, and food in the pantry ... And closer still, or so he feels, when he begins to fill the library shelves. He doesn't want his successor to subtract, for the purchase of books, so much as a peso from the funds to be used in fulfilling his sacred duty to assist the poor, so he buys enough reading material to last a lifetime. Choosing isn't difficult: classics, encyclopedias, novels, poetry, history, science. Arranging the thousands of volumes, he loses himself in daydreams about the future reader, and as he anticipates his tastes, his interests, his progression from one book to another, his reactions to this or that novel, to a line from a favorite poet or a philosopher's argument, he forms a clearer picture of the man for whom he is working, and feels that he can see him already, wearing the halo of sanctity prepared by his predecessor, adored by his parishioners upon whom he showers gifts of the purest, most abundant charity, keeping nothing back for himself (because all his needs have been met).

But the future has not arrived, not by a long way. Well before the completion of the house, the priest began work on its surroundings, which are at least as important, in his eyes, as the edifice itself. The planting of the gardens, under the supervision of expert landscape architects, began at the same time as the digging of the foundations. And now that the house is furnished and ready, he turns his attention to the outside. From the splendid curved staircases at the rear of the building, a formal French garden will stretch away for two hundred yards: carefully clipped pyramidal box plants, paths of fragrant herbs, flower beds, little round-topped trees alternating with statues, and, in the middle of the central roundabout, an imposing fountain with a profusion of crisscrossing jets and a large group of sculpted figures visible through the spray and the rainbows. Two long arbors open their arches like wings, giving onto the grounds proper, with their hectares of lawn, copses of exotic trees, bamboo thickets, flower-lined paths that wind among knolls made from earth dug up for the artificial lake, rocks transported from faraway places to create picturesque crags, and densely wooded tracts with undergrowth. Birds gladden these wild corners, and the priest populates the lake with carp, pike, and silvery trout.

Busy with these open-air tasks, he finds that he has more time, not because there is less work, but because the time of the plant kingdom, to which he attunes himself, is bountiful. Day-long walks on the thousand paths of the grounds compensate him now for the reclusion he imposed on himself while attending to the needs of the house. He stops here and there to admire a flower or a mushroom, to hear the trilling of a bird or meditate on the example of the laborious ant. And he is delighted to catch glimpses of the dream palace he has built, displaying its various aspects when seen from different angles, or modestly veiled and revealed by foliage.

But walkers naturally tend to range farther afield, and one day he reaches the outer edges of the grounds and continues until he comes to the houses (so to speak) of his parishioners. He is horrified by what he sees. He has been isolated for a long time, absorbed in his work, and although he has kept these poor people in mind as an objective or a mission, their concrete reality has become hazy. Now, with a shudder of surprise, he realizes that time has been passing for the poor as well, with devastating effects. Suspicious gazes, as dark as the shadows they inhabit, emerge from the black holes of the huts, along

ACTS OF CHARITY   313

with the stench of human and animal cohabitation. Women aged by deprivation, physical abuse, and constant childbearing run away to hide their ragged clothing and their bare feet, gnarled by cold. Naked children with bulging bellies and fearful wide-open eyes watch him pass. The old (which, here, means people over forty) display the signs of their decrepitude: paralysis, blindness, dementia of various kinds. Sickness reigns, and those it doesn't kill are not strengthened by the ordeal, quite the contrary. Full of shame, the men avoid his gaze. Groans of suffering, tubercular coughs, and wails of mourning are the only music in these places of affliction. It seems to him that the conditions have worsened abysmally, although an exact comparison is impossible because so much time has passed since his last assessment and he has been so preoccupied with other problems in the meantime that his memories are rather confused. Reasonably, he reflects that, however it is measured, poverty is always poverty.

The shock caused by this vision, in contrast with the recent experience of seeing his work (the house) visibly there in a concrete, realized form, if not completely finished, makes him stop and think. It's true that for the price of just one of the expensive pieces of furniture in the house, one of the Bokhara rugs, a single painting or statue, even a single fork crafted by a Florentine silversmith, a whole neighborhood of decent little dwellings could be built, with sewage and heating. In his heart of hearts, he knows that he is doing the right thing, but he wonders if in the eyes of the world he might appear to be egotistical ...

Egotistical, him? Everything he's done has been for someone else. His bowels writhe at the thought of that monstrous accusation. And an evil or mischievous inner spirit tempts him to even greater self-mortification, for fear that, of all people, his successor, the beneficiary of all his efforts, might reprove him on precisely those grounds ... And yet, in the depths of the anxiety provoked by this speculation, he finds the way out: he has never intended to explain himself, for example by leaving a message for his successor; the true nature of his work is not to be disclosed; all its merit shall remain a secret between himself and God. What does imperfect human justice matter? But he backs away from these thoughts, not wanting to fall into the trap of sanctimonious pride or the temptation of martyrdom.

He also backs away from the vision of those harsh realities whose contemplation posed a threat to his equanimity. He returns to his house, where there is still quite a lot to do, and the wretched of the earth will be hidden from his sight.

There really is something missing from the house: that lived-in feel. He doesn't want his successor to move into an impersonal, purely material structure. Lived-in houses, full of things that have been used and loved, have a warmth that can't be faked. And that's what he decides to work on now; it's a restful way of passing the time, a reward for the long, exhausting tasks that went before.

As he lives his own life there, the priest discovers that certain things required for the future incumbent to be fully at home are still missing from the house, or perhaps from life itself. Small things, which become apparent only when the need arises. And supplying them, lovingly, one by one, occupies the rest of the earthly sojourn granted him by Providence. Every day he feels he is a little closer to that intuited center, a point in time, not space, which both encloses and reveals the mystery of Charity. He has come to identify that center with a man, the man he has created by thinking of him constantly, and, in a sense, obeying him. The house is full of that beloved, long-awaited stranger: it has all been done for him, so it's hardly surprising that his absence informs every nook and cranny of the house. Although he is a single man, he is many men in one, all men, in a way. Which is why nothing can be alien to him, a priori. Anything that happens to cross the priest's mind might be relevant. One day, for instance, a chance association of ideas leads him to chess ... What if his successor likes chess? Why not? And immediately he orders a board and a set of pieces and a little table, and even a timer in case the next priest is a serious player (why not?), and another portable, magnetic board, for traveling or taking on walks in the grounds, and a small but comprehensive set of chess books ... And since he wants it all to have been experienced already, he refreshes his knowledge of the game and starts playing ...

Death surprises him in the midst of another such task (although it's not really a surprise, because with the passing years he has gone into decline, the maladies of age arriving along with the inner peace that comes from having achieved one's goal). Ill now, confined to his room and his bed, he remembers that briefly, as a child, he was a passionate stamp collector. And since it has become second nature to turn every thought to the future incumbent, he thinks of what a joy it would be for that priest to find a fine stamp collection on arriving at the house, and how it would free him to spend more time bringing material and spiritual succor to the faithful. He contacts specialist dealers and acquires sets of stamps, collections from various countries, albums, tweezers, catalogs. With loving care, he files away those tiny squares of paper with their perforated edges, marveling at the colors, the figures, the way they evoke distant lands and, at the same time, recall his childhood. The final purchase: a Chinese chest with many drawers and compartments in which to keep the albums and boxes.

By the time the news of his death reaches the relevant diocesan authorities, his successor has already been chosen. Given the old priest's advanced age and the state of his health, known to be delicate for some time, preparations have been made. So the new priest arrives without delay. He is a young man, as young as his predecessor was when he arrived in the area. And he begins by doing the same things: observing the state of destitution in which his parishioners are living, imagining the effects of charitable action, like bounteous rain in a drought-stricken land. One thing, however, is not repeated: his own living arrangements have been taken care of, splendidly.

Except that they are rather more than "living arrangements" and they have been more than "taken care of." He realizes this as he visits the house, admires it, discovers its comforts and refinements. It's as if he had been there already, as if someone had examined his person with a microscope made of days and nights, of sleep and waking, in order to get to know him and communicate with him. You can get to know someone who's present simply by speaking and looking, but to get to know someone who isn't there, and may not exist (he estimates that the construction of the house began before he was born), a great deal more is required, as this enormous mansion shows, with its endless grounds and multitudinous riches.

Attending to his duties, he visits the neighboring village and is duly horrified by the poverty and neglect. Initially he is surprised and intrigued by the contrast between that wretchedness and the luxury of the house. Little by little, as the days go by, he begins to understand: he wasn't mistaken in feeling when he first entered the house that it was trying to tell him something. The house is a message, so is the garden, and every object they contain, a message personally addressed to him, addressed to that which lies deepest within him and participates in the divine being.

And the syntax of that message is so perfect that he finally succeeds in understanding it completely. He'd already realized, though without expressing it in words, that the house had been conceived and built for him. The words, once found and articulated, supply the motive: his predecessor, of whom he knew nothing before but is now, via the motive, coming to know a great deal, wanted him to have everything, so he wouldn't have to keep anything aside for himself and would be able to give it all to the poor. It's pretty obvious, really. It's self-explanatory. He feels a deep and growing admiration for the sacrifice made by his forerunner, who renounced the possibility of fulfilling his mission and thereby opening the gates of heaven, in order that the priest to come might do so. It's like one of those oriental fables, he thinks: unfathomably mystical and ingeniously constructed. Exploring the house and its treasures feels like entering the fable: a palace of déjà vu in which every step has already been taken and every movement made.

He is grateful, of course. How could he not be? How could he not feel beholden to that kindly genius who dedicated his life to smoothing the way for his successor? But he senses that there is something more. That he can do "something else." Accepting the gift just like that, as if he had earned it, would be unworthy of a man in whom such great hopes had been placed.

Gradually he clarifies his mission, with a certain number of hesitations, which are observed by the local poor who, ill clad and hungry, are enduring a cruel winter. He has plenty of money and no need to spend a peso on himself . . . It's a great temptation to shower his wealth on those who are silently beseeching him. But that's just what it is: a temptation. His determination to resist it, and the example set by his predecessor, prove to be stronger. What the dead priest did was so heroic, so saintly in its way, that it demands to be imitated. Also, simply to harvest the fruits of his action would be an injustice to him. These reasons, all of which are valid, are strengthened by an irresistible force, to which the new priest attributes a higher cause.

So he, too, decides to prepare the way for his successor's action, choosing self-sacrifice, forbidding himself to use the money at his disposal for charity, and spending it on the house instead ... He is excited by the prospect of working for a man he hasn't met and will never know, guessing his tastes, his habits, even his little quirks, and responding to them in advance. It's like having company, one of those "invisible friends" that children entertain, but without the fantasy. And bequeathing a matchless legacy to that friend: the unmatchable gift of being able to give.

It's not an easy decision to make. In his excursions beyond the limits of the property, he can see for himself the extremes of suffering produced by child malnutrition, inadequate housing, and untreated illness, where poverty rules. What if he put aside a part of the money? No. Again he is tempted. But he realizes that it's all or nothing. He cannot serve two masters.

Another and more serious objection is that the house is there already, and the needs of its inhabitant have been provided for. But it's very easy for him to brush this objection aside. In spite of the supposed exhaustiveness to which his predecessor dedicated his life, and all the love he put into his work, it's all too obvious that a great deal is missing ... At least it's obvious to him, for two reasons: First, as time goes by, and people have access to more information and therefore have more opportunities for consumption, needs increase and diversify, as do the ways of satisfying them. The touching attempt to prepare a response to each of his desires in advance has turned out to be woefully inadequate. The second and more important reason is that he can benefit from his own experience as a receiver of the gift and act in consequence, whereas his predecessor had to rely almost entirely on intuition and guessing.

So he wastes no time in getting to work. The first task, imposed by a particularly cold winter, is to replace the now obsolete heating system with a more modern one, equipped with temperature controls. This provokes the first of a very long series of reflections concerning his successor. Will he be someone who feels the cold? The mere supposition is enough to give the priest the sense that he is in touch with the man who will take his place, and has already begun to accompany him, mute and inexistent but eloquent nonetheless; and he sees himself reflected in this situation, an imagined, inexistent figure accompanying the priest who originally built the house … The whole edifice, down to its most hidden corners, is affected by the installation of the new thermostat-controlled boilers and the system of pipes. As the work proceeds, the priest takes note of various improvements and additions that are either necessary straightaway or logical steps in the process of perfecting the house for its future resident. The general theme of heating suggests the idea of supplementing the comforts of the house with a conservatory. Like a new Janus, the priest looks back at his predecessor ("How could he have overlooked this?"—a question he will ask again and again) and forward to his successor ("He might be a flower enthusiast"). He fills the conservatory with orchids, dwarf palms, and bromeliads, creating a tropical enclave: colors, scents, and forms that open and close in a tableau of unfamiliar beauties.

Since the new system of boilers is more than powerful enough to heat the house, he decides to exploit its excess capacity by putting a heated swimming pool in one of the basement rooms. To complement the pool, he builds a glass solarium. Maybe the next priest won't want to swim, or sun himself; but maybe he will ...

As time goes by, and the priest identifies a possible interest here, and another there, the figure of his successor becomes more clearly defined. When he thinks that he was once the successor himself, he is overtaken by a strange dizziness, which compels him to continue. Everything he can see in the house, and the house itself, was conceived and made in accordance with a hypothesis about him, and now he is repeating that process, completing it, perfecting it.

Internal walls are torn down and expanses of masonry replaced with large windows to convert a whole string of attic rooms—the ones with the best exposure—into a studio that could be used for painting, or sculpture, or any other art or craft ... To keep all the options open, the priest fills that ample space with easels, drawing boards, clay-firing ovens, stretchers, paper, brushes, and chisels. Persisting in the artistic vein, he sets up a space for music downstairs, on the *piano nobile*, with a soundproof acoustic chamber, for which he orders a Bösendorfer piano, an Érard harp, violins and cellos made by the finest luthiers, and various exotic instruments—stringed, wind, and percussion—including a beautiful samisen. Next to this space, made by joining two interior rooms that he judged to be superfluous, is a little theater, opened up in the same way, with thirty seats (upholstered in wine-colored Venetian velvet), rococo decoration, and a stage equipped with the latest systems for changes of scenery and lighting.

At a certain point, before these renovations are completed, he begins work on the grounds, for which he has grand plans. The first is the construction of a tea pavilion, to which he commits himself heart and soul, determined to make it an epitome of refinement and comfort. He decides on a light, ethereal structure, a little house of dragonfly wings, continuous with its natural environment, as a contrast to the house's majestic solidity. He approaches this task with the deepest seriousness; the pavilion is to be the alternative to the house in every respect. He rejects the designs submitted by a series of well-known architects until one set of plans, produced and modified according to his instructions, finally meets with his approval, and then the building begins. Bricks and mortar are ruled out; the whole thing is made from bamboo and rare timbers, fabric, glass, and paper. It's a fairy-tale retreat, its spaciousness dissembled by the surrounding vegetation, the flowering vines that appear to be extensions of the structure, and the various hidden levels within. Although it has a studied austerity, the interior contains many little salons looking out onto different parts of the grounds, and an abundance of sliding panels, raffia mats, and rugs. The visitor enters via a broad, elevated veranda, suggestive of tropical colonies.

As one season gives way to another, the grounds begin to preoccupy the priest, and he spends a lot of time on them, without neglecting the house, in which there is always something to be done. In addition to replanting copses, laying out avenues of statues, introducing topiary, fountains, arbors, and a grotto, he undertakes more ambitious projects. He populates the gardens with deer, of a delicate and decorative breed, like the pheasants and peacocks that he also imports, which provide fleeting, sumptuous flashes of color among the plants. Specially trained staff are employed for the care and breeding of these creatures.

Neglecting the category of animals was, he thinks, a major oversight on the part of his predecessor. When considering an unknown future man, and trying to cover all his needs, animals to live with might be a priority. Or not. You never know. But since those humble, quiet companions have been a consolation and a joy to so many people, they cannot be ignored. For his successor they might be especially important, and the cost of acquiring them and providing an adequate habitat would reduce what he could give in aid to the poor. So the priest sets about building stables and kennels amusingly designed to resemble medieval castles, Hindu temples, and Mayan pyramids, all to scale, and fills them with handsome Arab steeds, greyhounds and mastiffs, Pomeranians and lapdogs. A tall columbarium on the top of an artificial hill beyond the lake is filled with doves imported from distant lands. And inside the house there are various aquariums of different sizes, to soothe the eye with mobile, live decoration, culminating in an enormous tank that takes up a whole wall, in which a big golden manta ray from the Indian Ocean glides among yellow longnose butter-flyfish, little red fish as bright as rubies, slimy octopi, and sea-horses riding on transparency like marionettes.

Time goes by and the priest grows older, work and hope occupying his days. There is, he feels, something microscopic about his work. The house has been left to him entire and complete, but from the moment he decided to decline the invitation to sainthood and pass it on to the next priest, he started finding little cracks to fill in that apparent completeness, and even after all this time and everything he has done, he's still finding them. Each addition and improvement defines a new characteristic (always in the form of an alternative, a choice among possibilities), enriching the figure of the priest who will come to open the gates of heaven for him and his predecessor with the golden keys of Charity.

For he has not lost sight of Charity. Quite the contrary: it is the center and motor of his striving, although he will not be the one to practice it, which grieves him deeply. In his visits to the areas where the poor people live, he must close his eyes to the wretchedness of a situation that he cannot remedy: he has come too soon. He consoles himself with the thought that it makes no difference whether action is taken now or a generation later: by their very nature, desperate situations of that kind tend to perpetuate themselves. And when he returns to the house and its grounds, to that splendor built in the name of Charity, he sees it transformed into the enormous good that his successor will be able to do.

Protected by hope, then, he continues with his work, and, as with the previous incumbent, his excursions become less frequent until one day they finally cease altogether. Age, he feels, is bringing him closer to the man who will come to fulfill the promise. Old now, he approaches the young man to whom he has devoted so much thought, whose reactions he has tried to anticipate, guessing his preferences for this or that color, for a style in furnishing, or a way of spending his evenings. At certain moments, in the fuddled ramblings of senility, he believes that his successor is there already, opening the door and walking in, wet from the rain and ruddy-cheeked from the cold, exhausted after a day spent in the shacks of the local people, comforting the sick, taking food and clothing to the destitute, supervising the building of a school ... The new priest wants to relax now, and for that he has his comfortable abode ... but perhaps what he needs to complete his satisfaction at that imagined moment is a pipe to smoke, a harmless indulgence for an active man ... but there's not a pipe in the house! Emerging from his somnolence, the old priest orders a set of pipes, in various woods and meerschaum, with mother-of-pearl and carving, and revolving pipe racks, and a set of pipe tools ...

These increasingly minor and intimate additions occupy the final days of his life. When the new priest arrives, he admires the house and is horrified by the terrible poverty surrounding it, as if he were performing a ritual. Just as his predecessors anticipated, the contrast intensifies his determination to act, and he is about to start handing out milk and diapers for the babies, medicine for the sick, blankets and fuel for the rudimentary huts that offer scant protection from the winds of a harsh winter. If he delays, it is not for want of initiative, but because there is so much to do. There is so much poverty, he doesn't know where to start: the urgent needs compete among one another fiercely. And this delay, though meant to be brief, is long enough for his intention to deviate. Prompted by a natural curiosity, he visits the house, the gardens, the tea pavilion, the deer park; he only has to live there for a day, or an hour, perhaps just a minute, to catch the echoes of a former future of which he is the incarnation, and he begins to understand what motivated the builders. The sacrifices they have made for him are sublime, and it seems mean to take advantage of them ... He will be followed by another, and he is inspired by the idea of working for that other because, as he gradually sees and understands everything that has been prepared for him, he notices all the things that could be perfected and added for the next priest ...

There is no need to pursue the series: it would take us too far, all the way to an eternity that has been lying in wait from the outset. Let's just say that the successor to this third priest, and the one who takes over from the fourth, and all those who follow, decipher the message and accept the challenge. The house continues to be completed and beautified, in splendid isolation, an oasis of perfection in a desert-like world devastated by egotism and indifference. In its permanence, the house becomes a symbol of the virtuous soul, the divine soul, and its comforts are progressively refined by the unbroken chain of just men, the golden thread that runs through History, in the name of the redemption that Charity will bring.

AUGUST 1, 2010

Cecil Taylor

DAWN IN MANHATTAN. IN THE FIRST, TENTATIVE LIGHT, a black prostitute is walking back to her room after a night's work. Hair in a mess, bags under her eyes; the cold transfigures her drunkenness into a stunned lucidity, a crumpled isolation from the world. She didn't venture beyond her usual neighborhood, so she only has to walk a few blocks. Her pace is slow; she could be going backward; at the slightest deviation, time could dissolve into space. What she really wants is sleep, but she's not even conscious of that anymore. The streets are almost deserted; the few people who usually go out at this time (or have no indoors to go out of) know her by sight, so they don't examine her violet high-heeled shoes, her tight skirt with its long split, or her eyes, which wouldn't return their glassy or tender gazes anyway. It's a narrow street, with a number for a name, and the buildings are old. Then there's a stretch where they're more modern, but in worse repair: stores, fire escapes dangling from sheer façades. Farther on, past the corner, is the place where she sleeps till late, in a rented room that she shares with two children, her brothers. But first, something happens:

five or six guys who've been up all night have formed a semi-circle on the sidewalk, in front of a store window. The woman wonders what they could be looking at that has turned them into figures from a snapshot. The group is absolutely still; not even the smoke of a cigarette is rising. She walks in their direction, watching them, and, as if they were a fixture to which she could attach the thread that is holding her up, her step becomes somewhat lighter. It takes her a few moments to understand what is going on. The men are in front of an abandoned store. Behind the dirty window, in the dimness, are dusty boxes and debris. But there is also a cat, and facing it, with its back to the window, a rat. Both animals are staring at each other without moving; the hunt has come to an end, and the quarry has nowhere to run. Sublimely unhurried, the cat tenses its every nerve. The spectators are not simply statues now but beings of stone: planets, the elemental cold of the universe … The prostitute taps the window with her purse, the cat is distracted for a fraction of a second, and that is enough for the rat to escape. The men emerge from their reverie, look at the black accomplice with disgust; a drunk spits on her, two others follow her as she walks away … before the darkness has vanished altogether, an act of violence will take place.

One story is followed by another. Vertigo. Retrospective vertigo. There's an excess of continuity. Narrative traction cannot be suspended, even by inserting endings. Vertigo creates anxiety. Anxiety paralyzes … and saves us from the danger that would justify vertigo: approaching the edge, for example the edge of the chasm that separates an ending from a continuation. Immobility is art in the artist, while all the events treated in the artwork take place on the other side of the glass. Night comes to an end, so does day: there's something awkward about the work in progress. The opposite twilights drop like tokens into slots of ice. The eyes of statues closing when they open and opening when they close. Peace in war. And yet there's a movement that's out of control, and all too real; it makes others anxious and provides the model for our own anxieties. Art figures it as Endless Revolving Growth, and it gives rise to libraries, theaters, museums, and whole universes of fantasy. It may stop, but if it does, an enormous number of remnants are left. After a while, the remnants begin to revolve and breed. Multiplication multiplies itself . . . But, as we know, there is only "the one life." From which it follows that an artist's biography is hard to distinguish from the trials of its writing: it's not simply a matter of representing representation (anyone could do that) but of creating unbearable situations in thought. That's why biographies are usually so long: nothing is ever enough to appease the mobile impulses of immobility. The stories try desperately to coalesce, they wrap themselves in pearly teleological scruples, the wind ignites them, they fall into the void . . . But maybe no one cares.

And why should anyone care? Biographies are the lives of others. Children read the illustrated biographies of famous musicians, who are always child prodigies, possessed by a mysterious genius. They understand the music of the birds and fall asleep to the murmur of streams. The obstacles that stand in the way of their careers are not placed there by reality but by the story's didactic design. These lives are strikingly similar to those of the saints: persecution and martyrdom are the instruments of triumph. Because all the saints have succeeded. And not only the saints and the child prodigies: all the subjects of biographies have succeeded; they have won the competition. Of the numberless people who have lived, History saves only the winners, even when it is inspired by a humanitarian moralism. Because of their essential banality and their immutable conventions, these life stories don't remain in the memory for long (they end up blurring into one another), but that doesn't prevent them from distorting it, inserting definitive, iridescent slides that go from point A to point B, and then from B to C, and when the lights go out, the points are illuminated; they are the beautiful souls who have risen to heaven to make up constellations and horoscopes. How could we regard those books with anything but suspicion, especially since they were and are the fundamental nourishment of our past and future puerilities? "Before" there is the future success; "after," its delicious rewards, all the more delicious for having been the object of remarkably punctual prophecies.

Let us examine a particular case, to refine the demonstration. For example, one of the great musicians of our time, whose existence is unquestionable. Cecil Taylor. Born into jazz, he remained faithful to its outward forms: the clubs and bars and festivals at which he performed, the instrumental groups he put together, even the odd vague (or inexplicable) declaration of an influence (Lennie Tristano, Dave Brubeck). But his originality transcended musical categories. His thing was jazz, but any other kind of music too, broken down into its individual atoms and reassembled, like one of those celibate machines that produced the dreams and nightmares of the twentieth century. According to the legend, Cecil made the first atonal jazz recording, in 1956, two weeks before Sun Ra independently arrived at the same result. (Or was it the other way around?) They didn't know each other, nor did they know Ornette Coleman, who was doing similar work on the other side of the country. Which goes to show that beyond the genius or inspiration of those three individuals (and Albert Ayler and Eric Dolphy, and who knows how many others), causation was operating at some higher level.

That level is History, and History has an important role to play, because it allows us to interrupt the infinite series that are generated by the art of thinking. This is how interruption loses its false prestige and its insufferable preponderance. It becomes frivolous, redundant, and trivial, like a muffled cough at a funeral. But its very insignificance gives birth to Necessity, which makes the rule of History manifest. Interruption is necessary, though it may be a momentary necessity, and the moment itself is necessary too, and often sufficient, which is why we say that a moment is "all it takes."

In the end, biographies are literature. And what counts in literature is detail, atmosphere, and the right balance between the two. The exact detail, which makes things visible, and an evocative, overall atmosphere, without which the details would be a disjointed inventory. Atmosphere allows the author to work with forces freed of function, and with movements in a space that is independent of location, a space that finally abolishes the difference between the writer and the written: the great manifold tunnel in broad daylight … Atmosphere is the three-dimensional condition of regionalism, and the medium of music. Music doesn't interrupt time. On the contrary.

1956. In New York City, there lived a man named Cecil Taylor, a black musician, not yet thirty years old, a technically innovative pianist, a composer and improviser steeped in the century's popular and highbrow traditions. Except for half a dozen musicians and friends, no one knew or could understand what he was doing. How could they have understood? It lay beyond the scope of the predictable. In his hands the piano was instantly transformed into a free compositional method. The so-called "tone clusters" that he employed in his evanescent writing had already been used by the composer Henry Cowell, but Cecil took the procedure further, complicating the harmonies, systematizing the atonal sound current into tonal flows, producing unprecedented results. The speed of it, the interplay of different mechanisms, the insistence, the built-in resistances, the repetitions, the series, everything, in short, that contributed to the turn away from traditional harmonic structure erected majestic, airy ruins, on the far side of any recognizable melody or rhythm.

He lived in a modest sublet apartment, on the Lower East Side of Manhattan. The place was rife with black mice, and there was a floating population of cockroaches. Doors ajar, the routine promiscuity of an old apartment building with its narrow stairs and its radios playing. That was the kind of atmosphere. He slept there through the morning and part of the afternoon, and went out at dusk. He worked in a bar that was part of the scene. He'd already made a record (*Jazz Advance*) for a small independent label, which hadn't distributed it. A date to play in the bar, which for various reasons hadn't worked out, had given him the idea of asking for work, and he'd been there for a few months, washing dishes. He was waiting for offers to play in places that had a piano. Given the number of night spots with live music in the city at the time, and the constant turnover of famous and unknown performers, opportunities were bound to come up. It was a time of renewal; there was a hunger for novelty.

He knew, of course, that because of the demanding and radical nature of his art, he could forget about being suddenly or even gradually discovered, his reputation spreading like ripples when a stone falls into a pond. He wasn't that naïve. But he was perfectly justified in hoping that sooner or later his talent would be acclaimed. (There's a truth here, and an error: it's true that now he is celebrated all around the world, and those of us who have listened to his records for years, gaping in admiration, would be the last to question that; but it's also fairly easy—almost too easy, in fact—to demonstrate that there's an error in the reasoning. It could, of course, be objected that such a demonstration is no more than a flight of literary fancy.

Which is true, but then it's also true that stories, once they're imagined, acquire a kind of necessity. A strange and rare kind, whose strangeness has an influence, in turn, on the imagined story. The story of the prostitute who distracted the cat wasn't necessary in itself, which doesn't mean that the virtual series of all stories is unnecessary as a whole. The story of Cecil Taylor calls for the illustrative mode of the fable; the details are interchangeable, and atmosphere would seem to be out of place. But how can we hear music except in an atmosphere, since the sounds are transmitted by air?)

The bar in which his first performance finally took place (it wasn't strictly speaking the first, because there'd been one already, but Cecil chose not talk about it) was a dive where music was secondary, a background to waiting and drug deals. But drugs, and waiting too (they went together), were so intimately related to time that the artist felt he should be able to arouse some interest; all he knew for sure was that he wouldn't cause a scandal, which was a pity in a way, because a scandal is an intensification of interest, but it wasn't in his gentle, contemplative nature; and in a place like that, where people were risking everything, they would hardly be shocked by one more disruption of the dominant key. He prepared himself by imagining indifference as a plane and interest as a point: the plane could cover the world like a paper shade, but interest was punctual and real like a pair of neighbors wishing each other good day. He readied himself for the inherent incongruence of the higher geometries. The unpredictable clientele could provide him with a modicum of attention: no one knows what grows by night (he would be playing after midnight, the following day, in fact), and when tomorrow appears today, it never goes totally unnoticed. Except for this time. To his astonishment, this time turned out to be precisely "never." Invisible ridicule melting into inaudible giggles. It was like that all through the set, and the proprietor canceled his date for the following night, although he hadn't paid for it. Cecil didn't talk to him about his music, of course. He couldn't see the point. He just went back to his room.

Two months later, his erratic work routine (he'd gone from washing dishes to working at a dry cleaner) was enlivened once again when he agreed to perform in a bar, just one night this time, in the middle of the week. It was like the previous bar, though maybe slightly worse, with the same kind of clientele; there was even a chance that some of those who'd been present the other night would hear him again. That's what he got to thinking (what a dreamer!), misled by his own repetitions. His music reached the ears of fifteen or so drunks, and maybe those of one or two women dressed in silk: small, black, beautiful ears, each adorned with a golden bud. There was no applause, someone laughed stupidly (at something else, no doubt), and the owner of the bar didn't even bother to say good night to him. Why would he? There are times like that, when music meets with no response. He made himself an idle promise to come back to the bar some other time (he'd been there before), to put himself in the situation, or rather the position, of someone listening to music and knowing that it's music, so that he could imagine what it would be like: the consummate pianist intuiting each note as he plays it, the slow succession of melodies, the reason for the atmosphere. But he never did; it wasn't worth the trouble. He considered himself unimaginative, unable even to imagine the reality surrounding him. After a week, the mental image of this latest failure blended with that of the previous one, which left him feeling somewhat bewildered. Could it have been a repetition? There was no reason why it should have been that simple, but sometimes simplification works in tandem with complication.

One autumn afternoon he was walking home, mentally humming something that he would translate into sounds as soon as he sat down at the piano (he paid by the hour for the use of a Steinway upright in a music school, after the lessons), when he ran into an ex-classmate from the New England Conservatory. As soon as he saw and recognized him, the music in his head fell silent. The reality of that individual—son of Norwegian immigrants, big nose, little ears—contaminated the street, the cars, even Cecil himself with empirical details. They started chatting; they hadn't seen each other for eight years. Neither had betrayed his calling as an avant-garde musician: the Norwegian was making ends meet by giving lessons to children; his constructivist pieces for chamber orchestra hadn't been performed, even privately; he was still playing the cello; and he had spoken with Stravinsky. Cecil let him talk, nodding sympathetically, though he made fun of Stravinsky in private. He paid more attention when the cellist said, in conclusion, that the career of the innovative musician was difficult because, as opposed to the conventional musician, who had only to please an audience, the innovator had to create a new one from scratch, like someone taking a red blood cell and shaping it with patience and love until it's nice and round, then doing the same with another, and attaching it to the first, and so on until he has made a heart, and then all the other organs and bones and muscles and skin and hair, leaving the delicate tunnel of the ear with its anvils and miniature hammers till last … That was how he might produce the first listener for his music, the origin of his audience, and he would have to repeat the operation hundreds and thousands of times if he wanted to be recognized as a name in the history of music, with the same care every time, because if he got a single cell wrong, a fatal domino effect would bring the whole thing crashing down … The metaphor struck his drowsy interlocutor as suggestive, if a little extreme, and provoked a vague reply. The constructivist was impressed by Cecil's sibylline presence, his whispering, his woolen cap. Had he made something of his life, instead of being a nonentity, he would have recorded the meeting in his memoirs, many years later.

A year earlier, Cecil had done some arrangements for the famous jazzman Johnny Hodges, who, in return, had offered him a contract for five nights at a hotel, playing piano in his band (which didn't usually include a piano). The first four nights he didn't event touch the instrument. The only one who noticed the silence was the trombone player, Lawrence Brown, who, before the start of the fifth performance, smiled at him and said: Hey, Cecil, I don't know if you've noticed, but that piano has eighty-eight keys. How about you hit one?

The story came up late one night, at a table in the Five Spot, and though it wasn't exactly proof of his credentials, and had to be explained, the upshot was an offer to play there one night during the week, as support for an avant-garde group. It was a heaven-sent opportunity, and he treated it as such. He gave up his job at the dry cleaner, bought a piano with a providential loan, and practiced almost nonstop, only breaking off to reply to his neighbors' complaints with polite explanations. He had moved from the rundown tenement on the Lower East Side to a poky room on Bleecker Street.

The cream of the jazz world went to the Five Spot, so he would have an audience of connoisseurs. He convinced himself that the jolt of his playing could transform that audience and produce the applause that he had been denied until then. The theory of cumulative units that his ex-classmate had propounded was precisely that: a theory, an abstraction, nothing more. In reality, there was something magical about an audience, like a genie appearing from a lamp.

The night in question arrived; he climbed onto the stage, sat at the piano, and began. The amplifier died almost straightaway—a technical fault, supposedly. It didn't matter to him. But his performance was cut short by condescending applause. When he looked up, disconcerted, he saw the avant-garde musicians coming forward with their instruments and their simian smiles. He went to sit at a table where there were some people he knew; they were talking about something else. One took hold of his elbow and, leaning toward him, slowly shook his head. Laughing cheerfully, another came out with a supposedly apt remark: "It's okay, it's over now." And that was all; they stopped talking to listen to the next number.

Someone came up to him and said: "I'm a poor black autodidact, but I have a right to express my opinion, and in my opinion what you do isn't music." Cecil just nodded and shrugged, as if to say, What can you do? But the self-proclaimed autodidact wasn't content to leave it at that. "Don't you want to know the reasons for my opinion? Are you so vain, do you really think being an artist makes you so superior that you don't care what a fellow human being thinks?" "I'm sorry, I didn't ask because I didn't realize there were any reasons, but if there are, I'd be interested to hear them." A satisfied smile from the autodidact, as if he had scored a point. He explained: "It's very simple: music is a whole made up of parts that are also musical. If the part isn't musical, the whole isn't either."

The argument didn't seem irrefutable, but it wasn't the time or the place to go into it. And there was a more general problem too. Cecil kept thinking about this experience over the following days, as he went distractedly about his business; he replayed what had happened step by step and tried to find an explanation. He thought perhaps the explanation would occur to him once he'd forgotten what had happened, but in the meantime he couldn't help remembering. He mentally reconstructed the club, the movements of his fingers on the keyboard, the words and reactions of the others ... and the reconstruction was accompanied by a slight sense of incredulity, the feeling inevitably provoked by whatever has, in fact, occurred.

Like a naughty child caught in the act, he confessed that he'd been hoping for a response from the musicians. The way he played might have sounded strange. Hyperharmonic piano percussion, spatial intentions translated into time, sound sculpture ... (there are always plenty of formulae to account for an extraordinary phenomenon), and someone who wasn't working in the field could well have been disconcerted. But the professional musicians who went to the Five Spot to keep up-to-date were aware of Schoenberg and Varèse, and they used formulae themselves, all the time! The only explanation he could come up with, borrowing an argument from the crazy autodidact who had accosted him (maybe he wasn't so crazy after all), was that "musicians are part of music": because they couldn't get outside it, they couldn't offer any explicit recognition.

Actually, he wasn't so sure that any of the musicians he thought he'd noticed had really been there, because he was very short-sighted and wore dark glasses, which, combined with the subdued lighting, made it just about impossible to see. He promised himself, as he usually did, to come back later and assess the situation more objectively. He usually failed to keep those promises, and this time, preoccupied by other things, he let several weeks go by. He took a job as a night watchman at a supermarket and then as a cleaner in a bank, and both changes obliged him to rearrange his routine and his habits. Finally he went back to the Five Spot, to hear a singer he passionately admired, and was surprised to find a job offer waiting for him.

It turned out that a rich lady who lived on Fifth Avenue was hiring pianists for her bohemian dinner parties, and recruiting them from the Five Spot, as a kind of guarantee of quality. He never found out if they did it on purpose, to him or to her. In any case, she was paying a hundred dollars, up front. Cecil prepared some lyrical improvisations (he recorded his ideas in a little notebook, using a personal system of dots). He walked in the park until the sun went down, in a state of mind hovering between "What do I care?" and a detached optimism. Squirrels were running about in the trees, as if the law of gravity had not yet come into effect. The sky suddenly turned an intense turquoise, the breeze died away, and there was a silence in which a plane could be heard flying over the city. He crossed the street and told the doorman who he was.

He entered the penthouse through the servants' quarters, where he spent the best part of an hour drinking coffee with the staff. Finally, a valet dressed in black came to tell him it was time, then took him across the salon to the piano, a full-size grand, already open. He barely glanced at the guests, who were drinking and chatting, light years away from any conceivable music. He looked down at the keyboard and peered at the strings, shining like gold. It was a first-class piano, and seemed to be brand-new.

He played a note with his left hand, a deep B-flat, which reverberated with slow submarine convulsions ... And that was all, because the lady of the house was standing beside him, closing the lid over the keys with a movement so smooth and effective it seemed to have been rehearsed.

"We'll do without your company for today," she said, looking around the salon. There was applause and laughter, but only from the guests who happened to be nearby. The room was very large.

Cecil was still perplexed hours later, talking it over with his lover. How could a single note possibly have such an effect? But had it been just a single note? He honestly couldn't remember. He could have sworn it had been just the one, but perhaps within the dream of that note, he had played one or several of his famous "tone clusters," or launched into some scales, or put his hands into the entrails of the piano.

No matter what exactly had happened, he should have expected some such reaction, from snobs like that with no knowledge of music. But he might have expected the opposite too, because his music, unable to break through their shell of ignorance, could have spread over its surface like Vaseline and facilitated a superficial penetration.

Time went by, but brought no changes. That winter there were a number of notable opportunities. A bar with a bad reputation took him on for a week to provide some late-night variety (he was to start at two a.m.). The bad reputation was due to the dealing done in the back room. The owner, who was also the dealer, was Irish; he went to see Cecil personally and ex-

plained what he wanted: real, innovative music, not just wallpaper. Cecil asked if he'd heard about his playing. He didn't quite
dare ask if he'd actually heard him play. The Irishman nodded
without elaborating and offered him twenty dollars a night.

The place was seedy. The clientele was made up of black
drug addicts, and a significant number of old ladies with resigned expressions, waiting in the corners. Two cobwebby pianos were standing guard at the back of the room. No one was
paying any attention to the banjo trio and its messy chords.
Paradoxically, there was a good ambience, a certain excitement
in the air, almost like a prior music.

He sat down at one of the pianos ... He wasn't sure which
one, he wasn't there long enough be sure, because he'd only
played a pair of chords or bursts of notes when the owner of
the bar tapped him on the shoulder and, with a worried look
on his face, told him to wrap it up. Cecil took his hands off the
keys and the downward pressure on his shoulder became an
upward-pulling grip that lifted him to his feet. One of the old
black ladies had appeared on the other side of him, and, as if
she'd been waiting for a sign, slid into his place on the stool and
began to play "Body and Soul."

The Irishman showed him the way out, still looking worried.
The speechless pianist was wondering what there could possibly be in his music to worry a man who dealt every day with
the dangerous suppliers and buyers of hard drugs. The dealer
held out a ten-dollar bill but, just as Cecil was about to take it,
pulled his hand away.

"You weren't playing some kind of joke, were you?"

There was a menacing gleam in his squinty eyes. Cecil wondered whether there had really been two pianos. That character had been dealing in danger so long, he had absorbed it and become danger in person. He would have weighed two hundred pounds, more than twice as much as the pianist, who didn't wait around for further denigration.

Cecil was a kind of sprite, always stylish in spite of his limited means, wearing velvet and white leather, and pointed shoes that complemented his compact, muscular physique. He didn't exercise, but the way he played the piano engaged every movable molecule in his body. Sweating had become second nature to him. He could lose as much as ten pounds in an afternoon of improvising at his old piano. Extraordinarily absentminded, whimsical, and volatile, when he sat down and crossed his legs (in his loose pants, immaculate shirt, and knitted waistcoat) he was as ornamental as a bibelot. His continual changes of address protected him; they were the little genie's suspended dwellings, and there he slept on a bed of chrysanthemums, under the shade of a droplet-laden spiderweb.

That night he walked the deep streets of the island's south, thinking. There was something odd: the attitude of the voluminous Irish heroin dealer was not substantially different from that of the lady who lived on Fifth Avenue, except that she didn't seem worried, though perhaps she was just hiding it. And yet the two individuals were not at all alike. Except in that one respect. Could it be that the propensity to interrupt him was the common denominator of the human race? And he discovered something more in the Irishman's final words, something he began to reconstruct from the memories of all his ill-fated performances. People always asked him if he was doing it as a joke. Some people, of course, the rich lady for example, didn't deign to ask, but their behavior presupposed the question. And he wondered why the question applied to him, but not to others. For example, he would never have asked the lady, or the Irishman, if they did what they did (whatever it was) seriously or as a joke. There was something inherent in his work that raised the question.

Another rich lady, Mrs. Vanderbilt, figured in a famous anecdote, mentioned in virtually all the psychology books written around that time. She once decided to liven up a dinner party with some violin music. She asked who the best violinist in the world was. Why would she settle for second best? Fritz Kreisler, she was told. She called him on the telephone. I don't give private concerts, he said: my fee is too high. That's not a problem, replied Mrs. Vanderbilt: How much? Ten thousand dollars. All right. I'll expect you tonight. But there is just one thing, Mr. Kreisler: you will dine in the kitchen with the servants, and you must not mix with my guests. In that case, he said, I'll have to alter my fee. That's not a problem, how much? Two thousand dollars, replied the violinist.

The behaviorists loved that story, and they would go on loving it all their lives, telling it to one another tirelessly and transcribing it in their books and articles. But what about *his* anecdote, the one about Cecil Taylor? Would anyone love that?

Would anyone tell it? Anecdotes had to succeed too—didn't they?—for someone to repeat them.

That summer, along with a horde of other musicians, he was invited to participate in the Newport festival, at which a couple of afternoons would be given over to the presentation of new artists. Cecil thought about it: his music, which was essentially new, would be a challenge to that festive, seaside atmosphere. All the same, it was a change from the smoke and chatter of bars: he'd be performing for jazz fans, who'd paid for their tickets and come to listen and judge. And yet, although he prepared for the event with his customary dedication, when the day came, his performance was an absolute fiasco. No one interrupted him this time, but the listening was interrupted: the audience walked out, which didn't stop the critics and journalists among them having an opinion. Not even an opinion about him; they used it as a pretext to settle scores with the organizers, who were so lacking in judgment that they'd invited people who didn't even play jazz, or any kind of music. The closest thing to criticism came from the *Down Beat* journalist. Without mentioning Cecil by name, and adopting an ironic tone, he trotted out a version of the Cretan liar paradox: If someone were to hammer a piano with his fists and say, "I am making music..." Music, thought Cecil as he read, can't be paradoxical, because of its nonlinguistic nature, and yet what is happening to me is a paradox. How can that be?

He couldn't come up with an answer, then or ever. Over the following months he performed in half a dozen bars, always a different place because the result was always the same, and he received two invitations, which reopened the wound of anticipation, one from a university and the other from the organizers of a series of avant-garde events at the Cooper Union. He took up the first with some hope, which turned out to be misplaced (within a few minutes, the room was empty; the professor who had issued the invitation came up with complicated excuses and hated him ever after), but at least it served to provoke a reflection, which might have been misplaced as well, not that Cecil cared anymore: an educated audience was equivalent in every respect to an uneducated one. They were the same, in fact, except that they were looking in opposite directions, facing away from each other. The pivot on which their seats turned was the hoary old tale of the emperor's new clothes. For one group the obscene and shameful thing was nakedness; for the other, it was clothes.

His experience at the Cooper Union was even less gratifying. They used a blackout as a pretext to stop him halfway through; there was vigorous booing, and from what he heard later, his performance left the audience wondering about the limits of music, and whether he had meant it as a joke.

Cecil gave up another of his temporary jobs, and, with some money he'd saved, spent the winter months studying and composing. In spring, a contract came up for a couple of dates, in a bar in Brooklyn, where they laughed in his face and threw him out. As he was traveling home in the train, the rocking movement and the stations sliding by put him in a meditative frame of mind. It struck him that the logic of his predicament was in fact perfectly clear, and he wondered why he hadn't seen it before: in all those edifying tales about pianos and violins, there was always a musician whose talent wasn't recognized at first, but in the end it was. That was where the mistake lay, in the transition from failure to triumph, as if they were two points, A and B, joined by a line. In fact, failure is infinite, because it's infinitely divisible, unlike success.

Let's suppose, said Cecil in the empty carriage at three in the morning, that in order to be recognized I have to perform for an audience whose coefficient of sensitivity and intelligence has a certain threshold value, x. And let's say I start off performing for an audience with a coefficient of $x/100$, then I'll have to "go through" an audience whose coefficient is $x/50$, then one with a coefficient of $x/25$ ... and so on. There was no need to reinvent Zeno's famous argument: it was all too obvious.

Six months later he was hired to play in a dive frequented by French tourists: existentialists, who came to the city of jazz in search of powerful emotions. He arrived at midnight, as agreed, and they took him straight to the piano. Sitting on the stool, he stretched his hands out toward the keys, and launched into a series of chords ... There were a couple of unemphatic bursts of laughter. With a cheerful look on his face, the master of ceremonies was waving him off the stage. Had they already decided that it was a joke? No, they were actually quite indignant. To ease the tension, an older pianist took his place immediately. No one said a word to Cecil; still, he hoped they'd pay him a part of the promised sum (as they always did), and he stayed there watching and listening to the pianist. He could hear the influence of Ellington and Bud Powell ... The guy wasn't bad. A conventional musician, he thought, is always dealing with music in its most general form, as if leaving the particular for later, waiting for the right moment. And they did pay him: twenty dollars, on the condition that he would never show his face there again.

Translator's note

"The Spy" has been translated for this volume from the revised version of the text in *Relatos reunidos* (Mondadori, 2013). Likewise, "Cecil Taylor" has been translated from the revised version, published as a book by Mansalva in 2011 with illustrations by El Marinero Turco.

31172094500964

"Logic-defying brilliance."
—*Publishers Weekly*

"Argentine author César Aira is an exquisite miniaturist who toys with avant-garde techniques. His work has drawn comparisons to Vladimir Nabokov and Italo Calvino for its gleeful literary gamesmanship and stories-within-stories."
—*The Wall Street Journal*

"His novels are eccentric clones of reality, where the lights are brighter, the picture is sharper, and everything happens at the speed of thought."
—Jacob Mikanowski, *The Millions*

"What a gift: to look forward to reading a new Aira novel from New Directions every year for the rest of one's life."
—Thomas McGonigle, *Los Angeles Times*

"Irreverent inventiveness ... without analogue in contemporary literature."
—Megan Doll, *San Francisco Chronicle*

"One of the most celebrated authors in Latin America."
—*New York Observer*

"A quixotic chemist."
—Michael H. Miller, *The American Reader*

"The novelist who can't be stopped. Aira's novels are dense, unpredictable confections delivered in plain, stealthily lyrical style capable of accommodating his fondness for mixing metaphysics, realism, pulp fiction, and Dadaist incongruities."
—Michael Greenberg, *The New York Review of Books*

"Outlandish B-movie fantasies are all part of the game. His best-known works are nonsensically hysterical. To love César Aira you must have a taste for the absurd, a tolerance for the obscurely philosophical, and a willingness to laugh out loud against your better judgment."
—Marcela Valdes, *NPR Books*

"A distinctive hallucinatory style, which blends together reality and fiction, the waking world and the dream world."
—Chloe Schama, *The New Republic*

"César Aira is the energizer bunny of Latin American literature."
—Tess Lewis, *The Hudson Review*